THE SECOND LIFE
OF NICK MASON

THE SECOND LIFE
OF NICK MASON

Steve Hamilton

G. P. PUTNAM'S SONS   NEW YORK

PUTNAM

G. P. PUTNAM'S SONS
Publishers Since 1838
An imprint of Penguin Random House LLC
375 Hudson Street
New York, New York 10014

ISBN 9780399574320

Printed in the United States of America
10 9 8 7 6 5 4 3 2 1

BOOK DESIGN BY MEIGHAN CAVANAUGH

To Shane

    who saw a better life, even when I couldn't

No man, for any considerable period, can wear one face to himself, and another to the multitude, without finally getting bewildered as to which may be the true.

—NATHANIEL HAWTHORNE, *The Scarlet Letter*

Everybody's got a secret Sonny
Something that they just can't face
Some folks spend their whole lives trying to keep it
They carry it with them every step that they take

—BRUCE SPRINGSTEEN, "Darkness on the Edge of Town"

THE SECOND LIFE
OF NICK MASON

| 1 |

Nick Mason's freedom lasted less than a minute.

He didn't see it then, but he'd look back on that day and mark those first free steps through the gate, after five years and twenty-eight days inside. Nobody was standing over him, nobody was watching him, nobody was telling him where to go and when. He could have walked anywhere in that moment. Pick any direction and go. But the black Escalade was waiting for him, and as soon as he took those thirty steps and opened the passenger's-side door, his freedom was gone again.

Mason had effectively signed a contract. When most men do that, they know what's expected of them. They get to read the terms, understand what the job's going to be, know exactly what they'll be expected to do. But Mason didn't get to read anything, because this contract wasn't on paper at all, and instead of actually signing anything, he simply gave his word, with no idea what would come next.

It was late afternoon, the heart of the day spent on processing and changeout. The daily discharge from USP Terre Haute. Typical prison operations, hurry up and wait, the screws dragging their feet all the way to the end. There were two other inmates with him, both anxious to get outside. One of the men he'd never seen before. Not unusual in a prison with so many separate units. The second man was vaguely familiar. Someone from his original unit, before he made his move.

"You're getting out today," that man said, looking surprised. You don't talk about the length of your sentence with most men in this place, but there's no need to keep it a big secret, either. This man had obviously figured Mason for a longtimer. Or maybe he'd heard it from someone else. Mason didn't care. He shrugged the man off without another word and went back to his final-release forms.

When Mason was done with those, the clerk slid a plastic tray across the counter with the clothes he'd been wearing the day he processed in. It felt like a lifetime ago. He'd arrived here in this same room and been told to put his clothes in the tray. The black jeans and the white button-down shirt. Now, it felt strange to be taking off the khaki, like the color was a part of him. But the old clothes still fit.

All three men walked out together. The concrete walls, the steel doors, the two rows of chain-link fence topped with razor wire—all left behind as they stepped out onto the hot pavement and waited for the gate to grind open. There were two families waiting there. Two wives, five kids, all of them looking like they'd been standing there for hours. The kids held handmade signs with multicolored letters, welcoming their fathers home.

There was no family waiting for Nick Mason. No signs.

He stood there blinking for a few seconds, feeling the hot Indiana sun on the back of his neck. He was clean-shaven and fair-skinned, a little over six feet tall. His body was taut with muscle but lean like a middleweight. An old scar ran the length of his right eyebrow.

He saw the black Escalade, idling near the sidewalk. The vehicle didn't move, so he walked down to it.

The windows were tinted. He couldn't see who was inside until he opened the front passenger's-side door. Once he did, he saw that the driver was Hispanic, with dark sunglasses covering his eyes. One arm draped over the steering wheel, the other at rest on the gearshift. He wore a simple white T-shirt with the sleeves cut off, jeans and work boots, one thin gold chain around his neck. Dark hair pulled back and tied with a black band, and as Mason's eyes adjusted, he saw the gray threading through the man's hair and the lines on the man's face. He was at least ten years older than Mason, maybe a few more. But he was rock-solid. His arms were tattooed all the way down both arms to his fingers, and he had three rings in his right ear. Mason couldn't see the other ear because the man did not turn to him. "Mason," the man said. A statement, not a question.

"Yes," Mason said.

"Get in."

Out five minutes, Mason said to himself, and I'm already about to break my rules. Rule number one: *Never work with strangers. Strangers put you in prison or they put you in the ground.* A stranger already put me in the first. I don't need another stranger to put me in the other.

Today, Mason didn't have a choice. He got in and closed the door. The man still hadn't turned to face him. He put the vehicle in gear and accelerated smoothly out of the prison parking lot.

Mason scanned the vehicle. The interior was clean. The leather seats, the carpet, the windows. He had to give the man credit for that much. The vehicle looked like it had just rolled out of the show-room.

He gave the man's tattoos another look. No prison ink here. No spiderwebs. No clocks without hands. This man had spent a lot of time and money in the chair of a real pro, even if some of the color had faded over time. There was an Aztec lattice going all the way up the right arm, with a snake, a jaguar, a headstone, and some Span-ish words meaning God knows what. What was unmistakable were the three letters in green, white, and red on the shoulder—*LRZ*—La Raza—the Mexican gang that ruled the West Side of Chicago.

Another rule broken, Nick thought. Rule number nine: *Never work with gang members.*

They've sworn a blood oath of loyalty. But not to you.

An hour of silence passed. The driver hadn't offered so much as a sideways glance. Mason couldn't help but wonder what would happen if he turned on the radio. Or actually said something out loud. Something made him stay silent. Rule number three: *When in doubt, keep your mouth shut.*

After driving past every exit on US 41, they finally pulled off. For an instant, Mason wondered if this whole thing had been a setup. It was an unavoidable prison reflex, to be ready for the worst at any moment. Two hours away from the prison, somewhere in the middle of western Indiana, the driver could pull off on the most abandoned exit he could find, drive a few miles into the farmland, and then put a bullet in the passenger's head. Leave his body right there in the ditch beside the road. You wouldn't go to that much trouble to do something that could have been done already, on any given day standing around the prison yard, but Mason could still feel his body tensing as the vehicle slowed down.

The driver pulled into a gas station. He got out and pumped gas into the tank. Mason sat there in the passenger's seat, looking out at the little mini-mart. A young woman came out through the glass door. Maybe twenty years old. Shorts and a tank top, flip-flops on her feet. Mason hadn't seen a live woman dressed this way in five years.

The driver got back in and started the vehicle. He pulled out and drove back onto the highway, pointed north, and hit seventy on the speedometer. Dark clouds began to assemble in the sky. By the time they reached the Illinois border, it was raining. The driver turned on the wipers. The traffic got heavier and the lights from the other cars reflected off the rain-slicked road.

The tall buildings were lost in the clouds, but Mason would have known this place no matter how dark the sky or how low the clouds hung over the city streets.

He was almost home.

But first the long pass over the Calumet River, the cranes and drawbridges and power lines. The harbor was down there. The harbor and the one night in his life when everything changed. The one night that led him all the way to Terre Haute and to a man named Cole. Then, somehow, all the way back, a lot sooner than he expected.

He counted down the streets. Eighty-seventh Street. Seventy-first Street. They were on the South Side now. The rain kept falling. The driver kept driving. Garfield Boulevard. Fifty-first Street. You want to start an argument, you go into any bar around here, ask the regulars if Canaryville starts at Fifty-first or Forty-ninth. Stand back and watch the words fly. Then the fists, if it's late enough.

They passed the big train yard, a thousand boxcars waiting for an engine. Then the tracks running high along the eastern edge of his old neighborhood. Mason took a breath as they passed Forty-third

Street. His whole life came back to him at once in a sudden flood of almost random memories, both good and bad—Eddie's dad taking them to old Comiskey Park, the only game he ever got to see Michael Jordan play in person, the first car he ever stole, the first time he spent the night in jail, the party where he met a Canaryville girl named Gina Sullivan, the day he bought their house, the only place he could ever call home… it was all right here, wrapped up together in the city of Chicago. The alleys and the streets of this place ran through him like the veins in his body.

The lights were on at the new Sox park, but it was still raining too hard to play. The Escalade went all the way downtown, crossing the Chicago River. The Sears Tower—always and forever the Sears Tower despite whatever new name they try to give it—dominated the skyline and looked down at them through a sudden break in the clouds, its two antennae like a devil's horns.

The driver finally got off the highway and took North Avenue all the way across the North Side, until Mason could see the shores of Lake Michigan. The water stretched out in blues and grays forever, blending into the rain clouds. When they turned on Clark Street, Mason was about to say something. You bring me all the way up to the North Side for what, pal? A Cubs game maybe? Good luck with that one.

Mason hated the Cubs. He hated everything about the North Side. Everything it represented. When he was growing up, the North Side was everything he didn't have. And never would have.

The driver made his last turn, onto the last street Mason thought he'd see that day. Lincoln Park West. It was four blocks of high-end apartment buildings overlooking the gardens and the conservatory and the lake beyond. There were a few town houses between the apartment buildings, still tall enough to look down at the street and on everyone who passed by. The driver slowed down and stopped right in front of one of those town houses. It sat at the end of the block, rising three stories above the heavy front door and the garage bays, the upper-floor windows all covered with iron latticework. Built out to the side was another one story with a balcony on top, overlooking the cross street, the park, and the lake beyond it. Five million for this place? Hell, probably more.

The driver broke the silence. "My name is Quintero." He made the name sound like it came from the bottom of a tequila bottle. *Keen-TAY-ro.*

"You work for Cole?"

"Listen to me," Quintero said. "Because everything I'm about to say is important."

Mason looked over at him.

"You need something," Quintero said, "you call me. You get in a situation, you call me. Don't get creative. Don't try to fix anything yourself. *You call me.* Clear so far?"

Mason nodded.

"Beyond that, I don't give a fuck what you do with your time. You were inside for five years, so go have a drink, get yourself laid, I don't care. Just understand, you need to stay out of trouble. You get picked up for *anything*, now you've got two problems. The one you got picked up for... and me."

Mason turned and looked out the window.

"Why are we here?"

"This is where you live now."

"Guys like me don't live in Lincoln Park," Mason said.

"I'm going to give you a cell phone. You're going to answer this phone when I call you. Whenever that may be. Day or night. There is no busy. There is no unavailable. There is only you answering this phone. Then doing *exactly* what I tell you to do."

Mason sat there in his seat, thinking that one over.

"The phone is in here," Quintero said, reaching behind the seat and bringing out a large envelope. "Along with the keys to the front and back doors. And the security code."

Mason took the envelope. It was heavier than he expected.

"Ten thousand dollars in cash and the key to a safe-deposit box at First Chicago on Western. There'll be ten thousand more on the first day of each month."

Mason looked over at the man one more time.

"That's it," Quintero said. "Keep your phone on."

Mason opened the passenger's-side door. Before he could get out, Quintero grabbed his arm. Mason tensed up—another prison reflex, someone grabs you, your first reaction is deciding which finger to break first.

"One more thing," Quintero said, holding on tight. "This isn't freedom. This is *mobility*. Don't get those two things confused."

Quintero let him go. Mason stepped out and closed the door. The rain had stopped.

Mason stood there on the sidewalk and watched Quintero's vehicle pull away from the curb, then disappear into the night. He reached into the envelope and took out the key. Then he opened the front door and went inside.

The town house entranceway had a high ceiling, and the light fixture hanging over Mason's head was a piece of modern art with a thousand slivers of glass. The floor was large tiles laid diagonally in a diamond pattern. The stairs were polished cherry. He stood there for a moment until he noticed a beeping noise. He saw the security panel on the wall, took out the code from the envelope, and entered it on the keypad. The beeping stopped.

The door to his right opened to a two-car garage. In one space he saw a Mustang. He knew exactly what this was. It was a 1968 390 GT Fastback, a jet-black version of the car Steve McQueen drove in *Bullitt*. He'd never stolen a car like this because you don't steal a masterpiece and take it to the chop shop. You don't steal a car like this and drive it yourself no matter how much you want to. That's how amateurs get caught.

The other spot in the garage was empty. He saw the faint outline of tire tracks. Another car belonged here.

Mason opened another door and saw a full gym. A row of dumbbells, neatly arranged in pairs, ranged from nothing to the big fifty-pounders at the end. A bench with a rack, a treadmill, an elliptical trainer. A television was mounted high in one corner of the room. A heavy bag hung in another corner. The back wall was a full mirror. Mason looked at his own face from twenty feet away. Cole had told him he could go anywhere in the world with this face, but he never thought he'd end up in a Lincoln Park town house.

He went up the long flight of stairs to what was obviously the main floor. The sleek, modern kitchen had polished granite countertops, an island with a Viking stove and a restaurant hood hanging over it. The bar top looked out over a great open area dominated by the largest television screen Mason had ever seen. He was pretty sure the square footage of the screen was larger than the square footage of the cell he woke up in that morning. In front of the television was a U-shaped expanse of black leather with a large oak coffee table in the middle. You could easily sit a dozen people here. It made the quiet emptiness of the place feel like a sin.

The formal dining room had a table long enough to seat all dozen people that had watched the television in the other room. He left that room and went into what turned out to be the billiards room. An actual room for billiards, with a red felt table and a woven net under each pocket. There was dark paneling on the walls. A pair of stained-glass Tiffany lamps hung over the table. The far corner of the room was set up for darts, and yet another corner had two over-stuffed leather chairs with a three-foot-tall humidor between them. Looking through the glass at the selection of cigars inside, Mason remembered how a single cigarette could go for ten dollars in Terre Haute. A carton could get someone killed.

He went up another set of stairs to the top floor. There were bed-rooms on each side of a long hallway. When he got to the last door, he tried turning the knob. It was locked.

Mason went back downstairs and found a door on the other side of the kitchen. He walked through and saw another bedroom suite. There was an iron-framed bed topped with black linen, and on top of that were several shopping bags. He took a quick look through them. Pants, shirts, shoes, socks, underwear, belts, a wallet—every-thing a man could possibly need. Most of the bags had come from Nordstrom and Armani. One from Balani, the custom shop on Monroe Street. He did a quick check of the tags. Everything was his size.

I don't see my new friend Quintero doing this, he thought.

Mason went back out to the kitchen and opened up the refrigera-tor. After five years of prison food, Mason stood there staring at the salmon, at the cooked and chilled lobster, at the aged steaks. He didn't know where to start. Then he saw the bottles of beer on the lower shelf. He shuffled through the selection, mostly microbrews he'd never heard of. Then he found a bottle of Goose Island.

He opened the bottle and took a long swallow. It took him back to summer nights sitting out on his porch. Listening to a ball game with Eddie and Finn. Or listening to his wife and watching their daughter try to catch fireflies.

He found a take-out container of beef tenderloin with some kind of shiitake mushroom sauce, with angel-hair pasta. He went through the drawers until he found the silverware, grabbed a fork, and ate the entire dish cold, standing there in the middle of the kitchen. He wondered what the inmates in Terre Haute had for dinner that night.

Wednesday night, he said to himself. Usually hamburger night. Or, at least, what they called hamburger.

When he was done eating, he went to the black leather couch, found the remote control, and turned on the television. Leaning back and putting his feet up on the table, he took another long swallow from his beer, found the rain-delayed White Sox game, and watched the last inning. The Sox won. Then he spent a few minutes flipping up and down through the channels just because he could. You try doing that on the television in the common room and you'll start a riot. He shut the television off.

He went back to the refrigerator and took out another Goose Island, then went outside through the big sliding glass door off the kitchen. Still high above the street, with a swimming pool sunk into the great concrete monolith beneath the patio, the water surrounded by bluestone, lit up with underwater lights and glowing aquamarine in the darkness. A table, chairs, and a grill with a wet bar stood by, ready for an outdoor party.

Mason went to the rail and looked out at the park and, beyond that, the endless horizon of Lake Michigan. He could see the lights from a half-dozen boats on the water. He could hear the distant bass notes from a car cruising by on the street. A perfect summer night to be out on the town, no matter where you were going.

A breeze came off the lake and gave him a brief chill. Sixteen hours ago, Mason had woken up in a maximum security prison cell. Now he was standing in a town house in Lincoln Park, drinking a bottle of Goose Island and looking out at the lake.

I knew this man had power, he said to himself, but that was a *federal fucking prison* I walked out of today. How does one man make that happen?

Unless there's even more to him than I know . . .

As he was about to turn away, he looked up and saw the security camera, its little red light blinking. There was a similar camera on each of the other three corner posts. Someone, somewhere, was watching him.

This was his life now. It felt like he was holding his breath, waiting to see what this would truly cost him. How long until that happened?

How long until that phone rings?

When he finally went back into his room and lay down in his bed, he stared at the ceiling for a long time. He was tired. But his body was waiting for the guard to call lights-out. Waiting for the metallic click of his cell door locking shut. Then the horn, that lonely, far-away buzz, that sent him to bed, every single night, for the last five years.

He lay awake, waiting. The sounds never came.

| 2 |

The first time Nick Mason ever heard Darius Cole's name, he was four years into his twenty-five-to-life at USP Terre Haute.

It was a high-security facility, strictly segregated into six different housing units, a maze of one wing after another, with gray, featureless walls that seemed to stretch out forever. The whole compound was surrounded by a high fence topped with razor wire. Then a no-man's-land. Then another fence, with more razor wire. A guard's turret stood at every corner.

There were fifteen hundred other men in this place, including some of the most notorious inmates in the country. Serial killers, Islamic terrorists. A man who raped and killed four children. They had all been sent here, and the men in one housing unit were scheduled to die here, just like Timothy McVeigh did, strapped to a table and injected with potassium chloride, because Terre Haute was now the one and only facility designated for all federal executions.

The guards told you when to wake up and when to go to sleep. They told you when you could leave your cell or when you had thirty seconds to get back in it. They could search your body at any time. They could search your cell, come in and flip your bed and pick through everything you owned, while you stood still in the hallway outside, your face to the wall.

This was Nick Mason's life.

He was outside that day, the day he first met Darius Cole, sitting on the top of a picnic table and watching the Latinos play baseball. One of those perfect summer days that could really get to you if you let it. Mason had always lived by his own carefully constructed set of rules, refined over the years to cover any situation—to keep him alive and out of prison. But now that he was here, those rules had been stripped down to their essence. They were all about simple survival, getting through each day one at a time, holding on to his sanity, not thinking about how good life would be on the other side of that fence. Not thinking about the past or the people he left behind. The night at the harbor and how it sent him here. Not thinking about the future, how many endless days just like this one he had in front of him.

In fact, that was his new rule number one (prison edition): *Deal with today. Tomorrow doesn't exist.*

They did the head count at six o'clock every morning. There was a loud buzz at the end of the hallway and then the guards came around to make sure there were two men in every cell. You had until seven to be on your feet and dressed. That's when the cell door opened.

You filed down to breakfast. If you were near the end of the line, you had to eat fast because the work assignments started at eight. Mason was assigned to the laundry room. Supposedly one of the easier jobs, although Mason hated touching the other inmates' filthy clothing. The morning work period lasted four hours. Then lunch at noon, another rush if you were at the end of the line. Then an hour of classes or counseling sessions or just sitting alone in your cell. At two o'clock they finally let you outside.

That was a moment Mason lived for, every day, when he could escape from the gray walls and the artificial light, get outside and feel the sunlight on his face. See the trees in the distance beyond the fence. That's when he could stretch his legs and walk on the grass, remember these simple things he once took for granted. Or just sit at one of the tables and breathe.

Other inmates would often bring their mail outside with them. They would sit and read their letters from home and sometimes even share them with the other men sitting around them. It was just another way to pass the time.

Mason didn't bring mail outside and he had no interest in reading anyone else's. After four years of watching the mail cart come by, six days a week, he had learned not to expect anything. To feel nothing at all as the other men grabbed their letters and tore them open.

It was another hard lesson of prison life. If your hopes never leave the ground, they can never fall.

On this afternoon, he could hear a man reading something out loud, a funny story related to him by his wife. Mason was close enough to the field to see the ball game, but not too far away from the other white men at the tables behind him. It was something he didn't even have to think about anymore. The yard was always divided into three different worlds—at this time of day it was whites on the tables, blacks in the workout area, Latinos on the ball field— and you stayed with your own. The first time you strayed outside those boundaries, you got a warning. The second time, you deserved whatever happened to you.

A guard came up to him. He was one of those guys who walked around trying a little too hard to look like they owned the place.

Maybe because he was barely five and a half feet tall he had to put on the attitude every day, right after he put on his uniform.

"Mason," the guard said.

Mason looked at him.

"Take a walk with me. Somebody wants to meet you."

Mason didn't move.

"Let's go, inmate. On your feet."

"Tell me who we're going to see."

The guard took a step closer. His arms were folded across his chest. And with Mason sitting on top of the picnic table, the two men could look each other in the eye.

"We're going to go see Mr. Cole," the guard said. "Get up and start walking."

"Mr. Cole works here?"

"No, he's another inmate."

Whatever this was, it was not official prison business.

"I'll pass," Mason said. "Tell him I mean no disrespect."

The guard stood there, working it over in his head. He clearly didn't have a plan for no.

"This is not the way to play this," he said as he hitched up his pants. Then he walked away.

Mason knew that probably wasn't the end of the matter. So he wasn't surprised when he saw the shadow in the hallway later that day, just outside the door to his cell. What did surprise him was when the shadow gave way not to the same five-and-a-half-foot prison guard but to two inmates he'd never seen before. They were both black and they both looked like interior linemen from the Bears, six hundred combined pounds of prison khaki filling up the doorway and blocking out the light like a fucking solar eclipse.

Mason was determined to stay calm. It was his rule number two (prison edition): *Don't show them weakness. Don't show them fear. Don't show them shit.*

"Can I help you guys?" he said. He was sitting on his bed and he didn't get up. "You look lost."

"Mason," the man on the left said. "Mr. Cole wants to talk to you. Not a request."

Mason stood up. The two men remained polite and composed.

They walked on either side of him, drawing stares from every other inmate they passed. When the three of them were at the end of the cellblock, the guard took one look at them and let them pass into the connecting hallway. Mason felt vulnerable for the few seconds they were alone there. The two men could have stopped at any time and taken him apart piece by piece. But they kept walking, and Mason stayed between them. He didn't say a word. It was his one rule from the outside that was just as good on the inside, rule number three: *When in doubt, keep your mouth shut.*

They passed another guard. Mason was now in the Secure Housing Unit, a separate wing for what they called high-profile offenders. Men who were best kept separate from Gen Pop but with no special need to be isolated from one another once they were. Everything looked a little newer here—glass on the cells instead of bars, a central guard station on the second floor looking down over the common area. Men were playing cards at the tables. Others were watching the television. It seemed odd to Mason that the men weren't automatically separated by race here.

He saw whites and blacks and Latinos all sitting together, something you'd *never* see back in Gen Pop.

Mason was led to the cell on the far end of the second floor. The first thing he noticed as he got close enough was the number of books in the cell. One of two beds was piled high with them. The other bed was neatly made with a red blanket that was nicer than any other he'd seen in the prison.

He saw the bald head first. The man was standing with his back to the door, looking in the mirror. He was one of those men who might be fifty, might be sixty-five. There was not a hair on his head to give him away. His face was as smooth as his head. Not a wrinkle. But you'd see that with some of the lifers in here. All the years inside, away from the sun. Only his eyes showed age. He was wearing small, frameless reading glasses, pushed down on his nose.

Darius Cole's age might have been vague, but one thing that was perfectly clear was that he was black. Black as a mood, black as an Ali left jab or a Muddy Waters riff coming from the Checkerboard Lounge on a hot summer's night.

"Nick Mason." He had a smooth, quiet voice. Anywhere else, it would have been the voice of a peaceful man.

Mason kept looking around the cell, finding more and more violations. A corded lamp with an incandescent bulb. A laptop computer. A teapot sitting on a hot plate.

"My name is Darius Cole," he said. "You know me?"

Mason shook his head.

"You from Chicago, right?"

Mason nodded.

"My name still don't ring a bell?"

Mason shook his head again.

"You're not *supposed* to know my name," Cole said. "Not supposed to know anything about me. That's your first lesson, Nick. A man's ego will kill him faster than any bullet."

"No disrespect," Mason said, "but I don't remember signing up for any lessons today."

Mason waited for the two men to grab him. He was already an-ticipating how it would feel, the two sudden vise grips on either shoulder. But Cole just smiled and raised his hand.

"You need to carry yourself a certain way in here," he said. "I understand. You can drop it around me."

Cole pulled the chair away from his desk and put it in the middle of the cell. He sat and studied Mason for a long time.

"I pay that guard money every week, all he gotta do is get things done. Now you make him look like a little bitch. You think he's gonna forget that?"

Mason shrugged. "Guards don't forget anything."

"Musta seemed strange to you. Maybe that's why you said no. You wasn't curious at all?"

Mason took a breath while he put the words together in his head. "If I say yes to meeting you," he said, "there's a good chance you're going to ask me to do something. If I say no to that, then not only have I offended you, I've offended you to your face. So now I make you my enemy."

Cole leaned forward in his chair, listening carefully.

"If I say yes to what it is you want, there's a decent chance it'll be something bad, something I don't want to do. But maybe I feel like I need to do it anyway. So now I make enemies again. Maybe a lot of them."

Cole started to nod his head.

"So for me," Mason said, "the only right answer to meeting with you—"

"The only right answer," Cole said, cutting him off, "is not to meet with me at all."

Cole kept nodding his head. There was a smile on his face now. "You were supposed to go to Marion," he said. "I had you brought here instead."

Mason stood there trying to figure out what this man was saying. Marion was another federal prison. You draw federal time in Chicago, you go to Marion or Terre Haute.

"Take him back," he said as he gestured to the two men. "I'm done with him. For now."

He was still smiling as Mason was led away.

| 3 |

Mason woke up early, his body still on prison time. He got up, went outside, stood at the rail, and looked down at the quiet park and the sun rising low on the water. He looked up at the nearest security camera. That unblinking eye, watching him.

He went back into the bedroom suite, then into the bathroom. The shower was tiled floor to ceiling with natural lakeshore stones. He cranked the water, got in, and stood under the spray. For the first time in five years, there was no limit to the hot water. There was no limit to how long he could stand there. He could let it blast him until his skin was red and he couldn't see anything in the billows of steam. He felt the knots in his muscles going loose. Until one more prison reflex came to him and broke the spell. The sudden uneasy feeling, something he could never imagine leaving him—the instinct to always watch your back, even in the shower.

Especially in the shower.

He turned off the water and stood there, dripping. He opened the glass door and felt his way through the steam for a towel.

"You'll be wanting this," a voice said. It was a woman, looking away from him and holding out a towel.

Mason grabbed the towel and wrapped it around his waist. The woman was Mason's age, tall and lithe, dressed in a black business suit with a shirt the color of coral. Her dark hair was pinned up. She didn't wear much makeup. Nick's first impression was that she didn't need to.

Nick shook the water from his hair. "Who are you?"

"My name is Diana Rivelli. Nobody told you about me?"

"No."

She shook her head as she reached over to turn on the ceiling vent. "That figures."

"The room at the end of the hallway," Nick said. "The one that was locked."

"Yes," she said, looking a little unhappy with the thought of him trying her door. "That's my room."

I have a roommate, Mason said to himself.

"The clothes on the bed," he said. "You bought those for me. You didn't have to do that."

"Actually, I did. But you're welcome, anyway."

Mason had more questions, but she was already walking out of the room. He dried off and got dressed, trying on some of the new clothes. Jeans and a simple white dress shirt.

When he came out into the kitchen, he took another look around and found the walk-in pantry. At the back of it was yet another door. He felt the temperature drop as he opened it and stepped inside. He turned on the light and saw the wooden latticework along the wall, with a bottle of wine in each opening. There had to be at least three hundred bottles in here, with another dozen champagne bottles in a small glass-doored refrigerator on the table, next to the openers and decanters.

Mason's first cell mate made prison wine with fruit smuggled out from his kitchen job, some sugar, some toast, all mashed up in a plastic bag and kept warm for a week. From that world to this one in just twenty-four hours. Mason shook his head, turned off the light, and went back out to the kitchen.

He found a frying pan in the cabinet below the kitchen island, got some eggs and cheese from the refrigerator, then cut up some onions and peppers. Diana came back down the stairs.

"You want an omelet?" he asked.

She sat down on the other side of the island and looked around at the mess. "That's the wrong pan. If you're making an omelet, you use the omelet pan. And you've got it way too hot."

Mason worked the spatula around the edge of the omelet and saw that it was already burning. "It's been a while."

She looked away and tucked a stray hair behind her ear.

"Where do you work?" he said.

"I manage a restaurant on Rush Street. Antonia's. Come by tonight, have dinner, see where you'll be working."

Mason stopped dead. "Where I'll be working?"

"You're an assistant manager," she said. "Take the omelet out of the pan... or the scrambled eggs...whatever you'd call that."

Mason scooped it onto a plate.

"You won't be cooking," she said. "No offense."

"Cook, assistant manager, like it even fucking matters. What do I know about restaurants?"

Eddie would be able to fake his way through this, he thought. He'd always been the great improviser ever since they were kids.

How many times had they done jobs together, Eddie acting like he really belonged somewhere, and getting away with it?

"You'll get a pay stub in case somebody needs to see it. The IRS, whoever else. Other than that, your official job description as assistant manager will be to stay the hell out of everybody else's way."

Mason took a bite of his omelet. "What can you tell me about Quintero?"

"I don't think we've ever spent more than a minute in the same room. I wouldn't mind keeping it that way."

Mason looked her over. He couldn't figure out how she could be so matter-of-fact about this, a convict released yesterday and today standing in her kitchen.

I wonder if I'm the first one, he thought. Maybe they come through here like a regular changing of the guard.

"What's your story?" he said. "Why are you here?"

"I told you, I run a restaurant."

"Does Cole own it?"

She hesitated. "Not officially. Not on paper."

"How long have you known him?"

She hesitated again. Maybe she's another devoted follower of my rule number seven, Mason thought. *Keep your personal life and your professional life separate.* As separate as enriched uranium and those mullahs over in Iran.

"I've known Darius a long time," she finally said. "My father was one of his first business partners. It was my father's restaurant."

"Where is he now?"

"He's dead," she said, looking away from him. "He said the wrong thing to the wrong person. Darius dealt with that person. And everyone else who was involved."

Mason studied her carefully. She was talking about something else, something that went beyond the restaurant business or buying him clothes. She lived in Cole's town house and obviously had a history with the man. She called him by his first name.

"You've been living here," he said to her, not even a question, "ever since he went to Terre Haute."

This was a classy woman, Mason thought. Smart enough to know how attractive she was, smart enough to know that with her body and brains, she could do and have pretty much anything or anyone she wanted.

But she stayed here.

Her eyes met his. "We don't need to talk about that," she said. "I need to get to work."

Mason could understand this need to compartmentalize. To set everything else aside so you could focus on the one thing you had to do. For Mason, it was stealing a car, or knocking over a drug dealer, or, eventually, breaking into a building and drilling open a safe. But then he'd come home when it was done and he'd leave that work behind him. He'd have money, he'd have time, he'd have a way to keep living until it was time to work again.

He could see the same thing in Diana. That same need to focus on her job, to keep everything else separate. Her father is killed and Cole "deals" with it. She lives here with him and then stays here, for years, after he's gone. She gets up every morning and goes to work.

She does her job.

Now if Mason only knew what his job would be.

"What can you tell me about what I'll be doing here?" Mason said. "Besides staying out of your way at the restaurant."

"That's between you and Darius," she said.

"I hated prison, but at least you knew what to expect there. Right down to the minute. Here, I've got no idea what's going to happen next."

Mason thought about the twenty-year "contract" he had signed with Cole and how Cole was the only man who really knew what was written in it.

"When the time comes," Diana said, "just do exactly what you're told. Nothing more, nothing less. Trust me, that's the only way to play this."

"Those cameras outside," Mason said, nodding toward the pool. "Don't they bother you?"

She looked outside and shrugged. "I don't even think about them anymore."

"He could have put me anywhere," Mason said. "Why here? So you can keep an eye on me? Is that part of your job?"

"Maybe it's part of *your* job to keep an eye on *me*." She gathered up her purse, took out her keys, and went down the stairs.

| 4 |

After five years without a visit or a phone call, Nick Mason didn't even know if the life he'd left behind would still be there, but he had to try.

He went through the clothes in his room and put on a black sports coat over his jeans and white dress shirt. When he went down to the garage, he found the keys to the Mustang in the ignition. He hadn't driven a car in five years. He opened the garage, put it in reverse, backed out into the street. Then he headed south.

If you grow up in Chicago, you know it's a city of neighborhoods, a great patchwork of separate communities, spreading out in three directions from the shores of Lake Michigan. Each neighborhood has its own rhythm, its own way of life, and its own food—from the deep-dish pizza in Streeterville to the pierogies in Avondale to the fried rattlesnake in La Villita.

And if you grow up in what they officially call New City, like Nick Mason did, you know it's really two separate neighborhoods in one: Back of the Yards and Canaryville. Back of the Yards is where you find the kids with the Polish last names, the grandchildren of the men who worked as meatpackers in the Union Stock Yards. On the other side of that is Canaryville. That's where you find the Irish kids. Like Eddie Callahan. Or Finn O'Malley. Or a half-Irish, half-whatever kid named Nick Mason.

Of the three, Eddie was the smartest. He was a short, redheaded kid with freckles, built as solid as a fullback. Surprisingly fast when he had to be. He didn't always talk like a kid from Canaryville. He even had both parents at home most of the time.

Finn was tall and underfed, with a haunted look in his eyes that made him irresistible to some girls and unsettling to everyone else. His mother worked at the corner grocery, and his father was usually either missing or sitting at one of the bars on Halsted Street.

Nick's mother lived in one tiny apartment after another and sometimes relied on charity from St. Gabriel's. He had a vague memory of some men who'd come by to see her, but he couldn't remember any single man as his father no matter how hard he tried. It bothered him sometimes, but then he'd think, what the hell, it's probably just some local loser who may or may not be kicking around anymore. Sometimes he'd even wonder what would happen if he met an older man at the bar and saw enough resemblance in the face to make the connection. He honestly didn't know what would happen next, but it probably wouldn't be good.

A year older, Finn was the first one of the three to get drunk, the first to get laid, the first to steal a car. He was the first to get picked up by the police and held in a cell until his mother could get off work and come pick him up.

When Nick and Eddie followed Finn into the auto theft business, they discovered that they had a real talent for it. Something that

Finn would never have. They were a lot more careful, for one thing. They were more patient. They knew to walk away if everything wasn't right. Once they had that part figured, the rest was easy. It wasn't like breaking into people's houses. It wasn't that kind of personal invasion. It was just cold metal on wheels.

Eddie, in particular, got good at the technical side of car theft. He'd read the electrical diagrams on some of the models so he'd know where to find the wires to the main fuse, the ignition circuit, and the starter motor. Once you've got those three wires pulled out from the wiring harness and cut, you're in business.

It didn't take Nick and Eddie long to find the people who would buy the cars from them. If you did a clean job, and if you were willing to go out and find exactly what they wanted, there would always be people willing to pay you.

That's what Mason did instead of junior and senior year of high school. That's what he did instead of college. That was his job for six years. He got picked up a few times, but he was never charged. He was proud to say he'd never spent two consecutive nights in custody. The first time Mason and Eddie both got picked up together, Eddie's parents convinced him to join the Army. Mason was surprised when he agreed to it. He wasn't surprised when Eddie came back two years later.

"Turns out I can shoot a gun," Eddie said the first night Mason saw him again. "I mean, *really* shoot. And I loved it. But I couldn't take the rest of it, some asshole pounding on a garbage can lid and telling me to get out of bed."

"So two years of your life..." Mason said.

"Yeah, two years and I'm out," Eddie said. "But I can still hit anything inside a thousand yards."

Mason had never used a gun on a job before. You don't need one when you're stealing cars. But now with Eddie back, they had a new plan.

Robbing drug dealers.

It took less time than stealing a car, it paid twice the money, and nobody involved in this transaction had any interest in calling the police. The basic routine was to find a dealer, observe his routine, catch him when he was carrying the maximum amount of money. Do it quickly, decisively, and then get the hell out. The risk was a lot higher, so that meant some new rules. And when it came to the guns, they needed one very carefully thought-out rule that would keep everyone alive, including the dealers. A real cowboy like Finn would have come up with something straight and simple like *Don't bring out the guns unless you plan on using them.* But that's bullshit. Absolute suicidal bullshit. Because you *don't* want to use your gun. You just want the other man to think you will. The rule they came up with was *Act like you want to shoot the man. Act like it's the one thing you want more than anything else in the world.*

It was a rule that worked, because if you could sustain that belief within yourself, then the man you were robbing would believe it, too. No dealer wanted to die over a few thousand dollars. Not if it was money he could make back the next day.

Of course, you could only do that kind of job so often. It wasn't like stealing cars, with a fresh supply lined up and down the street every single day. You knocked over dealers and they started putting extra men on the corners. So you backed off and let things go back to normal. Then you hit them again.

The business stayed profitable for two years. Then one night they had a house lined up in Roseland. Abandoned for months, it became a place for users to score, but within another couple of days the op-

THE SECOND LIFE OF NICK MASON

eration would be moved to yet another house. All they had to do was wait for the right moment, enter in front and back to introduce themselves, take the money, and say good night.

They were just getting ready to move when another vehicle pulled up on the other side of the street. A big Ford Bronco. Three white men got out. One of the men went around back. The other two went to the front. Their guns were out before they even hit the door. It was as if they had borrowed the same plan and then executed it exactly as Nick, Eddie, and Finn would have.

They were back out of the house within two minutes. One of them was carrying a grocery bag. They got in their Bronco and took off.

"You know who that was?" Eddie asked.

Nobody answered. The way these guys looked, the way they moved, the fact that they didn't care about being seen . . . that was Mason's first encounter with dirty cops. It wouldn't be his last. But, for now, it meant one thing: when the cops take over your business, it's time to find a new one.

After six years of stealing cars and two years of taking down drug dealers, Nick Mason graduated to high-end robbery. He got his first job through one of his old chop shop contacts, who told Mason about a business supplying and servicing video poker games in bars. The bar customers weren't supposed to be playing for real money, of course, but the owner had been overheard complaining about how the "not real" money was piling up and he didn't want to put it in the bank and have to account for it on the books. So it was all just wads of cash that barely fit into the hiding places all over his shop. He hadn't spent any of that money on a safe.

As soon as Mason shared this with Eddie and Finn, Finn wanted to bust right into the place and put a gun to the man's head and ask him where the money was hidden. But Mason knew this was an opportunity to learn how to do this kind of job right. Like a pro.

Mason watched the place for a few days. It dealt with more than just the video poker. It was a "vending and amusement supply company," for cigarette machines, pinball machines, video games, you name it. There was always someone in the building from eight in the morning until six in the evening, at which point everything was locked up and the alarm was turned on. There was a side window with thick iron bars, but Mason could look through and see the work area in the back of the building. Mason made detailed notes so he'd be sure to have a plan once he got inside, along with the proper tools.

Meanwhile, Eddie was learning everything he could about the alarm system. He was the one who knew how to hot-wire cars, so he was the natural choice for alarm man. The sticker in the front window told Eddie what kind of system it was. All he had to do was figure out how to disarm the system within the thirty-second delay after the front door was opened.

When the night came, the three men broke the glass on the rear door and were inside in seconds. Eddie went straight to the security panel in the front of the building and disabled it, which for that particular model meant grabbing it and pulling the entire old-school landline piece of crap right off the wall. Mason started searching through locked metal cabinets, using the large bolt cutters he had brought with him. He came up empty every time. Eddie joined him and started going through the hollow consoles of the vending machines and video games. Finn just poked around, getting more and more anxious.

"I told you how we should have done this," Finn said just as Mason pushed up the ceiling tiles and pulled down a bundle of money.

The three of them spent the next few minutes pushing up every ceiling tile in the storage area. When they were done, they had a garbage bag full of cash, over twelve thousand dollars for one night's work. One week if you counted the prep work. They had learned some good lessons that were useful on their next job. And the job after that. The ideal target was anyplace where a large amount of cash was put to bed for the night. Eddie learned a little more about alarm systems with each job. Mason learned about cheap safes and how to drill them open.

The last job the three men did together, years before getting together again one more time at the harbor, was another cash business with a drillable safe. By then, Mason wasn't relying on anyone else for the setups. He'd learned how to recognize the easy targets. In this case, it was a car audio store, and as Mason stood at the counter, he could see the safe in the back room, a model he knew he could drill in ten minutes. It was practically begging to be opened.

He spent an hour watching the customers. Half of them wore gold chains and all of them wanted their rides to have the biggest subwoofers on the road. A lot of cash went into the register. Not many credit card receipts.

He kept watching the place. A few more days to learn the routine, to find out when they'd bag up the money and take it to the bank. Eddie learned about the alarm system, and on a Sunday night they broke in through the back door. Eddie disabled the alarm, Mason plugged in his industrial drill with the diamond-tipped bit, and Finn stayed at the front window to watch the street.

Mason went right through the face of the lock until he got to the drive cam. Then he used a long punch rod to push it out of the way. He opened the safe and stuffed everything into a trash bag.

As he stood up, he saw Finn coming toward him. "Cops," Finn

said, although the look on his face had already made that obvious, not to mention the flashing red lights that were suddenly reflected in the front window.

Mason told him to get down and to stay quiet. He went close enough to the lobby of the store to see out the window and caught sight of the back half of the patrol car. It was parked twenty feet from the door.

"We gotta get the fuck out of here," Eddie said from behind him. The only other way out was the back door.

Mason ran the odds through his head. Go out the back, get in the car, drive around the other side of the building, hit the street...

In that moment, Mason felt his whole life slipping away from him. The alarm was disabled, the safe was drilled open, the money was stuffed into a trash bag. This would be the easiest bust of the year for these guys. The only question would be what kind of deal they could make, three guys with some history but no felony convictions, now facing burglary and probably Class 3 larceny, depending on how much money was in that bag.

"I told you we should have brought guns," Finn said, his hands shaking and his eyes as wide open as a junkie's. "Did I not fucking say that?"

Mason wanted to slap him hard across the face. For all of his rules, Mason had one blind spot—this one man who had been like a brother to him for as long as he could remember. Seeing him like this made Mason reconsider. Maybe he needed one more rule about working with guys who lose their shit and start talking about guns when they're backed into a corner.

Mason took a breath and went over to the small side window, peering out at the parking lot. He saw the front half of the patrol car.

And then another car. An old beater with four male occupants. It had pulled over into the lot and was parked directly in front of the patrol car.

It was a traffic stop.

Mason kept watching out the window as the four high school shitheads were taken out, IDs checked, beer bottles dumped, and the empties lined up on the roof of the car. He let out his breath and whispered to Eddie and Finn that they weren't all about to get arrested after all.

But now they'd have to wait to get out of there.

Parents were called and brought down to the scene of the crime. Another patrol car pulled in to help out. Thirty minutes passed and the three men were still trapped inside the store. Then an hour. Finn was getting anxious again.

At one point, one of the patrol officers actually came over to the store and looked in the front window. He cast a long shadow that reached all the way across the counter and into the back room. Mason, Eddie, and Finn all held their breath and made sure they couldn't be seen. Then the shadow left the window and the cars started to pull out of the lot.

Except for the one patrol car.

Mason could imagine the two cops calling in on their radio, requesting backup. After all this time waiting, he thought, maybe we really do have to go out that back door and try to outrun them.

But then the car finally turned onto the street and drove away.

As soon as it was out of sight, they went out the back door and got in their car. Eddie carried the trash bag.

"Let's get the fuck out of here," Eddie said as Mason started the car and hit the gas. When they counted the money an hour later, it turned out to be just over nine thousand dollars. Three thousand per man. Not nearly enough money for what they had risked.

It was time to take a break. And then, when they got back together, to make a decision. Either go bigger or get out.

But then Finn did something stupid, even by his own standards. He took a girl to a bar in McKinley Park and got in a fight with one of the locals who said the wrong thing to her. Bad enough to take her out of Canaryville in the first place when there were perfectly good bars on your own home turf and nobody's calling the cops as long as it's a fair fight. But Finn was a stranger in McKinley Park, so a patrol car did show up and Finn ended up hitting the first cop who put a hand on him. That cop got a concussion and Finn got eighteen months for aggravated assault and obstruction. When he was released, he didn't even bother coming back to Canaryville to face Mason and Eddie. He went to Florida instead.

It felt like one more sign. Then Eddie met Sandra. Mason got back together with Gina, and if there was still any question left, she answered it for him.

It was time to get out.

Mason turned thirty and he was trying to settle down, trying to stay straight. He was married to Gina by then. Adriana was four years old. Finn had been in Florida for a few years and had just recently returned to Chicago. He got picked up again on his first night back in town. Two days later, he found Nick Mason.

"Got a job for us," he said.

"I'm out, Finn. Forget it."

Nick had the house on Forty-third Street and he was doing whatever straight jobs he could find. Manual labor, construction, driving a delivery truck. The same kind of working-stiff jobs everyone else in their neighborhood did.

"You don't look retired to me. You look busier than ever, getting up early every morning to drive that truck around."

"It's called working for a living. You should give it a try. Just once in your life."

"You have to hear me out," Finn said. "This is a onetime thing and then you're set."

"No."

"You take care of your family. You buy a nicer house. You change your whole life."

"I said no."

"Don't you get it, Nickie? This is your walkaway job. A half million dollars for one day's work."

That stopped Mason dead.

"Half a million split four ways," Finn said. "There's a shipment coming in through the harbor."

"A shipment of what?"

"Shipment of I don't know and I don't care. That's not the point. The point is, someone needs four men to unload it and then drive two trucks to Detroit. That's all we're doing and then taking half a million for our trouble. Hop on a bus back home and have a fucking party."

"Who are the four?"

"You and me and Eddie. And this other guy."

"What other guy?"

"This guy I met in custody."

"An ex-con."

"He's not an ex-con. He never went away. He was in the holding cell when I got picked up again. They had to let us both go the next morning. But we're talking and he asks me if I knew two other good men."

"Answer's still no," Mason said. "I've got too much to lose."

"I know that, Nickie. You do this for them. Your family. Think of what that money could do for you guys."

"Find somebody else."

"Just meet him," Finn said. "What would it hurt? Meet the man and hear what he has to say. If you don't like it, you leave."

Mason thought about it. "What's this guy's name?"

"McManus. Jimmy McManus."

Jimmy fucking McManus. That was the moment. Five and a half years ago. Mason could have walked away right then. He never would have met the man. He never would have made the biggest mistake of his life.

Mason wouldn't have gone to prison. Finn wouldn't have gone into a cheap pine box.

As he drove through his old neighborhood, Mason was replaying that day, and a thousand others, in his head. He was recognizing every tree and every fire hydrant. Every narrow lot with every house packed in tight with only inches between them. This place where everyone lived on top of one another, where there were no secrets, where outsiders were noticed immediately and watched until they were gone.

Mason drove down one block, threading his way through the cars that lined each side of the street. He came to a stop sign, then drove down another block. Then he was there.

Five years after leaving this house, Nick Mason was back, sitting at the wheel of a restored 1968 Mustang, a car more expensive than any car he'd ever stolen. A car more expensive than all the cars he'd ever owned himself put together. Hell, maybe more than he paid for this house back when he actually lived here.

He sat there and watched the summer day go by on his old block. A woman was walking a dog. Across the street, a little girl was riding a bicycle. She must have been about five or six. She was good at riding her bike. It made Mason remember the week Adriana learned to ride without training wheels. He looked out the car window at the exact spot where she fell. *Right there.* She got up and fell again in the same spot. She got back up and this time she kept going.

The ghost of his former life, right here in front of him, playing across four seasons. Hanging the Christmas lights, building a snowman. That almost level front porch that he built with his own hands.

Actually, the porch looked dead true. It had a natural stain before. Now it was painted bright white.

The front door to the house opened. A man came out onto the porch. A stranger. For one instant, Mason was already reaching for the car door, getting ready to confront the man. What are you doing in my house? Where's my wife and daughter?

But then the man called to the girl who was riding the bike. This man had fixed his front porch and had painted it. God knows what else he'd done to the place. But he has every right, Mason said to himself, because he lives here. Because this is his house.

Mason was startled by the sudden rapping on his window. He looked up and saw a man standing there by the driver's-side door. Mason used the old-school 1968 crank to slide his window down. When he looked up, he saw a familiar face.

Quintero.

"The fuck you doing here?" Mason said. "Are you following me?"

Quintero didn't speak. He handed Mason a piece of paper. Mason took it from him.

"What is this?" Mason said.

"What you're looking for."

A car started honking behind them. Quintero's Escalade was double-parked, blocking the entire street. Quintero gave the driver a look and the honking stopped. Only then did he return to his vehicle. He got in and drove off.

Mason unfolded the paper. There was an address written down. In Elmhurst, of all places.

Elmhurst?

He looked out his windshield at the Escalade's brake lights as the vehicle slowed at the stop sign, then disappeared down the street.

You know where they live, he said to himself. I shouldn't be so surprised, but you know where Gina lives. You know where my daughter lives.

The man standing on his front porch was eyeing him now. Mason couldn't blame him. A strange man in a strange car parked on his street. Then a gangbanger pulls up behind him in a gangbanger Escalade, blocking the whole street. If it were Mason on the porch, he'd already be wandering down to the street for a little chat. *Can I help you out, friend? Are you lost, buddy?*

Mason pulled away from the curb. When he got to the stop sign, he saw two kids in an old beater slowing down at the intersection, checking out the black vintage Mustang. They were eighteen years old, maybe nineteen. Tough Irish kids like a thousand others Mason grew up with. Like Eddie, like Finn. Like himself. Mason could see their eyes following the smooth lines of the car, then coming up to meet his.

He could tell what they were thinking. This guy must have taken the wrong turn on the expressway and found himself on the wrong street. *You have no business driving down this street,* those eyes said to him. *This is our neighborhood. You do not belong here.*

Looking back at them, Mason wondered which one of these kids would fuck up his life as badly as he had himself. Maybe both of them.

He hit the gas and headed to Elmhurst.

Detective Frank Sandoval had worked a hundred brutal homicides with his old partner Gary Higgins, but he'd never seen fear on the man's face. Not once.

Until today.

Sandoval had come up here to this little inland lake west of Kenosha, Wisconsin, not knowing if he'd found the right place until he had walked around to the lake side of the house and had seen the old Crown Vic, pulled around back so it couldn't be seen from the road. The sun was going down by then. Sandoval held up a hand to shield his eyes and saw the silhouette on the dock. He walked down the trail, moving fast. Sandoval was built short and compact, with Latin features, and dark piercing eyes that took in every detail around him. He was a man doing the one job in the world that could contain all of his energy.

When Sandoval was close enough, the silhouette resolved into a man he would have recognized anywhere. Late fifties, with wide shoulders and not much hair left on his head. One of the most decorated homicide detectives in the city, with a list of high-profile arrests that would run off the page.

Sandoval thought back to the first time he'd ever seen this man. It was his first day as a detective at Area Central Homicide. The commander had partnered him with Gary Higgins. First thing Higgins told him was shut up and listen. Keep your eyes open and watch me. Learn how this really works before you start thinking you know something.

It was a six-man team, working under one sergeant. It didn't take long for Sandoval to see how the other men took their lead from Higgins. Always the first man through the door. Knew when to lean on people and when to hang back. Knew which questions to ask and the right time to ask them. If Higgins hadn't been a cop, he would have probably been a professor of human psychology.

He did it hard. He did it right. Most of all, he did it clean.

Everything Sandoval knew about being a good homicide detective, about being a good cop, he learned from Gary Higgins. But now, as he looked down the dock, he saw his old partner sitting motionless on a folding chair between the last two pilings. The water was as flat and still as a mirror. When Sandoval took one step onto the dock, Higgins turned around quickly. The surprise on his face gave way to anger.

"Whatever answers you thought you might be getting on the drive up here," Higgins said, "you can forget it. You'll get nothing from me."

"We have to talk, Gary."

Higgins stood up and came down the dock toward Sandoval. He'd seen this man just a few weeks ago. How could he be so much thinner? He looked like a man who'd aged ten years.

"Who'm I talking to?" Higgins said as he grabbed Sandoval by the shoulders and began to pat him down. "Who else is listening?"

"Take your fucking hands off me," Sandoval said, pushing him away. "You think I'd come here *wired*?"

He studied Higgins's face. The lines around his mouth, the dark bags under his eyes. From two feet away, he could smell the alcohol on his breath.

"Raise your arms," Higgins said.

"Fuck you. I'm not wearing a wire."

"How did you find me?"

"I remembered you talking about this place," Sandoval said. "It's still in your father-in-law's name, so I came up here and took a shot."

"Who else knows you're here?"

"Nobody. I came on my own."

"You should have stayed in Chicago, Frank. They could have followed you. They're probably watching us right now."

Sandoval looked around at the empty lake. There were other houses all along the shoreline, but he couldn't see another soul. "Jesus," he said. "What's the matter with you?"

Sandoval watched Higgins, waiting for the rest of his old partner to come back. The man who could never stop talking when they were on the job.

"I was your partner for six years," Sandoval finally said. "You never took money, never crossed the line. I know you're not jammed up, so you tell me what kind of deal you made to put Nick Mason back on the street."

"I got nothing for you, Frank. You're wasting your time here."

"Thirty years," Sandoval said. "You expect me to watch you throw that away, not say a fucking word? Give me a name, let me start helping you."

"You can't help me."

"Give me one name."

"I can't."

"Okay, I'll give *you* one. Darius Cole."

Higgins looked away. It was a fraction of a second, but it was all Sandoval needed to see.

"Yeah, now we're getting somewhere. Darius Cole, who happened to be in the same block with Nick Mason, down at Terre Haute. Of course, you already knew that much, right? And Mason's got what, twenty years until his first parole hearing? At least two decades before he's out, Gary. You know where he is right now?"

Higgins didn't answer.

"He's in a five-million-dollar town house in Lincoln Park. Which I'm sure is owned by guess who. I haven't dug into it yet, but I don't have to, because you know it's one shell company that owns other companies, one for the restaurant, one for the town house, and who knows what else. But if you follow the money, it all flows back to Darius Cole. So Nick Mason's out of prison and soaking in a hot tub and getting ready to do . . . what? Cole knows. Maybe *you* know. What horrible thing is he out to do, Gary? Whatever it is, you're going to be wearing it. How's that sit with you?"

Higgins looked at him.

"He killed a federal agent, Gary. Now he's out."

"We never put that gun in his hand."

"The fuck does that matter?" Sandoval said. "You know it's felony murder as long as he's there. Who cares if he pulled the trigger?"

Higgins put his hand on Sandoval's chest and drove him backward, into the piling. Sandoval felt the rough wood digging into his back.

"You think I don't know this?" Higgins said, his face two inches away. "All of this? I know what I did, Frank. I know what I fucking did. Every night, I gotta drink myself to sleep so I don't put a bullet in my head."

"We can climb out of this. Together."

"You don't know these people," Higgins said. "You don't know what they'll do to you. Is this worth your life, Frank? Your family's life? That's what the risk is here if you don't stop. You say you want the answers, but you don't. Believe me, you fucking *don't*."

Sandoval had seen enough pain in his life. How many times had he answered a homicide call, met the wife or the parents, and seen a whole world of it? More than one person should be asked to bear? You never get numb to it. It's new every time.

He was seeing that now, that same kind of pain, staring back at him through his partner's eyes.

"I'm done," Higgins said. "I'm over. You don't have to be. Go back to Chicago and forget you ever saw me."

Higgins let him go. He turned away from him and went back to the end of the dock.

"I'm not going to let this go," Sandoval said to his back.

Higgins didn't turn. He kept walking away.

"No matter what you say, Gary, I'm not going to stop."

| 6 |

Nick Mason was staring at the house that contained his wife, his daughter, and another man who was apparently fulfilling his role as a husband and father.

He was in Elmhurst, a suburb west of Chicago. He was parked on the street, looking out at a big Colonial, some shade of beige or taupe or desert sand or whatever the hell it said on the paint can. Black shutters, white trim. Everything just so. Probably three thousand square feet, with big bedrooms. It was the kind of house he would have laughed at back when he was in the market for a house himself. This *McMansion*. But if you had injected him with truth serum back then, he would have confessed his secret longing to live in a place just like this. To watch his daughter grow up here.

The big sloping front yard was a half acre of perfect grass. It would take you an hour to cut it with a push mower, but Mason knew this guy had a rider mower with the snowplow you could put on the front for a Chicago winter.

One bay in the three-car garage was open. He could see a bicycle parked inside. He could see a soccer net and a ball. Around the far edge of the house, peeking out from the backyard, a swing set. Not cheap metal, but cedar, with the clubhouse connected to it, green flags at the corners of its roof and a slide going out its door.

Mason unfolded the piece of paper and checked the address. He couldn't help wondering if Quintero had come here himself. If he had sat in his Escalade, in this exact spot, watching Mason's daughter cross the front yard. The man's eyes hidden behind his sunglasses, a ghost sitting behind the tinted windows of his big black vehicle.

Then, as if conjured from his imagination, he saw the black Escalade roll past him. Quintero had followed him all the way here. The vehicle didn't stop. It kept going down the quiet streets of Elmhurst and then disappeared after a left turn at the next corner.

Mason tightened his grip on the steering wheel. He closed his eyes for a moment. Everything is wrong, he said to himself. Every reason for getting out of prison, for signing that invisible contract with Darius Cole, it's all falling apart right in front of me.

He waited for his heart to stop pounding. Then he got out of the Mustang and walked up the driveway to the house. He went to the front door and stood there for a few seconds. Then he rang the bell. Four notes chimed from somewhere deep inside the house.

When he first met her, her name was Gina Sullivan. She had dirty-blond hair and green eyes. They were kids back then. Gina was eighteen and just out of high school. Nick was nineteen and already on his own most of the time, crashing at Eddie's house some nights, other nights at Finn's house. Other nights, wherever he landed.

There was this party they had all gone to. There were a dozen girls there, and this one in particular. Young Gina asked young Nick what he did for a living, already guessing he wasn't Sigma Phi Epsilon. Nick said he stole cars. Gina thought he was joking, so he told her to pick out a car and he'd steal it for her. She did and he did. They ended up in the backseat a few hours later. Not long after that, Gina confessed to him that the car he had stolen was her father's.

Gina went away to Purdue University that fall. When she came back, they picked right up where they had left off. She went away again that next fall, but only lasted another semester and came back to the family home up on the north end of Canaryville. After getting thrown out of the house, she lived with relatives for a while and in the midst of all that she broke up with Nick, then they were back together, then they broke up again. He was past auto theft and on to high-end work by then. Nick had written his rules, a whole set of them, refined through experience, and by learning from Finn's mistakes.

Gina had one rule for Nick. The only rule she needed. *The straight life with me or the life you're living without me.*

Nick chose life with Gina Sullivan. Because nobody on planet Earth could ever push his buttons like this woman could. Nobody could make him happier. Nobody could make him crazier. Even when he was trying to settle down. Trying to be a normal working stiff. Even then, maybe it was still more crazy than good most of the time.

But when it was good, man, it was fucking great.

They got married. They bought the house on Forty-third Street. They had a daughter. Nick kept his promise.

Until the harbor job.

Five years and a month later, he was standing at her door, waiting for someone to open it. He was starting to think nobody was home.

Then the door was pulled open and Gina looked out at him.

She hadn't changed. Not really. It was the same dirty-blond hair, even if she had it cut at an expensive salon. They were the same green eyes. Mason saw the spark of recognition in those eyes just for a fraction of a second. That old fire that had burned so bright between them. But then it was gone just as quickly.

"What the hell are you doing here?" She came out onto the porch and looked up and down the street like her neighbors would all be out in their yards, watching them.

Mason had seven or eight questions to ask her. He couldn't decide which one should come first.

"You're supposed to be in prison," she said. As soon as those words were in the air, she covered her mouth. "My God, you escaped! Then you came *here*?"

"No," Mason said, reaching out to her with one hand.

"Get away from me," she said, taking a step backward.

"I didn't escape," he said. "Will you fucking listen to me? I got out yesterday."

"That's not possible. You're in for another twenty years. At least."

"The conviction was overturned. They had to let me go. I swear, Gina, I'm telling you the truth."

He was watching her as she talked. The movements of her mouth. He could practically feel the heat of her body. He wanted to grab her, wrap her around himself.

God, he wanted that so bad.

"That's bullshit, Nick. Nobody told me anything about letting you go."

"They didn't have to. I'm not out on parole. I walked out of there a free man. They said if anybody else needed to know about it, it was up to me to tell them."

"Then how come you didn't tell me?"

"Here I am," Mason said. "Now you know."

She looked away from him, rubbing her forehead. "I don't get it," she said. "I mean, wait. Just stop it. This isn't happening. There's no way they overturned your conviction."

"Clean record," he said. "Like it never happened. I even have a letter of apology from the prosecutor. You want to see it?"

She turned and looked at him again. "Nick, if this is really true..."

"You never came," he said. "Not once."

"Nick..."

Five years, he thought. Five fucking years to finally say that to her.

An inmate at Terre Haute is allowed seven visits per month. He gets three hundred minutes of phone time. So out of a possible four hundred and twenty visits, Gina had used exactly zero. Out of a possible eighteen thousand minutes of phone time, zero.

Mason had tried calling her. He had written to her. It wouldn't have been that hard for her to drive down there. Bring Adriana, sit in the visiting room for a few minutes. Just let him see their faces, say a few words to them.

Even a quick phone call. Five fucking minutes.

It would have given him so much. But it never happened.

"Not once, Gina. No visits, no calls, no letters. Just *nothing*. Like I was dead and gone."

"I did what I thought I had to do, Nick. For Adriana."

"Where is she?"

"She's at practice," Gina said. "With Brad."

Mason worked over the name in his head for a moment. Brad. Bradley. He wasn't sure which was worse. "Are you two..."

"We got married, yes."

Mason felt those words washing over him. He knew Gina had divorced him. That was the one small bit of contact he'd gotten from her—or, rather, from her lawyer—seeing those papers come through and having to sit there in his prison cell and sign them.

But now, he said to himself, she's living in this house. And, of course, she's remarried. She stood in front of a judge and said all the words and she lives here with her new husband and is going to bed with him every fucking night.

Somehow it wasn't really true until this second. When she said those words.

Cole must have known this, he said to himself. He made this deal with me, knowing I would try to get this part of my life back. Something that could never happen.

"Okay," Mason said, measuring his words, "so my daughter is at practice with your new husband, Brad. What kind of practice?"

"Nick..."

"When will she be back?"

"Why are you asking me that?"

"Because I want to see her."

"Listen to me," she said. "Think about what you're asking me here. Please, Nick, think about it. Your daughter's in a good place. She goes to a great school. She has a great life. The life we both wanted for her, remember? She's got that now. And you're going to come around here, straight out of prison, and mess that up?"

"You don't get to pick your parents, Gina. She got *me*. And I'm not leaving until I see her."

"So how exactly do you think this is going to work? Are you going to come visit her every weekend? Have cookouts with us in the back-yard? Are you going to come with us to the parent-teacher conferences? Or career day at the school, maybe? 'Hi, this is my dad. He's going to tell you how to steal a car.' Is that how you think this is going to work, Nick?"

Mason listened to her. He was holding on to himself, keeping his cool. He knew making a big scene here wouldn't help anything. But, God damn, even now she could still push his buttons. "You never brought her to see me," Nick said. "My own daughter. Not one time in five years."

"Because you broke your promise," she said. Her voice was low, barely above a whisper. "Because you're a criminal and you always will be. No matter what your piece of paper says."

She stopped to wipe her eyes.

"I bet on you," she said. "I bet everything I had on you. Look what I got. The best thing you can do for me, and for your daughter, is to just stay away."

It hurt him to hear it. He could see it hurt her just as much to say it. He was trying to think of something to say right back, something to convince her that she had it all wrong. That he really was innocent and never should have been in prison in the first place. But the truth was, another man had made his conviction disappear, and, without him, Mason would still be in a prison cell.

There was nothing Mason could say to her. Not one word.

Gina was crying. She couldn't even look at him anymore.

She reached out to touch his chest. One touch. For one second. All of the years they had spent together, the fighting, the making up, the sitting on a porch at night. All of the years trying to make a life. After everything, this was all she had for him now.

She pulled away from him, went back in the house, and shut the door.

| 7 |

Darius Cole was born on the streets of Englewood. In the
suburbs, you inherit wealth. In Englewood, depending on which
block you live on, and which side of the street, you inherit a gang's
colors. By the time he was thirteen, he was on a corner. This was
back in the 1970s, when the city saw a thousand homicides every
year.

Young Darius was given a bag of money one day. Take this to the
laundry, he was told. If there's one dollar missing, we'll find out in
two minutes. You'll be dead in three.

He took the money to the laundry—actually, it was a laundromat—and that's where he met the man who kept a little office in the
back of the place. It was one of several cash-based businesses the
man owned all over the city. Laundromats, car washes, restaurants.
Anyplace that handled a lot of bills, and even loose change. The man
would take money from guys like Darius Cole and he'd mix it up
with the cash from the businesses and like some kind of magic trick
he'd somehow make it all come out clean.

The man at the laundromat told Darius Cole that this was a trick invented in Chicago, by Al Capone, back in the Prohibition days. Later, Cole learned about Meyer Lansky, the criminal mastermind and financial genius who was a hell of a lot smarter than Capone. Lansky financed the National Crime Syndicate, held points in every casino from Vegas to London, and transferred every dollar he made to his own personal bank in Switzerland. He never spent one day in prison.

Cole didn't want to be just another kid working a corner. He wanted to be the black Meyer Lansky. No more drug addicts. No more gunfights on the streets. If you clean the money, you get clean yourself. You wear a suit like a legitimate businessman. Fuck that, you *are* a legitimate businessman.

By the time he was twenty, Cole had a minority share in a dozen restaurants. In barbershops. In car washes. Even a few laundromats. Any business that handled cash, with minimal recordkeeping, Cole wanted a piece of it. He'd mix in drug money with the cash proceeds and deposit it all as legitimate income.

The entire time, he kept a low profile. No flash. He paid federal agents to keep him out of the files. FBI, DEA, ATF, IRS, even Interpol. Cole stayed invisible.

He bought more businesses all over the country. Better restaurants, nightclubs. If the bartender would take a hundred-dollar bill from you without blinking, Cole wanted to meet the owner.

He got so good at it, he started handling other people's money. Not from rival gangs, of course. Some lines don't get crossed. But there were plenty of other criminal enterprises with money that needed cleaning. He didn't get nervous about taking that money from white men in suits and giving most of it back to them. In fact, he would use the opportunity to learn everything he could about their operations, every last detail, until he could take over from the inside, like a Greek soldier from a Trojan horse, eliminating anyone who dared stand in his way.

By the time he was thirty, Cole had grown smarter and even more powerful. He expanded overseas, first in the Cayman Islands, then in Mexico, Brazil, Russia, Poland, Belarus—any country with soft banking laws. He always kept the money moving, more and more of it, faster and faster, in amounts small enough to avoid suspicion, but times a hundred, then a thousand, using accounts in other people's names. People he could trust. People who knew the penalty for betraying him. The money would be round-tripped from one "smurf" account to another, Kraków to Rio to Jakarta, before coming back to Chicago.

When the time was right, he moved back into the drug business, but he did it the smart way, on the wholesale end. There was already a direct pipeline from the Mexican cartels to Chicago—Cole took this over and made life easier for the Mexicans by giving them one single contact to work with. Then he supplied the product to high-level dealers who would move it throughout the entire Midwest. So instead of having a thousand customers, he had twenty or thirty, all men he could trust. This was how he managed the risk and maximized the revenue. Then he channeled that money into more and more legitimate businesses.

He hired the best accountants. He hired the best attorneys. And he paid off the dirtiest cops. He grew his business into an empire.

Most cops know how to follow criminals. Only a select few of them are good at following money. Cole stayed ahead of them for years until they finally brought him down on a federal RICO case. He'd been here in Terre Haute ever since.

It was a story Mason never thought he'd hear. Not from Darius

Cole himself. He never thought he'd make a second trip to the Secure Housing Unit. Or that the third trip would be permanent.

The same two men came to get him that day. Mason ignored the
stares and followed them out of the cellblock. As he walked between
them, he had time to think it over. It must have been a hell of a first
conversation or there wouldn't be a second. But what did Cole really
want from him? If he wanted Mason's ticket punched, that would
have happened already. Out in the yard or in the cafeteria. You
wouldn't walk the man right to your cell.

When he got there, Cole was sitting at his desk with his back to
him. He turned and gave Mason a quick nod. He was wearing the
same rimless reading glasses that made him look like a prison librarian.

"Why am I back here?" Mason said.

Cole turned in his chair and took off the glasses. He didn't look
like a librarian anymore. "You're back here," he said, "because you
got something I wanna know more about."

"Look, Mr. Cole..."

"Read up on you," Cole said. "Got some questions."

Cole reached behind him and grabbed a folder from the desk. As
he opened it, Mason saw his own mug shot from four years ago on
the top page. This was his criminal file.

"You're dialed in," Mason said. "You've got this whole place wired.
Is there anything the guards *won't* bring you?"

"You're a Canaryville boy," Cole said, putting his reading glasses
back on and starting to flip through the pages. "'Father unknown.'"

Mason didn't respond to that. He didn't like seeing this man
reading through his file, but once again figured it was probably a
great time to keep his mouth shut.

"Tough way to start your life," Cole said. "Don't learn how to be a man, sometimes, until it's too late. You put work in on the streets for over fifteen years, never spent more than one night locked up."

Mason watched Cole flip back to the first page.

"'Possession of a stolen vehicle,'" he said, reading from the page. "Got a few of them here. You work for one shop? Freelance? How'd that work?"

"Whoever paid. I moved around."

"'Possession of burglary tools'? Man's branching out. But that one got dropped, too. Nothing ever sticks to you."

Cole kept reading the file.

"You work alone sometimes," Cole said, flipping to the next page. "Sometimes with a crew. All over the city. Sometimes you go in hard. Sometimes on the sly."

He flipped back to the first page.

"Thirty years without going down. But then they get you and you don't just go down, you go down *hard*. Some men wouldn't handle that so well."

"This is starting to sound like a job interview," Mason said.

"That's exactly what this is."

The two men looked each other in the eye. Cole waited for Mason to say something.

"I handled it," Mason said. "What choice did I have?"

"You always got a choice, Nick. Even here, *you always got a choice*. Like when I wanted to meet you."

"Look, if we're gonna do this again..."

"How come you didn't give them up?" Cole said. "Twenty-five-to-life, you're looking at. Hard federal time, Nick. But you keep your mouth shut."

There was a long silence, finally broken when two inmates walked by in the hallway outside Cole's cell. Their conversation ended as soon as they saw the look on the bodyguards' faces, and the two men moved quickly away.

"One of your men got killed that night," Cole said, looking back down at the papers. "Finn O'Malley. He a friend of yours?"

"Yes."

"Two other men got away. Were they friends, too?"

"One was a friend. The other was a piece of shit."

"But you didn't turn on either of them."

"I turn on the piece of shit, he turns on my friend. I'm still heading down here, either way. No matter what I did."

"You had a wife," Cole said, looking at the sheet again. "And a daughter."

"I'm outta here," Mason said.

"You don't talk about them. They don't belong in this place, right?" Cole leaned forward and studied Mason carefully for a long time. "What happens when they come to visit you?"

Mason looked away without answering. Cole shuffled through the papers again and found something interesting on one of the last pages.

"They don't," Cole said. "Ever. So you don't talk about them. It's, like, a rule you made up. To keep your mind right."

Mason stared at Cole. He'd never mentioned his rules to anyone in here. It was an essential part of him that nobody else had ever seen.

"That's right, Nick. You know what I'm talking about. You wanna hear one of my rules?"

Mason didn't respond.

"I'm here for two lifetimes, Nick. But just because I eat here and I sleep here, does that mean I *live* here? Fuck that. I'm still back in Chicago, where I belong. Most guys hear that, they think I'm crazy. But maybe you understand what I'm saying."

Mason looked at one bodyguard, then the other, wondering if they had to hear this bullshit every day.

"It's a state of mind," Cole said, tapping his temple with one index finger. "You look at it right, it's just a problem of geography."

A problem of geography, Nick thought. The man actually just said that.

"That's just one of my rules," Cole said. He picked up the file and opened it again. "I already know a couple of yours. Don't sell out your friends. Keep everything separate. Keep your family inside you. I'm seeing a picture here."

"You hear my name," Mason said. "Now you read a file. And you think you know me?"

"I want to know what's *not* in the file."

"I do my time," Mason said. "I mind my own business. I don't fuck with people and people don't fuck with me. I don't need to make friends here. When you make a friend, that man's enemies become your enemies. I don't need that."

Cole listened to him carefully, slowly nodding his head.

"That doesn't mean I don't look out for people," Mason went on. "I look out for them, they look out for me. That's how you survive. But I don't owe them anything else. I don't belong to anybody in this prison, Mr. Cole. And even though I can see you've got lots of power here and you can drag me down here anytime you want, I'm not going to belong to you, either. Nobody owns me."

Cole kept looking at him, still nodding his head.

"You don't always have to be that way," he finally said. "People in my neighborhood, they have a problem, they don't call nine-one-one. They call me. I'm the police, the fireman, and the judge."

"Yeah, that's *your* neighborhood. It's not mine."

Cole smiled at that. "How long you been here, Nick?"

"You saw the file. Four years."

"Four years down, twenty-one to go if you're lucky. So we got time to get to know each other. My boys will help you pack your stuff."

"Excuse me?"

"You're coming to SHU, Nick. Better food, better equipment . . . You'll like it here."

"What if I say no?"

"It's already done," Cole said.

| 8 |

Mason left Elmhurst and gunned the Mustang down
North Avenue, driving like a man with no family to live for.

He blew through every yellow light, made one turn and then another, with no idea where he was going. Finally, he stopped at a bar on a street he didn't know. In a part of the West Side he'd never seen before. It was a building made of concrete with glass blocks rounding off the corners. No sign. No name. An anonymous place for the local daily drinkers who all knew the bartender and one another. Mason opened the door and stepped inside into the darkness, feeling the cold blast from the A/C.

He went to the bar, put down a twenty, and told the man to line them up. There was another man drinking at the other end of the bar. Another two men in one of the booths. A television was on over the bar, but the sound was off. A half-dozen backlit beer signs glowed on the walls.

Mason downed the first shot of rail whiskey without even tasting

THE SECOND LIFE OF NICK MASON

it. It burned halfway down his throat. He drained another before easing up and taking a long breath.

"What did you expect?" he said to himself loud enough for the man at the end of the bar to look up at him. "What did you really think was going to happen?"

Mason picked up the third glass and weighed it in his hand. He looked at the cheap, watered-down whiskey and then threw it back.

Mason thought about all the guys he'd met inside, guys who'd been there for big chunks of their lives. He'd overhear them talking to one another, how life was going to be when they get out, how they got this woman out there, their old girlfriend from high school, hottest thing on two legs back then. They're gonna get out, go find her, have some fun for a while, but then make it real. Get married, have a family. Make up for lost time. This whole picture they create, lying in their cells at night, staring up at the ceiling. Mason would hear them talking about it at the lunch table, during work detail, whenever they had a few minutes and a sympathetic ear, and he'd think some of these poor bastards in here have no idea how life really works. That girl from high school? Probably married and already has three kids. Or something a lot worse, depending on the neighborhood. Dead and gone. Or maybe even in the women's penitentiary herself. No matter what, she sure as fuck wouldn't remember some loser boyfriend from high school who went away all those years ago. You go find her, pal, assuming she's alive. See how that little reunion turns out.

But Mason had to ask himself how his expectations were any different. Maybe it was only five years, but did it turn out any better? Getting married, having a kid together, it didn't mean shit in the end. The Earth turns and everybody moves on with their lives.

Everybody forgets you.

I didn't even see her, he said to himself. I didn't even get to see what my own daughter looks like now.

"Line 'em up again," he said to the bartender.

"Hope you're not driving," the man said.

"Pour me a real drink, I might have a problem."

"Seriously, friend..."

"I am not your friend," Mason said. He was already adding it up in his head—two behind him, one to his left, this clown in front of him. If they all wanted to give him a problem at once, it might get interesting.

"Maybe you should leave," the bartender said. "We don't need trouble here."

Mason remembered what Quintero had said to him about what would happen if he got into trouble. Not even twenty-four hours had passed.

Mason waited a few more beats. Then he got up and left.

He stood on the sidewalk for a moment, blinded by the setting sun. The world became clear again and he went to the parking lot. He got in the Mustang, started it, put it in reverse, and pointed it at the street. A man walking by chose that moment to stop directly in front of his car, blocking the exit. He was dressed in black, head to toe, his shirt tight enough to show off his biceps. He had gold chains around his neck and a pair of screw-you mirrored sunglasses to complete the look.

"All right, auto show's over," Mason said out loud. He didn't bother cranking down the window. "You got your look, now get your ass out of the way."

The man didn't move. Mason revved the engine.

"I will seriously run you over," he said. "Today is not the day to fuck with me."

The man stepped aside finally. As he barreled out of the parking lot, Mason looked up and saw the man taking off his sunglasses. He saw the man's face for one fraction of a second. Full lips, crooked nose, hair thinning on top yet somehow the rest of it tied back in a ponytail.

Their eyes met. A spark of recognition.

Mason was a hundred yards down the street when it hit him. That was Jimmy McManus.

Mason doubled back in the black Mustang to the same parking lot. He even got out and went inside the bar, hoping that McManus really was a regular there.

The bartender was yelling something at him as he walked back into the place, but Mason didn't hear a word. He scanned the room for McManus.

He wasn't there.

Mason got back in the car and drove across town. Seeing that man, at least, was a wake-up call. There was no time to feel sorry for himself. He had bigger problems.

He wasn't going to get Gina back. He had to accept that. Even seeing his own daughter was going to be a lot harder than he ever could have imagined. But he still had a deal to live up to. He still had a job to do. He had to be ready for that phone to ring even if he had no idea what would happen next.

He took out the cell phone and put it on the seat next to him. I don't even know what the ringtone sounds like, he said to himself.

The next morning, he would find out.

| 9 |

Detective Sandoval's hunt for Nick Mason had brought
him to one of the most expensive streets in Chicago. Sandoval
parked a few doors down from the town house and double-checked
the address. Lincoln Park fucking West, he said to himself. With the
park right across the street. The gardens, the conservatory, the zoo.
A great view of Lake Michigan. This is the place. This is where Nick
Mason lives now.

Sandoval remembered Mason's last address. Or rather his last
address before USP Terre Haute. It was a little shitbox in Canaryville, one of those houses they built right on top of one another
with barely enough room to walk between them. Forty-third Street,
if his memory was right. He'd seen it a few days after that night at
the harbor. He'd just recently been partnered with Higgins back
then, still getting the hang of the guy. Higgins was at the peak of his
career, with a winning streak of big busts that would have made
most cops insufferable. But Higgins wore his success well, with just
enough self-confidence to believe he could solve any murder in the

city. That's how they ended up on the Sean Wright case. It was a "heater case," with a mandate from the superintendent's office. A federal agent had been killed. They needed to solve it and solve it quickly.

They started with the one dead suspect, a man from Canaryville named Finn O'Malley. A perfect name, Sandoval thought, for a mick from that part of town. O'Malley had a long record of minor incidents, some pickups on more serious charges that never went anywhere, until an aggravated assault on a police officer put him away for eighteen months. They went to O'Malley's last-known residence and asked around. They got nothing. Sandoval was ready to take it personally, all the locals closing ranks on him. But Higgins kept his cool and dragged him back to the station and they spent a full day going through old arrest records. If they couldn't find any known associates who also went away to prison, they could at least find some other men O'Malley might have been picked up with even if everybody eventually walked.

That's how they came up with two more names. Eddie Callahan and Nick Mason. They'd been picked up together and then released, on two separate occasions, a few years apart. A long-standing relationship.

Sandoval and Higgins went out looking for both men. They found them in Canaryville—Eddie Callahan at his fiancée's apartment and Nick Mason at the house he shared with his wife and young daughter. Both men denied any involvement in the harbor job. Both men claimed they had been straight for years. Both men admitted that they had seen Finn O'Malley at Murphy's bar on the night in question but that he had left the bar long before Callahan and Mason went home.

The two detectives checked out their story at the bar. The bartender on duty that night confirmed that O'Malley had been there, had left early, and that Callahan and Mason had stayed.

"You trust that guy?" Sandoval said to Higgins as they walked back to their car. "Who's the guy who killed Lincoln? John Wilkes Booth? If he's a Canaryville guy, this bartender's fucking great-grandfather swears Booth was at the bar all night. Never went near that theater."

"Went deep for that one," Higgins said.

"Am I wrong?"

"You're not wrong."

The next day, a stolen car was found in a parking lot a mile down the road. The blood was tested and found to be consistent with Finn O'Malley's.

"Somebody brought that blood home," Higgins said.

"Only been a few days," Sandoval said. "If either guy's in his own car that night..."

Higgins looked at his partner. They both knew what would happen next. Warrants were served. The cars were impounded. In Mason's car, they ended up finding trace amounts of Finn O'Malley's blood on the right armrest of the driver's seat. Callahan's car was clean.

When Mason was brought in, Sandoval and Higgins sat there in the interview room for a while. Higgins had already told Sandoval to do the talking. He had a gut feeling that Mason wouldn't say a word to either one of them, but at least Sandoval was the same age. He might have a slightly better shot at him.

Sandoval kept watching Mason, waiting for the pressure to build. For most guys, it doesn't take long. You just have to sit there and wait for it to become real to him.

I'm sitting in a room with two cops, the guy will say to himself. There can only be one reason for that. They've got me nailed.

But Sandoval wasn't seeing this on Mason yet. All the signs you look for. The way the eyes start moving around. Looking toward the door. Thinking about what you can say that will get you out of the room. Never mind where I go next, just get me the fuck out of here.

The hands coming together. The man instinctively protecting himself. Closing himself into a ball.

Or the legs starting to shake under the table. All that tension, it has to go somewhere. But no, not this guy. He wasn't giving them anything.

Not yet.

"Canaryville kid," Sandoval said, finally breaking the silence. "You go to Saint Gabriel's?"

Mason said nothing.

"Bet you're a Sox fan, too. I'm from Avondale, been a Cubs fan my whole life."

Mason stared past them at a spot on the wall.

"You go to Tilden High School? We played basketball there."

Mason kept staring at the wall.

"We saw your house there on Forty-third, Nick. Do a lot of work to the place? Me, I do all the painting at my house." He was still living with his wife and kids at that time and he really did do all of the painting. It wasn't a lie.

"Here's the thing," Sandoval went on. "I try to be clean, but painting's a fucking mess, you know? You do the painting at your house?"

Mason stayed silent.

"When I'm done," Sandoval said, "I got paint all over myself. My arms, in my hair. My face. So I go to the sink and I wash up and I think I'm nice and clean. Until my wife finds me and says, 'Hey, genius, what's this?' And she points to my elbows."

Sandoval stood up and came around to Mason's side of the table. He leaned close to Mason and showed him his right elbow.

"Right here," he said. "I can't see it when I'm washing. You know what I'm saying? So I miss it every time, Nick. Every single goddamned time. You think I'd know by now. Wash your elbows, Frank. And if I'm dumb enough to get in the car, what happens next?"

Sandoval put his arm down as if resting it on an armrest.

"Leather, you got a shot at cleaning that off. But I don't got leather seats, Nick. Can't afford it. I got cloth."

He got close this time. Just a few inches from Mason's ear. "Just like you."

They tried to convince Mason to turn on Eddie Callahan. They knew Callahan was involved. Confirming that fact would just be a formality. They also tried to convince Mason to give them the identity of the fourth man. Everything would go a lot easier, they told him, if he would just cooperate. Otherwise, the prosecutor would go for the max. It was a dead DEA agent, so everyone was out for blood. Mason shouldn't have to take it all alone.

Mason kept his mouth shut.

Even though Sandoval and Higgins made the arrest, the feds ultimately took the case away because it was a DEA agent who'd been killed. Neither man cared. What mattered was that Nick Mason drew twenty-five-to-life and went to Terre Haute.

But now, five years later, *sixty fucking months later,* Detective Sandoval was sitting here in his car waiting for Nick Mason to show up, a man who was free only because his old partner stood up in court and told the judge that he had taken blood evidence from the

THE SECOND LIFE OF NICK MASON

scene, brought it with him, carried it around for hours—*for hours*—then found some way to plant it in Nick Mason's car.

That's the way it was written. That was the official fucking record. And his partner's life was destroyed.

He felt his cell phone buzzing in his pocket. He took it out and read the text. It was Sean Wright's wife, Elizabeth, widow of a dead federal agent, single mother trying to raise two kids on her own, asking if the two families would still be getting together that weekend.

Sandoval texted back a reply. *Yes, looking forward to it.* Which was true. It was his one chance to see his own kids that week. His one chance to pretend the job hadn't cost him everything else in his life.

He took one more look at Nick Mason's new address. Then he drove away.

| 10 |

When the call Mason had been dreading finally came, he knew his life would never be the same. He just didn't know exactly what Darius Cole had in store for him.

The sun was just coming up as Mason left the car on Columbus Drive and walked toward Grant Park. He'd never seen the park this empty.

He saw Quintero standing on the lake side of the fountain. Lake Shore Drive ran behind him, and beyond that were a hundred tarp-covered sailboats all anchored in the open water. The breakwater formed a straight line behind the boats and then beyond that was the rumor of Lake Michigan, disappearing into the morning fog. The rising sun started to break through, painting the city behind them in brilliant hues of gold and blue.

Mason hesitated for a moment, looking up at the buildings, the reflections so bright they made his eyes hurt. He remembered the morning he and Gina flew back home from their honeymoon in Las Vegas, an overnight flight that circled the city and came around from the east just as the sun was coming up behind them. Gina was in the window seat and she grabbed Nick's arm tightly as the plane banked. He assumed it was her usual airplane jitters, but she gestured for him to look out the window. He pressed his face close to hers and saw that the city of Chicago was completely obscured by the morning clouds and yet somehow the reflection was still cast perfectly against the surface of the lake.

It was an amazing sight, the upside-down image of this city they both knew so well, where they'd try to find a real life together. So long ago, it seemed, even though barely a decade had passed. Now Mason walked here on the shore of the same lake, the same city behind him, glowing with the same colors, and yet everything else had been changed forever.

It was his own life that was upside down.

As he got closer, he saw that Quintero was wearing a black sweatshirt this morning. None of his tattoos were visible. His eyes were hidden behind dark sunglasses. He looked at his watch.

"I said five thirty," he said.

"I've got five thirty-two."

"That's not five thirty."

Mason looked out at the boats. "Which one of these is Cole's?"

"How about we make a rule here? Don't say his name out loud when we're on the street."

"Fine," Mason said. "I know all about rules."

"We both know who we're talking about. You make it a habit, then you don't fuck up when it really matters."

"Speaking of habits," Mason said, "how much time are you going to spend following me around?"

"I knew you'd be looking for your ex-wife and your daughter."

"Let me make this real clear," Mason said. "My ex-wife and my daughter have nothing to do with this. With *any* of this. To you, they don't exist."

"That's not how this works, Mason. You made this deal. You think you get to make the rules now? I'll go move into their fucking guest room if I want to."

Mason stood there for a moment, staring the man down. Then Quintero handed him a motel room key on an old-fashioned plastic key fob. The name and address of the motel was written on one side along with the room number: 102. On the other side was a promise to pay the return postage if you dropped the key into any mailbox.

"The room will be empty," Quintero said. "You go there and you park in front of this room. Nowhere else. Get there at eleven thirty p.m. No earlier, no later. Go inside and you'll find everything you need in the top drawer of the nightstand. Then go around and up the stairs to Room 215. Your man will be there. Call me when you're done."

Mason took a moment to process that. "Done with what?" he said.

"You're helping him check out. What the fuck you *think* you're doing?"

This is it, Mason said to himself. I made this deal. I didn't give him any exceptions. I didn't say there are certain things I will not do.

I just said yes.

He turned to face his city one more time. Then he turned back to the man who was telling him to do the one thing he never thought he'd do.

"Why don't you do it?" Mason said. "Something tells me it wouldn't be your first."

"I'm not doing it because it's not my job to do it. It's yours. We're gonna find out just how well you can handle things."

Mason stood there looking at the key. The sun kept breaking through the morning fog, making the glass on the buildings shine brighter and brighter. It was going to be a hot day.

"One thing I've never done," Mason finally said, "my whole life."

Quintero looked him up and down. He shook his head and there was almost a smile on his face. *"No mames,"* he said.

Mason didn't know exactly what it meant, but he'd heard a Mexican in SHU use the phrase now and then. He figured it must translate to something like "No fucking way."

"I know you're here for a reason," Quintero said. "Cole doesn't make mistakes. So you better get yourself ready, *cuate.*"

Mason put the key in his pocket and walked away.

"First one's a bitch," Quintero said to his back. "Then it gets easy."

| 11 |

"What do you know about the samurai, Nick?"

The two men were walking along the perimeter of the yard. A chain-link fence ran alongside them, ten feet high and topped with razor wire that gleamed in the sunlight. Beyond that there was the other fence. More razor wire. On the issue of which side a man belonged, there would never be any doubt in his mind.

"Not much," Mason said. "Why?"

"They got this code they live by. Called *bushido*. You ever hear of that?"

"No."

"*Bushido*," Cole said. He walked slowly when he was talking. "I like that word. I can look back on things in my life now, see how important that was, having a code like that. This shit goes back a thousand years, Nick."

Mason knew how many books Cole read. Between morning roll and lunchtime, that's when any man with sense left Darius Cole alone because that was the time reserved for reading.

Cole had an account with the Book Cellar in Lincoln Square and they would send him a new box of books every Friday.

The man read at least one book a day, Nick thought, but he couldn't shake the streets of Englewood when he spoke.

"You got some of that," Cole said. "What makes you stand out around here. You got yourself some *bushido*."

This is what they did. Every day, after Cole received his afternoon visitors, this was Mason's time to listen to him. Mason didn't have to say much in return. In fact, that was probably one of the things Cole appreciated the most, Nick realized, just being able to talk to somebody who knew when to shut the fuck up and listen.

"Don't have to know the word," Cole said. "Don't have to know anything about it. That don't mean you don't have it. You remember those first couple times you came down here?"

"I remember."

"What did we talk about? The rules you got for yourself. To keep your life in order. Keep your mind right. The way you handle things around here. I see you, you got this way of moving around the three worlds in here. White, black, Latino. Whenever you gotta leave your own world, make your way in another... You don't compromise yourself. You don't give up nothing. But you don't look for trouble, neither. I know you think it's no big deal. Just one day at a time. But when I see that, I see this *bushido*, Nick. You got that shit up to your eyeballs."

Cole had been reading everything he could find about Japan lately, a place that appealed to him somehow, even if it was ten thousand miles away. Maybe that was the reason right there, the fact that it was on the other side of the world, different from this prison in southern Indiana in every way you could imagine. A place where honor meant everything, where a man would rather drive a knife into his own gut than bring shame on himself.

But Cole was just about done with the books on Japan. Mason figured he'd hear about samurai and *bushido* for a few more days and that would be the end of it.

He was coming up on one year in SHU by then. His cell mate was one of the two big bodyguards who had originally brought him over for his first visit. Mixed-race roomies were something you didn't see anywhere else in the prison. In this block, it was commonplace. Just one more thing to learn about Cole, because Cole was unquestionably the boss of this unit. And that was why this was probably the most color-blind unit of any federal penitentiary in the country.

Mason would usually have lunch at Cole's table. Afterward, Cole would receive his visitors. He would mediate disputes. He would administer justice. There would be fines levied. Or restitution paid between one inmate and another. Sometimes justice would get a little more physical. Not right there in Cole's cell, of course. It would happen later, out in the yard or while waiting in line. It would be quick and severe and there would be no doubt in anyone's mind who sanctioned it.

Everyone called him Mr. Cole. Even the guards.

Mason kept waiting for the hook. He knew there had to be something asked of him in return for this new living arrangement. For all of this deferential treatment. Just listening to the man talk about books every day couldn't be enough. It would be Mason's turn to administer the justice, to find the man out on the yard. He'd grown up on the streets of Canaryville, so he knew how to fight. But Cole never asked him to do anything else. I never had a father, Mason said to himself more than once. Maybe this is what it feels like.

A few days after that walk in the yard, Mason was sitting in his cell. It was a tough day for him, tough in a way he didn't want to admit. Just the fact that it was this date on the calendar. Cole came in and stood over him. He had that way of walking right up to a man—any man in the block—just standing in the man's space, maybe putting an arm on his shoulder. Something only he could do.

"You're thinking about her," Cole said.

Mason looked up at him.

"Your daughter's birthday."

Mason didn't even bother asking him how he knew that. He didn't bother reminding Cole about his rule, either, that he didn't talk about his family here.

"Some days are harder in here," Cole said. "Can't help that."

Then Cole did something he'd never done before. He sat down on Mason's bed, a foot away from him. Mason saw the long scar on the back of Cole's right hand. He already knew the story behind it. Cole had gone to see a girl when he was seventeen years old, but she lived in the wrong neighborhood. He was two blocks past a line he shouldn't have crossed when two white men put a knife into the back of that hand. To this day, the jagged scar would be on his mind whenever he shook a man's hand for the first time.

"I saw you talking to Shelley the other day," Cole said. "Not thinking of getting ink, are you?"

Shelley was the man with the illegal tattoo gun. He'd made it with the motor from a CD player, an empty pen barrel, and a needle made by stretching out the spring from a stapler. He used burnt shoe polish for the ink. There's probably one such man in every unit in every prison in America.

"No," Mason said.

"Today's the kinda day you might do that," Cole said. "Get your daughter's name on your arm or something."

"I'm not getting a tattoo."

"That's all you need when you get outta here," Cole said. "Cheap prison ink all under your skin, turning green. Might as well write CONVICT on your forehead."

"If you hate tattoos so much, how come you let Shelley stay in business? One word from you and he'd be shut down."

"He can ink anybody else he wants," Cole said. "Just not you."

Mason stood up. He didn't mind listening to Cole most days. But today was not most days.

"No disrespect," Mason said, "I'm taking a walk."

"Sit down, Nick. You wanna be alone, I get that. But you should be talking to me about something else."

"Like what?"

"You're ready to hear this," Cole said. "Sit the hell back down."

Mason let out a breath and sat down on the bed.

"I'm going to ask you something," Cole said. "If you could walk out of here right now, go see your daughter, what would you say to her?"

"That's not going to happen."

"I'm saying if you could, Nick. How old is she?"

"She's nine."

"Nine years old," Cole said. "She hasn't seen you since—what?—four years old."

"That's right."

"You think she remember you?"

"Why are you asking me this?"

"Other day," Cole said, "you remember, we was talking about *bushido*?"

Mason took a moment, let out another breath. "I can't do this."

"Shut up and listen to me, Nick. Something you need to hear. There's more to that code than just having your mind right. You gotta have loyalty, too. You gotta be serving something. Somebody

THE SECOND LIFE OF NICK MASON

worth giving that honor to. So you get honor back in return. You hear what I'm saying? You know what a *daimyo* is, Nick?"

"No."

"A *daimyo* is the master. A *daimyo* is the boss. If a samurai don't have a *daimyo* to serve, he's just a *rōnin*. Like a homeless man. A vagabond. Wandering around the world, begging for food. No purpose in his life. Look around you, Nick. Look at all the men in here. How many of them does that describe to you?"

"I don't know," Mason said. "Most of them."

"Most of them, yeah. How about every man in here? I hate seeing you being one of those men when you could be doing something else. Something a hell of a lot better."

"What are we talking about here?"

"You could be a samurai, Nick. That's what I'm saying. I look at you, I don't see another inmate. I see a samurai."

Mason didn't know what to say. They had passed right by the usual idle prison talk, even by Cole's standards. Now they seemed to be heading into something else.

"Mr. Cole," Nick said. "I know you pretty well by now. You're always thinking eight moves ahead of everybody else. So if you've got something in mind for me, why don't you just tell me what it is?"

"Is that where you think I'm going with this? You think I need a samurai around this place? I got plenty of men who do anything I want. All I gotta do is say the word and it's done."

"Then I don't get it," Mason said. "What do you want me to do?"

"You know how I'm always talking about this place, how do I say it, being a problem of geography?"

Mason took one look around them. The cell just big enough to fit two men, a small desk, a toilet with no privacy. Beyond that, concrete walls and a thick pane of glass. Fluorescent lights buzzing over their heads. A dozen locked doors and then the fences and a small army of armed men standing between them and the world outside this place. Yeah, Mason said to himself, just a problem of geography.

"I still *live* in Chicago," Cole said. "That's the thing you gotta understand. It's still *my town*."

Cole leaned in toward Mason as he said this. He put out one hand like he was holding the city right there for Mason to look at.

"From there," Cole said, "I can do anything, Nick. Anything I need to do. But sometimes I need a good set of eyes on the other side of these walls. A good pair of hands out there."

"You don't have anybody on the outside?"

"Oh, I got people who work for me," Cole said. "People I can trust. But I need somebody special, Nick. I need a warrior. A man who can go anywhere. Do anything. I know I got myself stuck on this word, but it's the only word that really gets at what I'm saying here. I need a *samurai*."

"I can't help you," Mason said. "Unless you want to wait twenty years."

"Fuck twenty years, Nick. Do you really want to wait that long?"

"I don't see any choice."

"Listen to me," Cole said. "There's gonna be this man someday, he'll come to this prison to do your first parole hearing. Some fat white boy, civil servant type wearing a tie and glasses. You can see him, can't you, Nick? Like he's standing right here in front of us. Wanted to be a cop maybe, couldn't cut it, so now he's a parole officer. Only way he can have any kind of power over people. But that job, even that's too hard, chasing down convicts all day, so they ask him to serve on the board and he's all over that. Sit at a table, hear a man's story, how he's changed and found Jesus and he's ready to be a productive citizen again. It's all up to him. The man on the board. And if he got himself laid that morning, he puts down a big APPROVED on the file."

Cole made a fist and stamped an imaginary file.

"Or if his kid told him to go fuck himself, he puts down a big DENIED."

He stamped again.

"That man's never gonna sit in judgment of me, Nick. That day won't come. But that man's waiting for you. He's out there right now, but you know how far away he is? That man hasn't even signed up for the job yet. Hasn't even done his two years at the community college. He's sitting in some junior high school class, looking out the window. Don't even have hair on his balls yet."

Cole stopped for a moment, shaking his head, tapping his fist on the bed.

"That's too long to wait, Nick. Too long to wait for that boy to grow up to be the motherfucker who denies your parole."

"You're telling me all this for a reason," Mason said. "What is it?"

"I'm talking about *time*, Nick. What's it worth to you? Twenty fucking years. You'll be what, fifty-five? Your daughter'll be what, almost thirty years old? You miss her growing up. Maybe she even has kids of her own by then. You miss all of that. But what if that's just one story, Nick? What if there's another story where you get yourself out of here and she's still nine years old and you got a chance to be her father again?"

Mason looked at the man sitting on the bed next to him. He still didn't know what to say and it felt like a good time to be careful about that. Because none of this was making any sense.

"Listen to me." Cole stood up. He hooked one hand behind the back of Mason's neck and twisted his head so that it was inches from his. "You need to hear every word of what I'm saying to you. Because this is how it's going to work. Those two cops who put you away? One of them's a detective, who's gonna stand up in court and swear he put that blood in your car. The whole case gonna fall apart on them. They gonna vacate the conviction, Nick. That's what they call it. And that prosecutor, he won't want nothing to do with you. He won't touch a retrial because it's all gone to shit. You walk out of here twenty years early, Nick. Do you hear me? *You walk the fuck out.* No parole. No felony record. Like it never happened."

Mason knew about prison gangs. La eMe. La Nuestra Familia. Mara Salvatrucha. He knew they had power that extended outside the prison walls. He knew they could say one word and make things happen. But this... This was impossible.

"Remember what I do, Nick. What's my fucking specialty? *I make things clean.*"

"I'm not a wad of dirty money. It's not the same."

"I've been working on this," Cole said. "You'll be outta here by the end of the month. I'm setting you up on the outside. Everything you need, it's all taken care of."

"The end of *this* month?"

"What'd I just say? End of the month."

"Why are you doing this? Why me?"

"You gotta ask that question?" Cole said. "After everything we been talking about, this whole year? I watch you all the time, Nick. Every day. What I need out of a man, it's all right here. Right here inside you. Don't hurt that you're white, too. You look sharp, you look clean, no tattoos. I can send you anywhere in the world, Nick. You fit right in."

Mason shook his head as he looked up at him. "I still don't understand," he said. "You could have picked somebody who—"

"Just shut the fuck up," Cole said, "and trust me. I picked *you*. I'm trying to explain why, but maybe I can't. Not all of it. Maybe you'll have to find out for yourself what it is I see in you."

Mason took a moment to weigh those words. "If this really happens," he said, "what do I have to do?"

"All you gotta do is answer the phone, Nick. It rings, you answer. You do whatever you get asked to do. That's it."

The dinner horn rang and inmates started to move down the hallway. Mason stayed where he was, sitting on the bed. He couldn't help thinking about Gina. About Adriana.

"That night at the harbor," Cole said, still standing in front of him. "We both know what you lost that night. Your wife. Your daughter. Everything you had."

They were both right there in his head now. *Right there.* Close enough to touch.

"This is your chance, Nick. This is your chance to get it all back. All you gotta do is say yes."

I have to do this, Mason thought. I have to take this. No matter what it means.

"But hear me," Cole said, "before you say your next word. Make sure you understand what I'm saying to you. All that shit about nobody owning you? That's gone. It's a new fucking way of thinking for you. You make this deal with me, it's twenty years you don't have to be here anymore. But for those twenty years... your life don't belong to you."

Cole bent down close to Mason, close enough that his voice was a low rumble in Mason's ear.

"For the next twenty years, your life belongs to me."

| 12 |

As Nick Mason parked the Mustang outside Room 102, he tried to find the resolve inside himself to commit his first murder.

It was a motel like a thousand other run-down and forgotten shitholes all over the country. Shaped like an *L*, two stories high. A few blocks from Midway Airport, it might have even had some steady business back when Midway was the only game in town. Now the street was empty and there were maybe a half-dozen cars in the dark parking lot. Mason couldn't imagine anyone staying in one of these rooms and being happy about the way his life had gone.

It was 11:29. Mason took the key out of his pocket and unlocked the door. He pushed it open and flicked on the switch. A single light came on next to the bed. He checked the bathroom and the closet. The room was empty.

He went to the night table and slid open the one drawer. There was a Gideon Bible inside. Next to it was a gun and a pair of black gloves.

He put the gloves on first. The gun was a Glock 20. He checked the load. The magazine was filled with ten-millimeter shells. There was one in the chamber, ready to go.

The gun felt heavy in his right hand. He stood there looking at it. Stay in the moment, he told himself. Do one thing, then the next thing. Don't think about what this means. Or what kind of person you'll be if you really do this. Those are questions you can face later.

Then it all turned in his head at once. I'm not doing this, he said to himself. Samurai, my skinny Irish ass. There is no fucking way I'm doing this.

It turned again. Yes you are. You have no choice. Whoever's upstairs, waiting for you . . . It's not going to be the fucking Queen of England. Go upstairs and see for yourself.

He took one more long breath. As he turned, he caught sight of his face in the mirror hanging on the opposite wall. You made this deal, he told himself. You put Gina's life and Adriana's life on the line. You will do this.

You have no other choice.

Mason went back out through the door, shutting off the light behind him. He was wearing black jeans and a black jacket. He put the gun in the jacket's pocket and went to the stairs. The exit sign glowed a sickly orange. There were a Coke machine and a candy machine, both with crudely lettered signs indicating you were out of luck if you wanted either Coke or candy. An ice machine rattled, apparently still in business.

Mason heard a car moving somewhere, maybe a block away. He turned the corner. The balcony was empty. He walked slowly, feeling the slight sway of the concrete slab beneath him as he moved his weight from one foot to the other. He counted down the room numbers. 223. 221. 219. 217.

Mason could see the office below him, on the other side of the L.

He could see a dim light through the window, but he did not see an occupant.

He paused for a moment. Room 215 was ten feet away. His heart was pounding. Breathe in, he said to himself. Breathe out.

He took another slow step. Then another. He couldn't see any light coming from the room's window until he reached the center and there was a slight gap between the curtains.

The man in the room was stained blue by the glow of the television. He was sitting on the edge of the bed and he was a big enough man to make it sag halfway to the bottom of the frame. He looked at his watch, then stood up and brushed off the back of his suit coat, looking down at the bed like it had been a mistake to sit there. He was wearing a white dress shirt under his suit, no tie, but everything was perfectly pressed. His leather shoes had just been shined.

Mason's senses were so amped by adrenaline that every detail of the room, of the man, of everything else around him, was burned into Mason's mind in that one instant.

He closed his eyes and took one more deep breath. He took the gun from his jacket pocket and held it close to his chest.

A car turned onto the street below and its headlights swung across Mason's back. He froze for a moment. When the car was gone, he took the final two steps to the door. He knew one good kick would open it. But the headlights had set off a timer in his head and now that a full two seconds had passed the bell had started to ring. Yes, he told himself, the man may have seen your shadow against the curtains.

That's the exact moment when the door opened and the man came out and at Mason, moving impossibly fast for his size. He grabbed Mason by the collar and pushed him back against the balcony. For one sickening moment Mason felt the whole thing start to give. He could picture the two of them falling to the concrete below. But then the man pulled back like they were two wrestlers coming off the ropes and Mason was thrown into the room. The door swung closed behind them. The gun was wrenched from Mason's hand. He heard it land with a soft thud somewhere on the carpet.

The man's hands were wrapped tight around Mason's throat. Mason tried to dig his thumbs into the soft pressure points of the man's elbows, but the man was too heavy and strong.

The man pushed him back against the television set and it fell to the floor, plunging the room into almost total darkness. Mason brought his knee up into the man's groin and he felt the grip around his neck loosen and then give way. The man was breathing hard and making noises like a feral animal as he started swinging his fists. There was an explosion of light and pain when he caught Mason above the left eye.

Mason ducked and drove his shoulder into the man's gut. He drove him backward, past the bed and against the far wall. He felt the night table splintering and heard the picture frame sliding down the wall. The man tried to ram his head into Mason's nose, missed, but still caught him on the cheek, and another explosion went off as Mason felt himself overwhelmed once again by the man's pure physical mass.

After all of the fights Mason had been in, ever since he was kid, a ninety-pound weight advantage was the one thing he had no answer for. Now it seemed like the one final fact that would end his life.

The man was on top of him. Mason could smell the faint trace of alcohol on the man's breath, mixing with sweat and fear. He could already taste the blood in his mouth as the man hit him again. Then again. It was all going dark. And when the man hit him square in the throat, he took what would surely be his last breath. For one moment he saw the face of his daughter when she was four years old. He'd never see her as a nine-year-old. He'd never see anything else again, apart from the dark outline of the man above him, poised with his fist in the air, ready to drive it into Mason's head one last time.

Then he felt the hard metal of the gun butt just under the bed. He pulled it out and brought the barrel to the man's chest. He fired, the kick of the gun twisting it painfully in his hand, the body muffling the shot for everyone in the city except Nick Mason. It rang in his ears. And the ringing said to him, This is the first man you've ever killed.

Mason untangled himself from the man's dead weight. He went to the bathroom and flicked on the light. As he looked back, he saw the exit wound in the man's back. It was a ragged, softball-sized hole in the man's suit coat. And as he looked at the walls and ceiling, he saw the man's blood and tissue all over the place. He looked in the bathroom mirror and saw more blood on his face. His own blood, the man's blood—he didn't even know, or care, at that point. His cheek and eyebrow were already beginning to swell.

Mason wanted to take his gloves off to wash his hands and to feel the cold water against his face. But he knew he couldn't. He knew he had to get out of there and not leave a trace.

Breathe, he told himself. Breathe and move.

And don't make any stupid mistakes.

He took one of the towels and held it against his eye. Then he took a quick look around the room. He couldn't quite figure out what was missing until it finally came to him. There was no luggage in the room. The man checked in and he was sitting here, watching the television, but he had no luggage.

He was waiting for someone, Mason thought. Someone who could be here at any moment.

Mason put the gun in his jacket pocket. He gave the room one more quick look and that's when he saw the man's billfold, sitting on the bed.

He saw the glint of silver.

He went closer. He looked down at the star. There was no need to pick it up. No need to touch it. It was already telling him everything he needed to know.

Nick Mason had just killed a cop.

| 13 |

Mason closed the door to Room 215, trying to reconcile that there was a dead man—a dead cop—on the other side.

The towel was spotted with blood, so he put it inside his jacket as he stepped out onto the balcony and back into the stairwell. He stopped dead when he saw the security camera. It was mounted on this side of the concrete header over the entrance to the stairs. On his way up, there had been no way to see it.

Mason kept going. Down the stairs, still lit pale orange by the exit sign. He got in the Mustang, started it, backed up, and then gunned it onto the street.

Slow down, he told himself. It's time to be straight and correct.

He made himself bring the car to a stop as the traffic light went from yellow to red. He sat there idling for a moment, waiting for his heart rate to come down. Then he saw the flashing blue and red lights. The police car came around the corner, running silent and fast. The cop driving the car looked the Mustang up and down. Mason knew his face couldn't be seen through the tinted glass, but the car itself was unmistakable. Mason poised his right foot on the accelerator, ready to see what this thing could do from a standing start. But the police car kept going.

Mason let out his breath. The light turned green. He pulled out slowly and drove down the street, looking in his rearview mirror. There was nobody behind him.

He pulled out his cell phone and called Quintero.

"There was a security camera," he said as soon as Quintero answered. "I'm fucked."

"Relax," Quintero said. "Get a grip on yourself."

"I got spotted by a patrolman, too. If the guy knows cars, I'll stick in his head. When he finds out what happened at the motel, he'll remember he saw a 1968 Mustang one block away."

"I'm going to give you an address."

"That was a cop in the motel, by the way."

"The place will look abandoned, but we'll open up the door when you get there."

"Did you hear me?" Mason said. "That guy was a cop."

"You need to shut the fuck up and go to this address."

Quintero gave him an address on Spaulding, just over the river. Mason stayed off the highway, making his way down the dark, quiet streets. He crossed the river and spent a few minutes looking for the exact street and address. There was a huge storage warehouse and an asphalt yard locked up for the night. A half-dozen houses all boarded up, then at last another brick building with a large garage door being rolled up, a sudden bright rectangle spilling out onto the street. Mason turned into the opening. He saw Quintero standing there, his arms folded. The door was already rattling shut when Mason stopped the car and got out.

There were two other men in the garage. Dark-haired Latinos

like Quintero, except these men both wore gray coveralls. Banks of fluorescent lighting hung from the high ceiling, the area above them seeming to disappear into the darkness. There were workbenches and a lift and heavy welding equipment. Mason knew what this place was. He'd seen his share of chop shops.

"Tell me why I just killed a cop," Mason said.

Quintero didn't move. He kept his arms folded in front of his chest and said something to the other two men in Spanish. The men laughed.

"Tell me why," Mason said, "before I kick the shit out of you right here."

Whatever trace of a smile had been on Quintero's face disappeared in an instant. "Shut the fuck up, Mason. We got business to take care of. Take off your clothes."

"Excuse me?"

"We gotta get rid of them. You smell like a slaughterhouse."

Mason looked down at himself. It was his first good look in bright light. Even though his jacket and pants were black, he could see that they were soaked with blood. He took the towel from the motel bathroom out of his jacket. Then he took the gloves out of one pocket. Finally, he took the gun out of the other.

"Chingada Madre!" Quintero said. "The fuck is the matter with you? That gun is clean!"

"So what?"

"So you don't bring it with you, you stupid *pendejo*. You leave it in the room."

"Excuse the fuck out of me," Mason said. "I never shot anybody before."

Quintero took the gun from Mason as he said something else in

Spanish to the other two men. They already had both car doors open and were working on the seats.

"What are they doing to the car?" Mason said.

"What do you think they're doing?" Quintero said, taking the gloves and the towel. "Now take off your clothes. Unless you have any other surprises for me."

Mason took off his clothes. Quintero took them from him and put them in a garbage bag. Then he led Mason to a shower in the corner of the warehouse. He handed him a bar of soap and a large scrub brush.

"Every inch," he said. "No DNA, no fibers. We take no chances."

Mason got to work scrubbing himself down. When he was done, he stepped out of the shower. He grabbed the towel that had been put on a nearby worktable. Next to it were a pair of jeans and a shirt, underwear, socks, and shoes. He put on the clothes and looked at the rough mirror someone had screwed to the wall over the sink. The scrape over his left eye was still raw, and his whole face needed an ice bag. But he wasn't about to ask for one. He walked back to where the men were working on the engine of the Mustang. They already had the car seats out. Now they were pulling out the battery.

"You're not going to chop this car," Mason said.

They ignored him.

"They're not going to chop it," Quintero said from behind him. "They're going to fucking obliterate it. They're going to break it down to nothing like it never existed. That cop who saw the car? He saw a ghost."

Quintero took the wet towel from Nick and added it to the bag of clothes.

"Over here," Quintero said. He led him to the opposite side of the warehouse, where there was an incinerator. Quintero used a long pair of pliers with taped-up handles to open the door. Both men raised their arms against the sudden wave of heat. Quintero threw in the bag and it was instantly consumed by the flames. He nudged the door with the pliers until it was shut again.

"That camera at the motel," Mason said to him. "I didn't see it on my way to the room."

"What do you think I do?" Quintero said, throwing the pliers on the bench. "Just drive around and watch you? You don't think I had every angle at that motel taken care of? The feed on that camera was disabled. On *all* of the cameras, including the ones you *didn't* see. I even rented out every other room."

"What was his name?"

"Jameson. Sergeant Ray Jameson. Don't worry about it."

"Yeah, no big fucking deal."

"Listen," Quintero said, "you think that was Serpico you took out? I had to deal with that prick for years. Thought he could do anything he wanted, like he owned the whole fucking city. Whatever I paid him, he always wanted more. He was a piece of shit who happened to carry a badge in his pocket. Take away the badge and he's still a piece of shit. Just not as useful."

"If he's useful, why take him out?"

"He stopped being useful when he stopped doing the things we paid him to do."

"All right, hold on," Mason said. "You gotta understand something."

"What's that?"

"I can't do this shit."

"You can," Quintero said. "You just did."

Mason hesitated, because he didn't know how else to say it. He'd just killed a man, but there hadn't been a moment of truth. He didn't have to look the man in the eye. He didn't have to hear the man beg for his life or watch him piss himself. He didn't have to calmly pull the trigger and then walk away.

Instead, it all just happened in a rush. Hell, it almost felt like self-defense. But that was a distinction he knew Quintero wouldn't get. Mason was sent to kill the man. Mason came back. The man was dead. End of story.

Why me? That's the question Mason had asked Cole, sitting in that prison cell, right after Cole had made his offer to him. All those other men in that unit, many of them murderers. Multiple murderers. Men who could have killed that cop in the motel room without blinking. Why did Cole choose Mason?

It still didn't make sense.

"Your new ride," Quintero said. He led Mason to the farthest bay in the garage, beyond the reach of the fluorescent lights. They might as well have been on the bottom of the ocean. Quintero snapped on a light. The darkness separated in the glare from the caged bulb. There was something there, covered with a gray tarp. When Quintero pulled away the tarp, Mason saw a 1967 first-generation Camaro SS. It was painted jet-black, just like the Mustang. But where the Mustang was sleek and beautiful, this thing was just a beast. Twin pipes. A simple flat grille. This car was fast when it was made, too fast for any sensible person to actually drive on the street. Mason guessed it was just as fast now.

"How many cars like this are you gonna destroy?" Mason said.

"Maybe next time we won't have to."

Mason's heart rate was back to normal. He stood there looking at the Camaro and he thought about everything that had happened that night. This wasn't the right way to do it, he said to himself. Go into a motel room, kill the man with a gun, drive away in a car that was unlike any other car in the city. There were too many ways it could go wrong.

But maybe that was part of the test, seeing if Mason could deal with those problems. And then, once he did, proving to Mason that Quintero would be here for the cleanup, even if that meant destroying a car that belonged in a museum.

It was all part of the show. And both men had learned something important about the other.

Quintero took a set of keys from his pocket and tossed them to Mason. "Those bruises look good on you," he said. "Make you look humble."

"Open the door so I can get the fuck out of here."

Quintero hit a button on the wall and the bay door cranked open. Mason backed out the Camaro and took off.

He tried to keep it out of his mind as he drove back to Lincoln Park, pulled into the town house garage, and went up the stairs. The dark cherrywood was the same color as the blood-soaked carpeting in the motel. The television was on and Diana was sitting on the leather couch, watching a cooking show, magnified on the huge HD screen. She glanced up as she heard Mason and for one moment it looked like she might ask him why the hell he hadn't showed up at the restaurant like she'd asked him to.

But then she saw his face. She turned back to her show without saying a word.

Mason went into his bathroom and took off the clothes Quintero had given him. Even though he was probably the cleanest man in the world, he got in the shower and spent a half hour under the hot spray.

His own reaction was finally coming through to him now that he had stopped moving. He kept hearing the shot against the man's chest, kept feeling the weight of the man's dead body on top of him.

I always had rules, he said to himself. They never failed me until the day I started ignoring them. Now I need some new rules. New rules for new problems.

When he got out of the shower, he once again caught sight of himself in the mirror. The bruises were already looking worse.

He threw on some new clothes, went out to the kitchen, and filled a plastic bag with ice. He grabbed a Goose Island out of the fridge and sat down on the far end of the couch, holding the ice against his face. Diana didn't react. She didn't look at him. She didn't make a sound. She kept sitting there, watching the television.

It was a special break-in from the local news. A woman reporter was standing outside somewhere, holding a microphone. Behind her was a thin strand of yellow crime scene tape. Behind the tape was a line of doors. Above those doors was a balcony.

Mason knew this place.

The crawl across the bottom of the screen gave Mason the news he didn't need to read. Sergeant Ray Jameson, a highly decorated police officer, was killed by an unknown gunman. He leaves behind a wife and three children.

Mason looked over at Diana. She had her knees drawn up to her chest and she was hugging them. She kept staring at the screen.

Mason closed his eyes for a moment. He pressed the ice against his face. The cold was painful, but eventually it started to make him feel numb.

When he opened his eyes again, the reporter was signing off. Just before the camera cut away, he saw a plainclothes police officer stepping right into the shot, blinking at the glare of the camera lights. On the screen the man looked bigger than life and Mason knew him immediately even though he hadn't seen him in five years.

It was Detective Frank Sandoval.

| 14 |

When an SIS sergeant was killed forty-eight hours after
Nick Mason had been released from prison, Detective Frank Sandoval figured this was one crime scene he had to see.

As he ducked under the crime scene tape, a uniformed officer moved to stop him. Sandoval showed him his star and the officer stepped aside to let him pass.

He went up the stairs and down the exterior hallway to Room 215. He saw the blood on the walls first. Then the body on the floor. He took a step inside the room and looked at the exit wound on the man's back. A bullet goes in clean, but then it meets resistance. It flattens out, slows down, and pushes the tissue in front of it like a snowplow. By the time it comes out the back, it's not a clean missile anymore. It's a goddamned musket ball.

He looked up over his head. There was more blood on the ceiling. It had started to drip down onto the bed.

He took a glance into the bathroom. He counted three towels.

They were all clean. Sandoval knew there had probably been a fourth.

Sandoval came back out into the main room. He stepped back out onto the balcony. It was after midnight. There was one news truck below him, getting a jump on the other stations, and a half-dozen squad cars, the lights bouncing blue and red on every surface. Beyond the parking lot it was just darkness and quiet streets.

Another car pulled into the lot. A black Audi. He watched the driver get out and walk past the uniforms. They made no move to stop him. A few seconds later, he heard him on the stairs, then saw him coming down the hallway, moving with purpose. He was a tall man, with hard features, hair cut close and so blond it was almost white. His eyes were a pale, metallic shade of gray. Sandoval knew him by reputation only. It was Sergeant Bloome, one of the original members of SIS, one of the men who stood behind the mayor when they announced the big new initiative in Chicago's War on Drugs.

When they first put this team together, it was called Special Investigations Section. An elite task force of all the best narcotics officers in the city, handpicked by the superintendent himself. They were given their own floor at Homan Square, their own prosecutors and staff, anything they wanted. Their jurisdiction was the entire city of Chicago. They could go anywhere they wanted, talk to anybody at any time, take over any investigation. In a city overrun with drugs, they had been given a blank check from the highest levels to do whatever it took to bring down the dealers. They didn't have cases. They had targets.

They stood apart from every other cop on the force. You could see an SIS man from three blocks away, always in a dark suit, perfectly tailored, perfectly pressed. Expensive leather shoes. He had his pick of any car confiscated in a drug bust, so he always drove the best.

Nothing like the homicide-issued Ford Fusion that Sandoval was driving.

After two years in operation, you started to hear some things about these guys. Illegal seizures, low-level guys on the street getting robbed and beaten. Nothing to lose any sleep over, since they were making arrests every day, piling up numbers that a homicide detective could only dream of. The crime rate went down. The mayor was happy. The brass was happy. So the rumors were ignored, and every uniformed officer—like those guys standing down there in the parking lot, letting Bloome walk by with nothing but a nod—they all kissed SIS ass, because SIS was what every Chicago cop wanted to be. They were stars. Celebrity cops.

Bloome passed by Sandoval without even looking at him. He went into the room. Sandoval waited. A minute later, Bloome came back out. He leaned over the railing, breathing in the night air. Then he finally looked up and noticed Sandoval standing there.

"Who are you?" he said.

"Detective Sandoval. Area Central Homicide. Got a question for you."

"For *me*?"

"You're SIS," Sandoval said. "Jameson was SIS."

"Wow, you're some kind of investigator," Bloome said. "Whose dick did you suck to make detective?"

"Why was he here alone?"

Bloome took his arms off the railing and stood up straight. "Guy I worked with for twenty fucking years is dead on the floor in there," he said. "A friend. A great cop. So I'm not in the mood to answer your bullshit questions."

"You see a suitcase? He wasn't staying here. What was he doing, meeting a CI?"

"He was doing whatever the fuck he was doing," Bloome said. "Before somebody blew a hole in him. We're taking this case, by the way, so you can leave."

"It was never mine," Sandoval said. "Ryan's downstairs. He's caught it."

Bloome worked that over in his head for a moment. "Then what the fuck are you doing here?" he said. "That's a dead cop on the floor. You got no respect?"

"I'm working on something else," Sandoval said. "Thought it might be connected."

"Connected to what?" Bloome said. "What the fuck's the matter with you? Do you let guys off the street come walking onto *your* crime scenes?"

He stopped and looked at Sandoval's star again.

"Wait a minute," Bloome said. "You're Sandoval? Gary Higgins's partner?"

Sandoval nodded.

Bloome looked him up and down. "Here's what's gonna happen, Detective. You're gonna get the fuck out of here right now and I'm not gonna see your face again. Any crime scene. Anyplace got anything to do with me, with my men, with SIS. Just stay the fuck away from us so the real cops can do their job."

Sandoval nodded. "That's one way. Other way is I tell you to fuck off and I keep doing *my* job."

Sandoval turned and walked down the hallway. When he was in the parking lot, he looked back up at the balcony and saw Bloome watching him. Then he walked through the glare of the news team's camera lights, got in his car, and drove away.

| 15 |

Ten hours after committing his first murder, Nick Mason was desperate to find one good reason for it.

He had to see his daughter.

Mason went to the same house, the house where Adriana woke up every morning. Came home from school, did her homework. Went outside to play. Went to sleep. Did she still have nightmares? She had them two or three nights a week when she was four years old. How many more did she have when her father was taken away?

He took off his sunglasses and tilted the rearview mirror to look at himself. The scrape over his left eye was still an angry red, both cheeks were still swollen, and the bruises were turning every shade of black, blue, green, and even a little yellow. Mason had been in fights before, more than he could count, and he'd lost his share of them. But it had been a long time since he looked this bad.

When Diana had seen him that morning, she had put together another bag of ice for him, and she had stood over him for a few moments, getting a better look.

"Let me guess," she finally said to him, almost smiling. "I should see the other guy, right?"

"Yeah," Mason said. "Something like that."

The way he said it made her smile slip away. "Don't say another word."

She gave him some ibuprofen for the swelling. Then she went to work. Mason got in his new Camaro and came out to Elmhurst. It was becoming obvious that the house was empty. He put the rear-view mirror back in position and started the car.

As he was driving away, a couple of facts came together in Mason's mind. Gina had said that her husband and Adriana were at practice the other day. Mason remembered seeing the soccer goal in the garage, too. It was a Saturday morning in July. Maybe today was game day.

He'd seen the high school on his way here, so he backtracked and looked for soccer fields, but saw only a football field, and the whole place was deserted, anyway. He went up a couple of blocks and found Elmhurst College and a soccer field with players on it, but no young kids. He drove around for another few minutes and was about to give up when he saw a soccer ball sticker on the back of a mini-van. He followed it south, all the way to Oak Park, into a big parking lot where a half-dozen kids—all around Adriana's age and dressed for soccer—piled out.

Mason got out of the car and started walking toward the fields. There were three fields, with a couple dozen kids running around on each of them, all coed games, with a hundred adults standing around, watching and cheering. Or just standing and talking to one another, enjoying the summer day. He wandered around the perimeter of the first field, watching the kids chase the ball.

Mason wasn't sure if he'd recognize his daughter right away. Not after five years. More than half of her life. He kept looking at one young face after another.

Then he saw Gina.

She was on the far side of the field, standing with another woman, half paying attention to the game. A low stand of bleachers on this side of the field was half full of spectators. Mason was about to sit down, then stopped himself.

I have every right to be here, he thought, no matter what Gina might say to me. But maybe it would be better to stay out of sight.

He took a few steps back until he was standing against the backstop of the softball field. With his sunglasses on, he was virtually invisible, and yet he still had a good look at the field.

He kept scanning the far sidelines. He didn't see a man near her. Either the new husband was one of those guys who works even on Saturdays, Mason thought, or else he's one of the coaches.

Mason saw two men on the near side of the field, standing with the kids who weren't in the game yet. One looked a little too old. The other was tan and filled out his polo shirt like a man who ate right and took care of himself. That had to be good old Brad.

Mason turned his attention back to the kids on the field. That's why he was here, not to watch his ex-wife or her successful new husband, who swims his laps at the club every morning. He was just starting to scan the players when a girl in the middle of the field turned his way.

It was her.

It was his daughter. Adriana.

Nine years old, he said to himself. God damn, look at her. She was a younger version of her mother. Same dirty-blond hair, same build. Tall and rangy, with that dead-serious look of determination on her face. She was fast, too. Running circles around most of the boys.

He remembered the day she was born. Rushing Gina down to the hospital on Fifty-first Street, then waiting eighteen hours at her side until Adriana made her appearance.

Bringing her home. The room Mason had made for her. Painted green, the compromise when Gina took her stand against pink.

The first Christmas in that house. The tree in the corner. The first time she looked at him. Really looked at him. The first time she said, "Daddy."

The first time she walked across the room to him, her arms spread wide.

His chest felt tight. This was the exact moment he had been waiting for, finally being able to see her again, after five years.

It had been sixty months since the last time he saw his daughter. Over forty thousand hours.

But he couldn't talk to her. He couldn't explain things. Not yet.

A boy tried to take the ball away from her and knocked her to the ground. Mason was already leaning forward, like he'd actually go out there and do something about it, when the ref blew his whistle and gave her team a free kick.

"Shake it off, Aid!" It was the coach who was probably Brad yelling at her. Aid, he called her. Everything about this guy he already hated.

Mason watched his daughter play for the next half hour. He never took his eyes off her except for the few times he glanced over at Gina and saw her talking to her friend, barely paying any attention to this miracle that was happening on the field. This nine-year-old girl they created together who was so much faster, so much more graceful, than anyone else on the field.

At one point, the ball came over the line on his side of the field. Adriana came to pick it up and seemed to look right at him. They were still a good twenty yards apart, but he was about to lift his hand into a wave. Then she grabbed the ball and threw it back out on the field.

As the game was winding down, he started walking back toward the car. He passed a sheet of paper tacked onto the other end of the backstop. It was the league schedule. There were games every Wednesday and Saturday.

He was in his car before the rest of the kids and parents started streaming into the parking lot. He sat in the Camaro and watched his ex-wife and the coach, who was now confirmed beyond all doubt to be Brad, get into their Volvo SUV. Adriana followed after them, getting into the backseat. He watched them drive away. Back to their perfect house. Back to their perfect life.

He sat there for a few more minutes, thinking about what he had done the night before. It couldn't all be just for this, he told himself. This one chance to see his daughter, for just a few moments. Then to sit here and watch her drive away to another man's home.

Jameson chose his own fate, Mason said to himself. I chose mine. Now I just have to keep it all separate. Keep that part of my life as far away from her as possible. Keep doing my job. Keep living for moments like this. Because that's all I have right now.

Someday, I may have more. A lot more. Whatever I have to do to get there, that's what I want. A real life with my daughter. Then maybe, just maybe, this will all be worth the price I've paid.

| 16 |

Five years in prison had given Nick Mason convict eyes. It's a certain way of looking at the world, your primal reptile brain watching every movement, every change, measuring it for danger. The body language of a man approaching you in the hallway. Or the way his eyes track you across the yard. After a while, you don't even think about it. It's just a basic part of your awareness. Your survival.

He'd seen Sandoval sitting in his car a half hour ago, across the street from the town house. He'd just clocked him again in the restaurant parking lot. He knew he'd be walking through that door. Mason picked a table in the back corner, sat down so he was facing the door, and ordered a Goose Island.

He scanned the place while he waited, this restaurant where he was officially employed. It had once been a speakeasy, then they'd gutted the place and rebuilt it, leaving exposed brick on one wall. Another wall was dominated by the glassed-in wine tower, everything a contrast of old against modern, the natural cherry floors against the muted steel panels along the bar. There was a high cathedral ceiling, with pendant lights hanging from long braided cables. Red velvet upholstery on the chairs and in the booths, white tablecloths with votive candles. It all created an atmosphere of intimate sophistication. The windows overlooked Rush Street, where the streetlights were just starting to glow.

Mason knew this restaurant had to be a whole different world around lunchtime, with traders from the Chicago Stock Exchange, executives from the downtown banks, all walking up over the DuSable Bridge to sit at these tables, putting down their corporate credit cards and never thinking about the prices.

Right now, it looked like couples celebrating special occasions and some tourists out for a night on the town, maybe before catching a play at one of the theaters. There were a dozen high-end hotels within a few blocks of this place. Every concierge probably had Antonia's near the top of his call list.

The kitchen opened right into the dining room, so Mason could see the long prep tables, the stoves and ovens and walk-in freezer. The waitstaff and the chefs were all moving together in a perfect choreography. Then finally, at the center of everything, he caught sight of Diana. This woman who seemed so reserved and self-contained at the town house. She was unleashed here in this kitchen, totally in control and directing every movement around her.

Mason smelled the steaks broiling on the open grill. He checked the menu again, saw the four different cooking options for rib eyes, aged twenty-eight to seventy-five days in the cellar with Himalayan rock salt. He thought back to the last meal he had eaten at Terre Haute. The gray mass they passed off as meat, with rice and vegetables and bread that somehow all tasted the same. A cup of water to wash it down.

From that world to this.

. . .

About two minutes later, Sandoval came in. He gave the place a quick scan and spotted Mason, came over and stood by the table for a moment. Then he sat down in the chair across from him.

"Remember me?"

Mason didn't answer him. If his rule number three wasn't enough—*When in doubt, keep your mouth shut*—the extra rule number ten was designed to hammer home the point—*Never talk to a cop. Not one syllable.*

The rule applied universally, no matter what the situation, guilty or innocent, to formal questioning or just shooting the breeze. Never say one fucking word to a fucking cop because talking to a cop gets you on the cop's radar.

And once you're on a cop's radar, you will never get off.

"I arrested you," Sandoval said. "Five years ago."

Mason said nothing. Sandoval picked up Mason's menu and started looking through it. "Looks like a nice place. Food any good? You do work here, right?"

Mason didn't answer.

"Didn't know you were in the restaurant business, Mason. Real high-end place, too."

He looked at the menu again.

"Wow, fifty bucks for a steak," he said. "That's a little steep for a guy on a cop's salary. Maybe on my anniversary."

Sandoval leaned forward to take a closer look at Mason's face.

"What happened to your face?"

Mason stayed silent.

"All right," Sandoval said, putting down the menu. "You're not a chatty guy, I get it. How 'bout I just talk and you listen?"

The waiter came and gave Mason his beer. He asked Sandoval if he'd like a drink. Sandoval said, "No, thank you." The waiter left. Sandoval leaned forward on both elbows and looked Mason in the eye.

"Sean Wright," Sandoval said. "You remember him? Name might have got mentioned at your trial once or twice. He was the DEA agent who got killed that night at the harbor. Most of the time, you know, cops and federal agents, working the same town, you butt heads sometimes. Whether it's FBI, DEA, Homeland Security . . . they get in our way, we get in their way. Some of those guys are real jackasses, too. But here's the thing, Mason. One of those guys goes down . . ."

He paused and shook his head.

"Now we're the same," he said. "Cops, agents, don't matter. All the fucking same. So my partner and me, we got to the harbor and they're taking his body away. Wheeling him away with a sheet over him. They don't want to leave a dead agent lying there in the road. But I saw the pictures later. Read the reports. Man didn't even have his gun drawn. He gets out of the car and he's already dead."

Mason kept watching the man. He kept listening. He didn't react in any way.

"I know there's four of you in the trucks. Two trucks, two men each, one-in-four chance you pulled that trigger, right? One-in-four chance you gunned down a federal agent while you were running away. But you know it don't matter. I don't care. The law don't care. You're in the middle of a felony when he's killed, so it's felony murder. All four of you guys."

Sandoval paused to look around the restaurant like he was checking to make sure nobody else was listening.

"So two of you guys get away," he said in a slightly lower voice. "A third man gets shot in the truck. That leaves one man to stand up for everybody. That's you. Not how we want to close the case, but that's what we got. It was *something*, right? We got one guy who can be accountable. One guy I can take back to Sean Wright's family, say, Here, this guy's gonna pay for it. Your whole family got torn apart, and this don't bring him back. But here's one man. You can see him pay for it."

Sandoval leaned back in his chair and took a breath. Then he leaned forward again.

"Elizabeth Wright," he said. "That's his wife. Married seven years then. They got two kids. Sean Junior, he's nine years old. Sarah's eight. They're four years old, three years old when their father got killed. You can't imagine, Mason, what that's like, seeing those kids when we got that case. I got a boy and a girl, too. Exact same ages. My son and Sean, they play ball together now. This team I coach, I got Sean on there. I talk to him all the time, make sure he's doing okay. Sarah, I don't get to talk to. She still don't say much to anybody. Eight years old, Mason, girl just sitting there, staring off into space. Breaks your heart."

Sandoval leaned forward even farther and lowered his voice again.

"So here's what I wanna know, Mason. I see this family all the time. Five years later, I still see them. So what am I supposed to say to them?"

Mason picked up the glass of beer, but he didn't drink. Never talk to cops, he told himself. Never talk to fucking cops.

"Because as far as I know," Sandoval said, "they have no idea. I don't think anybody called them. And it didn't make the newspapers yet. The real crime reporters in this town are all dead or they took buyouts because nobody buys a fucking newspaper anymore, but someone will find the story eventually, go knock on their door with a camera crew... For now, that leaves me to give them the news. So how do I do that, Mason? How do I tell them you're out of prison already? You got any ideas for me?"

Mason held his glass and looked at the amber liquid.

"Yes?" Sandoval said. "You look like you wanna say something."

Mason put the glass back down.

This is why you stay off a cop's radar, Mason thought. Especially a cop like this. You give him any kind of reason and suddenly you're the one man he can't stop thinking about. When he's working another case, having lunch with his partner, doing his paperwork, waiting in line at the courthouse. Packing up for the day and going out for a splash with his cop friends.

Even at home, having dinner with his family, watching television, helping his kids with their homework. Going out to a Sox game on the weekend, having a hot dog and a beer.

You open up that guy's head at any minute and there you are, living somewhere inside it.

"Wasn't easy finding you," Sandoval said. "No parole, so no address. I looked in a few different places, nothing for Nick Mason. Nothing new. Then I remember this guy over at Social Security. They got this database, there's a new W-4 for Nick Mason, working at a restaurant. Let me guess, Darius Cole own this place?"

Mason looked at him.

"Got your address, too," Sandoval said. "I've been there, just taking a look, and you gotta be fucking kidding me, right? From federal prison to Lincoln Park West?"

Sandoval scanned the restaurant again, shaking his head slowly.

"You don't even have to hide it," Sandoval said. "This so-called job you got. That town house you're living in. It's all legit on paper. Hell of a nice life, huh?"

Yeah, Mason thought, hell of a nice life.

"If I'm in your place, I'm not sure how I sleep at night. But I guess you're a different kind of man."

"His name was Finn," Mason said, officially saying fuck you to rule number ten. "Finn O'Malley."

"The one who got killed?"

"Yes."

"Your friend, right? Grew up together in Canaryville. He's the one you left behind in the truck with a bullet in his head."

Mason took a breath. "Finn shouldn't have been there."

"Wrong place, wrong time, huh?"

Mason looked down at his beer.

"Did you kill that cop in the motel room last night?"

Mason looked back at him. "The fuck you talking about, Detective?"

"I know it was Cole. He's the one who got you out, he's the one who fucked my partner, and he's the one who told you to kill that cop. Just nod your head if I'm getting close here."

"If you could make a case," Mason said, "if you had anything real, you'd arrest me. What you have is bullshit."

The two men watched each other over the table for a moment. Then Sandoval stood up, took a few steps toward the door.

He stopped dead, then came back to the table.

"I don't have it yet," he said, leaning in close to Mason's ear. "But I'm gonna work this out, Mason. Every single fucking piece of it. You, Cole, anybody else who had anything to do with you getting out. I'll do it on my own, I don't give a fuck. No matter who tells me to leave it alone. I promise you, I promise me, I promise my ex-partner, Sean Wright, and his whole family… I'm not going to sleep at night until you're back in prison where you fucking belong. And Cole is out of business forever. You hearing me, Mason? You better get used to me because I'm gonna wake you up every fucking morning and I'm gonna put you to bed every fucking night."

He stood up straight and gave Mason a smile.

"Enjoy your dinner."

| 17 |

The bruises reminded Mason of what he had done in that
motel room. Even on the second day, as the bruises were beginning
to fade, he would replay the scene in his mind every time he looked
in the mirror. He wondered if that would ever change even when the
bruises were gone.

He went downstairs to the gym, put on some gloves, and worked
on the heavy bag. For the last year, he'd been keeping himself in the
best physical shape of his life, once he got into SHU with Cole. But,
even there, his workouts had been rushed, grabbing whatever reps
he could for the one hour the equipment was available. Now it felt
strange for Mason to take his time and to have so many options to
choose from. He didn't get on the treadmill, and he didn't even look
at the elliptical trainer, but when he was done with the bag, he did a
full-body workout with the weights, keeping everything in balance,
a push for every pull—back, chest, arms, legs—all good compound
movements. Deep into his head while he was doing each rep, Mason
shut out everything else in the world.

Keep moving, he told himself. Don't think. Move.

When he was done, he went outside. It was a choice he could make after five years of having no choices. A little breeze was coming in off the lake. He walked down the path, past the gardens, past the entrance to the zoo. He had a sudden ache as he walked past a father with a little girl up on his shoulders. The man was buying their tickets to the zoo, and as Mason looked at them, he couldn't help imagining what it would feel like to spend the day here with his own daughter. Maybe she was too big to ride on his shoulders, but they could still walk down the paths and look at all of the animals. She could ask him questions and he'd do his best to answer them, just like any father would. Yes, the giraffe has a long neck so he can reach the leaves on the upper branches. He'd give everything he had. Hell, he'd seriously consider going back to prison for the rest of his sentence if he could just have one day like that with his daughter. It would be something he could take back. Something nobody could ever take away.

That brought him back to the visit he'd gotten from Sandoval the night before. The story he'd told him about Sean Wright and his young family. And the promise that he'd be putting him to bed every night and waking him up in the morning. He looked behind him, expecting to see the man twenty feet away. But there was nobody following him.

Mason walked south down the beach path, the park on one side of him and, beyond that, the soaring buildings of downtown. On the other side was sand and water. People were wading in up to their waists and screaming about how cold it was. A few brave souls were in up to their necks. A woman came out of the water, dripping wet in her bikini. I have not touched a woman in five years, Mason said to himself. That is a fact.

He went all the way down to the south end, where men were playing beach volleyball. He looped around back under Lake Shore, past the ball fields. He stopped and watched a game of bare-handed softball—he knew it was a game that once ruled Chicago, but he didn't think anyone played it anymore. When the game was over, he kept walking.

I don't know what the hell I'm supposed to do on a day like this, he said to himself. Or how many days like this there's gonna be. All by myself, just waiting for that phone to ring again...

As he got closer to home, he hit another row of shops, all with blue canopies outside. Pricey salons, coffee shops, wine bars. Then he came to a pet shop. There was a dog sitting there, looking out the window. To Mason, it looked like part boxer, part pit bull, part dinosaur. He was about to keep walking, but the dog looked him right in the eye and started wagging its little stumpy excuse for a tail. Mason stopped and the dog sat down, still staring at him.

He went inside the store, feeling the instant chill of the A/C. There was a gated-off area by the front window, with separate sections for a half-dozen cats and the only dog in the shop, who now came over to Mason and did his best to body-slam the gate right out of the way.

"Easy there, Max!"

The voice came from the back of the store. A woman emerged from the storeroom, carrying a large bag of dog food. She put it on the counter and came over to Mason.

"He seems to like you," she said. She had short brown hair and brown eyes. Her cheeks were red from the summer sun. She was wearing jeans and a blue polo shirt with the name of the pet shop on one side of her chest. On the other was her name: Lauren.

He reached over the gate and rubbed the dog's head. The dog wagged his tail even harder.

"What kind of dog is he?" Mason asked.

"I'm guessing Cane Corso, mixed with something else. We don't usually sell dogs here, but he came in as a rescue."

"Cane Corso? Never heard of that."

"Smart dog. Athletic. Obedient."

"If I wanted this dog…" Mason said.

"I bet Max would like that very much. He's three hundred dollars."

Mason looked down at the dog. Max was sitting patiently as if waiting for the next chapter in his life to begin.

"Okay," he said, trying to convince himself.

"There's a twenty-four-hour waiting period," she said, "after we fill out all the paperwork."

He was already starting to feel the dog slipping away from him. Paperwork meant personal history. This might be a bad idea, he thought.

"He likes you," she said. "Come on over here and we'll get started."

He gave the dog one more look, then followed Lauren to the counter.

"Okay, I need your name and address," she said, picking up a clipboard with forms attached to it.

"Nick Mason." He gave her the address on Lincoln Park West.

"Wow, okay. I bet that's quite a place."

"I just moved in."

"Where'd you move from?"

Mason hesitated. "I'm from Canaryville."

"Canaryville to Lincoln Park," she said, nodding her head. "That's a change of scenery, I guess."

"Both places have lots of animals. They just keep them in the zoo up here."

"That's a good one," she said, nodding again.

"My name is Nick. It's nice to meet you."

"I'm Lauren," she said. "What happened to your face?"

The question surprised him. It was direct and honest and he thought carefully about how to answer. He liked her short hair and the color of her eyes. Most of all, he liked the way she stood her ground and waited to hear his explanation.

"I got in a fight," he said.

"What about?"

"Long story," he said. "But he was a bad guy. If that matters."

She looked at him and considered her answer.

"It matters."

"Does it matter enough that you might overlook it and let me take you to dinner?"

"You didn't come in here for this dog, did you?"

"I did," he said. "I'm taking the dog."

"Max."

"I'm taking Max. Max is going to have a great home. It's just when I saw you, I didn't want it to be one of those things I didn't do but wish I did for a long time afterward."

She looked at him carefully like a cop considering an alibi.

"You can come for Max tomorrow."

"Okay."

He turned and started out.

"And you can come back for me at seven," she said. "I'll be here, closing the store, if you still want to get something to eat."

"I'd like that. I'll see you at seven."

Mason went back outside into the hot sun. He was as surprised as Lauren was that he had asked her out. But it felt good to have something to look forward to that evening. This chance to connect with someone.

He wondered what her last name was, if she'd ever been married, if she had any kids. There'd be time enough to find out. He was open for anything.

He was still getting used to it, this thing that everybody else walking by on the street took for granted. Choice. He could go anywhere in Chicago, do anything he wanted. Until Quintero called again.

Forget about him, he thought, and the possibility that he may call at any minute. When it happens, it happens. For now, he had the rest of a summer afternoon to kill and he didn't want to go back to the town house and sit there by himself. He wasn't about to go to Elmhurst again. Not yet. The next soccer game was there on the calendar, waiting for him. Another chance to see his daughter.

For today, he had enough. One of the last things he ever thought would happen. A date for dinner with a woman not named Gina.

| 18 |

As Mason parked the car on Thirty-fifth Street, he re-membered an old joke. What's the difference between Bridgeport and Canaryville? People in Bridgeport take the dishes out of the sink before they piss in it.

Bridgeport's closer to the ballpark, closer to the river. There's a little more "diversity," meaning it wasn't just Irish American kids hanging out at every corner. There were Latinos and even an Asian community in this part of town. The houses were packed tight on narrow lots, just like in Canaryville, with the detached garages in back feeding out into the alleyways that run between the streets, but the houses were a little bigger and a little nicer. There were a few more neighborhood parks and a few more places to eat. Good deep-dish pizza and those breaded steak sandwiches they made here. That's Bridgeport.

Jokes aside, if you were honest about it, you'd have to admit it was a step up from Canaryville. You moved from there to here, you were moving in the right direction. Of course, you were still on the South

Side. That was important. You move to Bridgeport, it's not like you went too far north and started rooting for the fucking Cubs.

There was one house in particular that Mason was looking at. One narrow, two-story much like the others on the block, although this one actually had a little fenced-in strip of grass on one side. You couldn't just reach out from your window and borrow a cup of sugar from your next-door neighbor. Mason wasn't totally sure he had the right place, so he was sitting out on the street. The Camaro's engine was off but still ticking as it cooled down.

He saw a little boy come running out from behind the house and into the little side yard. The kid was maybe three years old. Red hair and freckles. He was wearing shorts and a White Sox T-shirt, and he had a big plastic baseball bat in one hand, a plastic ball in the other.

A few seconds later, another boy came running after him. He was an exact copy, same size, same red hair and freckles. He was also wearing a White Sox T-shirt, but a different variation. Maybe that was so people could tell them apart.

Mason watched the two kids for a while. The one with the plastic bat was about to hit the other one when a man appeared on the scene just in time to stop him. He was still short and as solid as a fullback. He had the same coloring as the kids, even if maybe he had a little less hair than he once did. Mason knew him immediately.

He got out of the car and shut the door. The man in the yard looked up when he heard the sound. He had the kid's plastic bat in his hand and he dropped it when he saw Nick Mason stepping over the curb and approaching the fence.

"Nick? Is that you?"

Mason stood with his elbows on the top of the fence. The two boys stared up at him, sensing something in their father and not sure how to react. Eddie Callahan opened up the gate and stepped out. He grabbed Mason by the shoulders like he was verifying the man was real flesh and blood, not some kind of hallucination.

"What the hell," he said. "I mean, *what the hell.*"

"It's good to see you, Eddie."

"What are you doing here?" Eddie said, taking a quick look up and down the street. "I mean, are you out?"

"I'm out."

"How did that happen?" Eddie asked, looking around again.

"It's a long story, Eddie. But I'm out."

Eddie's eyes settled on the car. "And what the hell are you driving?"

"A 1967 Camaro. I didn't steal it."

"Stop kidding around and tell me what's going on." He looked back at the two boys, who were standing at the gate. "It's okay, guys. Let's take you inside for a minute, okay. Let's go see Mommy."

He grabbed each of them by the hand and led them around back, taking one more look over his shoulder at Mason as he disappeared around the corner.

Mason stood there waiting for a while. Longer than it should have taken Eddie to put the kids inside. Meaning Eddie's wife was probably looking out the window at him and asking Eddie a lot of questions. She might even be calling the police, Mason thought, and it spooked him for half a second until he remembered he had nothing to worry about. From the police, at least.

Eddie finally came back out, looking like he'd just gotten an earful. "Sandra's a little concerned, Nick. Are you on the run?"

"Eddie, I'm not on the run. I'm not even on parole. I'm out clean. You got nothing to worry about."

"Okay," Eddie said, clearly wanting to believe him.

THE SECOND LIFE OF NICK MASON

"You gonna invite me in or not? Or are we gonna keep standing out here on the sidewalk?"

"Yeah, come on," Eddie said, opening up the gate. "Maybe in the garage? Would that be all right? We can talk there."

Mason shook his head and followed him. "This is the place you showed me. You told me you were thinking of buying it."

"This is the place," Eddie said. "It's got a yard, you know? Most places don't."

Mason looked around at the thin strip of grass running down the lot line. Just wide enough, maybe, to drive a car down. But Eddie was right, most houses in this neighborhood didn't even have this much.

"Bridgeport," Mason said. "You actually moved out of Canary-ville."

"Yeah, everybody's not all up in your business here. We really needed a fresh start. I mean, you know..."

Eddie cleared his throat and let that thought die in the air.

"What are your kids' names?"

Eddie stopped and looked him. "Yeah, they were born when you were... I mean, it's Gregory and Jeffrey."

"They seem like great kids."

"They're a big handful."

Eddie opened up the door to the garage and stepped inside, taking a quick look back at the house.

"Eddie, listen, I don't want to get you in trouble here. If Sandra doesn't want me here..."

"No, no, it's cool. Come on in and sit down. I got it all set up in here. Sandra calls it my man cave."

Mason stepped inside the garage and saw worktables along both walls. The tabletops were crowded with computer consoles and laptops. One table seemed to be set aside as Eddie's personal desk, with a nice computer monitor, keyboard, mouse, the whole works. A leather office chair was situated in front of it.

"This is what I do," Eddie said. "I fix them, I sell them. It's been pretty busy."

"I'm not surprised. You were always good with the technical stuff." Meaning hot-wiring cars and disabling alarms.

There was a tall safe set in the corner of the garage. Mason went over and tried the handle. It was locked up tight.

"I got a couple of rifles in there," Eddie said. "I still get to the range when I can, but too much other stuff going on, you know?"

Eddie rolled the office chair over to Mason. He pulled out a folding chair and set it up. Then he went to the little mini-fridge in the corner, opened the door, and took out two cans of Half Acre beer.

"You want one of these?"

"Sure."

Eddie gave him the can and sat down on the folding chair. Mason looked down at the man for a moment before sitting.

"Eddie..."

"Yeah, Nick?"

"You can relax now."

"I'm sorry, man." Eddie slinked down in his chair like somebody had taken half the air out of him. "I just don't know what to think. You show up like this, when you're not supposed to be out for another twenty years..."

"There was a problem with the arrest."

"I've heard of shit like that happening," Eddie said. "But I never thought—"

"Let's get this out of the way," Mason said, cutting him short. "I went away and you didn't."

"I know, man." Eddie looked at the garage floor.

"That's the way it happened. You wouldn't have given me up if it was you."

"I wouldn't have," Eddie said, looking back up at him. Mason could feel him grabbing onto this idea like a drowning man grabbing a lifeline. "I would have done the same thing, I swear."

"Okay, then, we're good."

"But I should have come to see you," Eddie said. "I was worried they would see my name and, I don't know, try to keep me there."

Mason took a hit off his beer. You feel really bad, he said to himself. And yet if I was still down there, you'd still be sitting here in Bridgeport, not coming down to pay me a visit. So you wouldn't have felt *that* bad.

"It's okay," Mason said. "You're married. You got kids. You gotta move on."

"I was gonna come. Really, I was. But Sandra, she just…"

She just wouldn't let it happen, Mason thought. I get it. The same woman who even now is making us sit out here in the garage instead of coming into the house. I should go in there, find her in her bedroom with both her kids hugged tight to her chest, tell her I just got done doing five years in a federal penitentiary and would have done a lot more. I never said a word about your husband being involved. Not one fucking word.

"So I heard about Gina," Eddie said. "I mean, I don't know if you've seen her yet. You knew she got remarried?"

"I heard," Mason said, trying to hide how much it still hurt.

He'd been keeping his cool. But it was getting to be a bit too much. He held on tight to his beer can and counted to three.

That "code" that Cole said he saw in Mason—all that *bushido* honor and *bushido* loyalty—maybe it really was a rare thing after all.

"I'm sorry, man," Eddie said. "It must feel like I forgot all about you in there. I really didn't. Every day, I thought about you in there and me out here."

Mason was quiet.

"We grew up together," Eddie said. "How many times did you save my ass, even before you went away? I should have been a better friend. After what you did for me."

"I said forget it."

"I'm turning this into a fucking soap opera, I'm sorry. Come on, let's drink to something, okay? You're out of prison." Eddie raised his beer. "To getting out. To freedom."

Mason raised his halfheartedly. The two cans clicked together. Mason wasn't so sure what they were drinking to. Whatever he had now, it wasn't really freedom. Like Quintero had said, it's *mobility*.

"To Finn," Mason said, raising his beer again.

"To crazy old Finn."

They clicked their cans one more time. Neither of them said anything for a while.

"I saw McManus," Mason finally said.

"How'd that go?"

"Could have run him over. Didn't even realize who it was until I was down the street."

"I'm surprised that asshole is still in town. If I ever see him, he's a dead man."

Mason took a hit off his beer.

"It's funny," Eddie said. "I think back to that night... That fucker was out of the truck before they even started shooting."

Mason nodded. He'd been thinking about it for years.

"He better not come to Bridgeport. I swear, I'll beat him to death. Right in the street."

Yeah, sure, Mason thought. While Sandra and the boys are watching you. That's exactly what you'll do.

"I saw Detective Sandoval, too," Mason said. "You remember him."

"Yeah."

"He might come by, ask you some questions, now that I'm out."

Eddie looked out at the house like he was imagining a detective on his front porch and Sandra answering the doorbell.

"Sandoval couldn't touch you five years ago," Mason said. "He can't touch you today. You got nothing to worry about."

"Right."

Eddie took a long sip off his beer and stared at the garage floor for a while.

"Hey, that reminds me," Eddie said. "I got something to show you."

He put down his beer, got up, and grabbed the stepladder from the far corner of the garage. He set it up and went into the rafters. He came down with a cardboard box. When he opened it, he pulled out a stack of newspapers. The first masthead read *Chicago Sun-Times*, and it took Mason about two seconds to understand what these represented. These were the newspapers from five years ago, all of the coverage from the harbor job, the dead agent, the apprehending of the suspect, the police superintendent standing on the court steps and saying that a federal agent's death has been avenged. The whole fucking circus.

"Eddie," Mason said, "why the hell would you save these?"

"I'm not even sure what I was thinking, but, I'll tell ya, when I'm having a bad day or something, I'll take out these papers and I'll remember what you did for me. How I'm here in this house with my wife and kids because you didn't give me up. How Finn never even made it back home at all. It just puts everything in perspective, you know?"

Eddie flipped through the pages, shaking his head as he relived the history.

"You should take these," Eddie said. "Read them, if you want. Burn them. I don't care. I just think you should have them. Now that you're out, I don't need them anymore."

Eddie put the newspapers back in the box. Mason took his last hit off the beer, then put the can down on the table.

"I'll get out of here," Mason said, "before I get you in any more trouble."

Eddie reached out and grabbed him by the shoulders again. This time, he pulled him close and gave him a hug. "It's good to see you, man. I still can't believe it."

"Take care of yourself, Eddie."

"Listen to me," he said, looking Mason in the eye. "If you ever need me, I'll be there. Anything, anytime. Whatever it is. I will be there."

"Okay."

Eddie took out a piece of paper from his pocket and wrote down his number. "Here," he said as he gave it to him. "I mean it, Nick. I owe you."

Eddie gave him one more hug. Mason picked up the box of newspapers and walked back down the narrow side yard, back to the street. He glanced at the window but didn't see Sandra looking out at him.

Mason put the newspapers in the backseat of the Camaro. Then he got in and left Bridgeport behind him.

| 19 |

As Nick Mason was nervously getting dressed for his first date, he silently prayed that Quintero wouldn't call him during dinner. He knew if he suddenly had to get up and leave, there wouldn't be a second date.

He showed up at the pet store at exactly seven o'clock. He was wearing his single-breasted Armani suit. A white dress shirt, no tie. Lauren was closing up the shop, but somehow she'd already changed into a summer dress.

"You look great," Mason said when he saw her.

"Thank you," she said. "So where are we going?"

"Maybe we just park on Halsted," he said. "Walk around."

Max was pawing at his gate the whole time. Mason went over to put a hand on his head, and Lauren kissed the dog on the nose. She stood up close to Mason. She smiled to break the tension. Then they both left the store and got in the Camaro. She knew enough about cars to be impressed.

"I can't imagine what it cost to restore this thing," she said.

"I wouldn't know," he said, leaving more questions than answers.

She looked over at him, her expression saying she still hadn't figured this guy out yet. Mason put the car in gear and they headed down the avenue. They parked in a lot, got out, and started walking north on Halsted Street. Tall brick buildings had shops and restaurants on the first floors, apartments above them. It felt a little strange to Mason because although this same street ran all the way down through the city, across the river, past Bridgeport, along the western edge of Canaryville, down there it was just a wide street with empty, weed-filled lots on one side, low, faceless buildings on the other. It's like he was in a different city now with a street name that made you think of home.

They walked under the El just as a train rushed by above them, then found a restaurant on the eastern side of the street and stepped inside. It looked like the right kind of place—a bar and some tables, nice enough without being too much, and mostly full. The greeter promised them a table if they wouldn't mind sitting at the bar for a few minutes.

Mason ordered a Goose Island. Lauren had the same. They sat there and clinked their bottles together and there was another awkward silence. Mason couldn't remember the last time he'd stood next to a woman in a bar and tried to make conversation.

That made him think about all the nights he was out with Gina, just standing close to her, the way they didn't have to say anything at all. And then when they got back home . . . No, he said to himself. Don't go there.

"So Max stays there in the store by himself?" he said to Lauren, looking for something, *anything*, to talk about. "Every night?"

"He's fine. The cats keep him company. And he guards the place at night."

"What happens when he comes to live with me? Who's gonna guard the shop?"

"It'll be a little strange not having him there," she said, "but he's going to have a new home. That's what he needs."

"He'll like the town house." Then he thought about Diana. Probably should have said something to her, he thought.

"Maybe I'll get the chance to come see him there. Or if you want me to just bring him over..." Lauren gave him a little shy smile and he was about to say something, but then the waiter came over and showed them to their table.

After fitting them with menus and lighting the candle, the waiter walked away and they were back to the awkward silence.

"So I've been trying not to ask," Lauren said, "but you live in a Lincoln Park town house and you drive around in a vintage Camaro. What exactly do you do?"

"I'm the assistant manager of a restaurant."

She looked surprised. "Which one?"

He fumbled on it for a moment, blanking on the name. That wouldn't be the greatest answer to give her. *Funny, I don't even remember.*

"Antonia's," he said. "On Rush Street."

"How's business these days? I imagine it might be tough for a high-end place."

"We're hanging in there."

She nodded and took a sip of her beer.

He took a long hit off his beer. "Okay, listen," he said, putting his beer down. "I gotta tell you something."

She put her arms on the table and leaned in to hear what he had to say.

"I'll just say it. I did some time in a federal penitentiary. Just got out. The part about me being an assistant manager, that's true. But I'm just starting there."

"Okay," she said, working it over in her head. "You get out of prison and you go right to one of the top restaurants in town?"

"The conviction was overturned."

"Oh!" she said, her face brightening. "You see that in the paper, somebody going to jail for something they didn't do. Finally getting out years later."

"It's prison, not jail. But, yeah."

"Prison, jail—what's the difference?"

"The amount of time you're there," he said.

"How long was it?"

"Five years."

"You're telling me you did five years for a crime you didn't commit? Are they gonna make that right? Pay you something?"

"No."

"They should," she said. "You lost five years of your life. They have to do something about that."

"Not gonna happen."

"What did they say you were guilty of?"

He hesitated.

"A robbery."

"They thought you were there," she said. "A case of mistaken identity."

"Something like that."

"It must have killed you going away like that for something you didn't do. I can't even imagine."

"You do the time every day," he said. "Or the time does you."

This is a mistake, he thought. I can't sit here and lie to this woman. One lie tonight turns into another lie the next time. How far could I take that?

What was I thinking? That I could have a normal relationship like a normal man?

"So what's it really like? You hear things about how it is in prison..."

"There are three kinds of people in prison," he said. "People who want to get out, people who never want to get out, and people who *know* they are never going to get out. You can't count the days. You keep quiet, keep to yourself. Don't go with anybody, don't owe anybody. You're all you got in there. The only thing you can count on is yourself."

Lauren was leaning over the table again. Her entire body language had changed. Mason remembered something Gina had told him once a long time ago. A boy wants a good girl who will be bad just for him, but a girl wants a bad boy who will be good just for her. Mason wasn't an ex-con—not officially, not on paper—but maybe that made it even better. He was bad, but not *too* bad.

Little does she know, he thought.

They ordered dinner. They had a few more drinks. When they were done eating, they went back outside into the warm night and walked up Halsted Street.

A few blocks up, he heard a band playing a Springsteen cover in a bar and slowed his pace.

Lauren noticed. "What?"

"I just like that stuff," Mason said.

"So do I."

"Yeah? You want to go in?"

"Yeah!"

They drank a little more. They stood close together while the band ran through all of Mason's old favorite songs. "Born to Run," "Thunder Road," then slowing down for "Meeting Across the River." It was good to feel her body close to his.

When it was after midnight, they walked back to the lot where he had parked his car. He could feel her shoulder brushing against his arm as they walked.

"Take you back to the store?"

She hesitated for a moment. "No, I don't have my car there. I take the train down most days."

"Okay," he said. "I'll take you home."

They got in the car and he asked her where she lived.

"I'm right up by the stadium," she said.

"Wrigley?"

"Yes. Two blocks away."

"You're a Cubs fan."

"Is that going to be a problem?"

"We were getting along so well," he said as he put the car in gear.

He drove up through Lakeview to Wrigleyville, shaking his head as he saw the stadium looming above them. Lauren started laughing.

After he parked the car, she took him into an old brick building and up a set of narrow stairs to her apartment. He turned her around and kissed her in the doorway. She wrapped her arms around his neck and kissed him back.

"How long has it been?" she whispered into his ear.

"A long time."

"How long? Tell me."

"Five years."

"Say it again. How long?"

"Five years."

"Show me," she said. "Show me what five years feels like."

He lifted her up and took her into her bedroom. They took off each other's clothes and came together while a fan blew back and forth across the room, cooling his back.

He went slowly, stretching her out on her bed and touching her, remembering what a woman feels like. Her neck. Her breasts. Her stomach. Her long legs. The wide curves of her hips.

He smelled her scent. He tasted her. Then she moaned into his ear as he entered her and the five years of waiting finally started to unwind inside him.

He took her hands and held them together on the pillow, above her head, as the passion worked its way through his body and into hers, and then back again, until it was too much to hold on to anymore. Five years of desire. Of hunger. Ready to be released.

Mason held on to her tight, trying to shut out everything else in the world outside that window.

The man who kills cops in motel rooms, he's not here. His past is not here, the things he's done, the things he may have to do tomorrow.

Tonight, you are someone else, Mason told himself. For these few hours, you can live inside a different life. He held on tight and dove into her again, this stranger beneath him.

The next morning, Lauren woke up to an empty space next to her. But then she smelled the fresh coffee and, two seconds later, Nick Mason came into the bedroom with two mugs. He was dressed.

"Cream and sugar," he said. "I hope that's how you take it."

She sat up and pulled the sheet up to cover herself. "Thank you."

"Listen, I just got a call," he said. "I have to go."

The message had been simple. Same place. 8:30.

"Are you married?"

"No," he said, taking a sip of his black coffee.

"Most single guys I know wouldn't bother to make coffee on their way out to an emergency."

"I'm not married, Lauren. I was before I went away. Now I'm not."

"Okay."

"I'll make breakfast next time."

"Is there going to be a next time?"

"Yes," he said, bending down to kiss her.

Mason left the room and put his mug in the kitchen sink. He went out the door, closed it behind him, and took the stairs down to the street. It was a hot morning, threatening an even hotter day.

Another lie already, he said to himself. And then another, every time the phone rings. He was looking for his car, squinting in the sunlight, when he felt a heavy hand on his back.

"Hey, Nickie boy."

Mason turned to see Jimmy McManus.

|20|

Nick Mason didn't want to talk to the man who put him in prison, the man who got his friend killed, but Jimmy McManus wasn't giving him any choice.

McManus wasn't dressed in his badass black today. Instead, he had on a gray ribbed muscle shirt and tight jeans. But it was the same jackass face, the same thinning hair tied back in a ponytail. His mirrored shades were perched on the top of his head.

"I thought that was you the other day."

"Take your hands off me." Mason could feel the nervous tension in the man, practically radiating from him like heat waves. It was the same hair trigger that made him come out of the truck, shooting.

"Hey, we're cool," McManus said, putting both hands in the air. "I just wanted to have a little chat. We're cool, right?"

"Are you fucking following me, McManus?"

"I was in the neighborhood," the man said, circling around to stand in front of Mason. "Call it a lucky accident."

Mason didn't respond. He waited for the man to get the hell out of his way.

"You gotta understand," McManus said, "last time I laid eyes on you, you were heading to prison. Parole was so far off, you were living on Buck Rogers time. But you ate your jack mack and did your time standing up with your mouth shut. I always respected that, Nickie. Same thing I would have done."

Mason stopped trying to step around the man. "You got two seconds to get the fuck out of my way."

"Easy, Nickie. Come on." He moved a hand toward Mason's chest but stopped just before touching him.

"One..." Mason said.

"I'm still connected, Nickie." He dropped his voice down and took a look around the street like he was sharing a big secret. "I know the people who fucking run this town."

"Two..."

McManus stepped back. "I just want to know what your angle is. How did you get out? What are you doing on the street?"

"I make you nervous?"

"Yeah, maybe, Nickie. That's not a good thing. I don't need any loose ends in my life. It's the loose ends that hang you."

Mason looked him up and down. If he was a real player, he wouldn't be dressed like some fucking Jersey Shore musclehead. He'd be clean and correct and he wouldn't walk around bragging about it.

"I'm gonna say this once," Mason said. "Then I never want to see your face again. I did five years. I didn't give you up then and I'm not gonna give you up now. As long as Eddie's around, I'm not gonna do anything that jams him up. So you better hope he lives a long life."

"I'm still nervous. Why don't you reassure me a bit more?"

"Fuck your reassurance," Mason said, pushing past him.

"I'll be seeing you," McManus said behind his back.

Quintero wasn't happy. Mason was late again.

"Maybe you work on early for next time," Quintero said as soon as Mason got to the park, "because this is the last time you'll ever be late."

Beyond him, the same hundred sailboats were anchored out in the open water. The fog had long burned off and it was a perfect summer day in Chicago—a cloudless cobalt sky, the lake glittering in the sunlight.

It was one of those days that feels like a gift. But here I am, Mason thought. This is how I have to spend it.

"I got held up," Mason said. "Not everybody's throwing a party about me being back on the street."

"We got a problem?"

"I'll let you know."

"You put some clothes together, so you're always ready," Quintero said. "You answer the phone and by the time you hang up, you're already out the door."

"Fuck that," Mason said, looking away.

Quintero shook his head and then pulled up the back of his shirt. For one second Mason thought he'd pushed him too far and was about to take one in the head. But it wasn't a gun in Quintero's hand. It was a manila envelope.

"You may have passed your first test," Quintero said. "With some help. This one's gonna be harder."

Mason took the envelope and looked inside. There were two sheets of paper. One was a copy of a police mug shot. A black man, front and side, holding a placard with his name on it. Tyron Harris. His hair was cut tight to his head and he had a small mustache. The look on the man's face was calm and cool like the whole experience was just a mild annoyance. On the second sheet of paper was a list of Chicago business names and addresses. Dry cleaners, liquor, electronics, and a half dozen more.

"Harris was the man who was scheduled to meet Jameson in the motel. I don't know where he lives, but here's a list of some businesses. He either owns them or has a piece of them."

"What's the job?"

"Find him," Quintero said. "Watch him."

Mason knew there'd be more to this job. He didn't have to ask.

"If you knew he was going to meet that cop in the motel room," Mason said, "and you wanted them both, why didn't you just wait? We could have taken them both out together."

I actually said that, Mason thought. This is how my mind works now.

"Harris would have come with at least four men," Quintero said. "Maybe five. Two men in the room with him, another on the door. One in the parking lot. Maybe one more on the street. He's still alive because he's careful. After what happened to his new business partner, he'll be even more careful. Get to work finding him. Call me on my cell, let me know what's going on with this guy."

Quintero took one step past him, then stopped. "One more thing," he said. "Let me know if the piece of shit following you is a problem. Your problems are my problems."

"He's nothing."

Quintero shook his head in disgust. "I'll decide if it's nothing."

"I'm more worried about Detective Sandoval," Mason said.

"How does a detective get on you that fast?"

"It's a personal thing. We have some history."

"You need to be clean when you're doing this next job, Mason. Every minute."

Mason looked out at the water.

"Now get to work," Quintero said. Then he walked away.

| 21 |

Nick Mason knew that Frank Sandoval was following him because Sandoval wanted him to know. At least for today, Sandoval was making no effort to hide the surveillance, hoping it would keep Mason on edge and force him to make a mistake.

Mason watched the blue sedan in his side-view mirror. He tried running a yellow light to lose it. He thought he was free, but then he saw it again. Or at least he thought it was the same car. It was later in the morning and there was plenty of traffic, and there were blue sedans all over the place.

He tried to loop around a block, watching carefully behind him, but there were too many cars and he couldn't get a clear bead on any one of them.

That's when he got the idea.

He drove down Rush Street to Antonia's. There was a car about to pull out of a parking spot right out front. The driver was taking his time getting into the car, starting it, maybe making a call on his cell phone. Mason stayed there in the street waiting him out, ignoring the honks from behind.

When the car finally pulled out, Mason took the spot. There on the street where anyone could see it. If you were looking for Nick Mason and you happened to follow him here, you'd have no doubt in your mind that this was his car and that he must be inside the place.

Mason went in through the front door and asked for Diana. The early-lunch crowd was just starting to sit down, so it wasn't too busy yet. Diana came out from her office, looking a little surprised to see him there. She was wearing another dark suit, with a lavender blouse. The color looked good on her.

"What's going on?" she said. "Is there a problem?"

"Where'd you park your car?"

"In the side lot, like always."

"I need you to move it," he said. "Go out and drive it down the street like you're going somewhere. Then come back around, away from Rush Street, and park behind the restaurant."

"I'm a little busy. I have a restaurant to run."

"Just do it and I'll let you get back to work."

When she left, he sat down at the bar and waited. The bartender asked him if he wanted anything. Mason said no, knowing today was a good day to stay sharp. He had the envelope folded up in his back pocket, so he took it out, unfolded the sheets of paper, and memorized the man's face again. Then he read down the list of businesses and addresses, trying to place them all on a city map inside his head.

It took Diana a few minutes longer than he would have figured, but that was probably a good thing. A sign that she knew how to do things all the way and not take any shortcuts. She came back into the dining room from the kitchen.

"Are you going to tell me what this is about?"

"I need your keys," Mason said. "And if somebody comes in looking for me, call my cell. Don't tell them I'm out."

She gave him a look. "Yeah, no kidding. I'll tell them you're in back doing something. Or in the office making a call that'll take a while. Stall them. Give you a call. You can decide if you need to get back here."

"And I was thinking it was an original idea…"

He took the keys from her and went out the back door to the little alley behind the restaurant. Her black BMW M5 was waiting there. Cole must have a thing for black cars, he thought. Or maybe she bought this herself. Who knows.

He got in and started it up. He pulled onto the side street and headed west, away from Rush Street. He stayed on the secondary roads for a while, then worked his way south. Most of the addresses on the list were on the South Side, so Mason knew he'd have no problem finding them.

He had the list on the seat next to him. While waiting at the bar, he'd put numbers next to each address. Go here first, then here, then here. Being smart about making one big loop through the South Side. No doubling back. No wasted effort.

He started in Avalon Park. The address turned out to be a restaurant. One Heart was a world away from Antonia's, a small place on the corner that seemed to specialize in fast Caribbean food. Busy, the height of the lunch hour, people were lined up outside the door. Must be some damned good jerk chicken in there. Mason was getting hungry. But there was no way he was getting out of the car. A white man in a BMW would get noticed and be remembered.

Mason watched the people going in and out of the place. He watched the cars going by on the street. Then he pulled away from the curb and went to the next address.

It was a barbershop, just a few streets away. It was one of those places that served as the center of the neighborhood. Two chairs, both occupied, two barbers in white shirts, snapping scissors, talking, listening. A half-dozen other chairs lined the wall and front window. Men sat waiting, flipping through magazines, shooting the shit. Other men stopped in to say a word or two, then continued on their way down the street. Mason sat there for a while and watched the place.

He moved on to a liquor store down in Roseland. It was busy in the way that all liquor stores are busy. Mason parked outside and started to wonder if he was doing this the right way. But he didn't think he could walk into any of these places and start asking questions.

Mason drove to Washington Heights and found a small grocery store. One of those places where you can buy everything, right down to the overpriced toilet paper, because you don't have a car and you don't feel like lugging a bunch of shopping bags on the bus. He didn't even bother parking and watching the place. He saw a McDonald's down the street and hit the drive-thru.

He decided to hit the first address last. It was on his way back north, anyway. When he crossed into Englewood, he started to think about Darius Cole and the stories the man had told him about growing up here, getting his start on a corner.

He found the laundromat. Right out of Cole's own life story, his first experience taking drug money to be made clean. Be a hell of a thing, Mason thought, if this was even the exact same place.

He could see it all happening through the windows, slightly fogged by the heat from the machines—a dozen young mothers, some grandmothers, sitting around waiting for their laundry, while their little kids ran laps around the place.

Then he saw the car.

The Chrysler 300—black, immaculately clean—was one of those boxy luxury sedans that looked like an old-school Cadillac. It was parked half a block down the street. Mason couldn't see inside the car. He was too far away and the windows had too much tint. But he thought he could make out the vague shadow of a driver sitting at the wheel.

That's his car, Mason said to himself. It's gotta be. So Tyron Harris can't be far away.

Detective Frank Sandoval sat in his car on the opposite side of Rush Street, looking across the traffic at the black Camaro parked outside the restaurant. He looked down at the pad on the seat next to him on which he'd written down the license plate number for the Escalade he'd seen at the park. He'd watched the man who met Mason at the fountain walk back to the vehicle and had just enough time to get the plate before picking up the tail on Mason.

He grabbed his radio and called in the number. Dispatch came back with an owner named Marcos Quintero. No warrants, no recent arrests. His record showed a gang affiliation with the West Side La Raza many years ago but no recent contact with the police.

Sandoval signed off and sat there for a while, thinking about how a gangbanger goes that long without even getting picked up. You don't leave that gang, Sandoval said to himself. La Raza is for life.

He watched the traffic go by. Watched the Camaro sitting there empty and his whole day circling around the drain. Then he got a call on the radio.

He picked up the transmitter, frowning with confusion. He knew he'd be transferring to the day shift soon, a fresh start for him after the business with his partner, but for now he was still officially on afternoons. So he had no idea who could be looking for him.

"Detective Sandoval, you're wanted at Homan," the dispatcher said. "See Sergeant Bloome at SIS."

Mason waited about ten minutes before three men came out of the laundromat. The two men on either side were big enough to remind Mason of Darius Cole's prison bodyguards. Both wore black T-shirts. One man had black track pants on, the other baggy blue jeans.

The man in the middle was Tyron Harris. Mason could see that in a second without having to pull out the mug shot. Dwarfed by the other two men, he wore a white summer dress shirt, untucked, over gray dress pants. He had a laptop bag looped over his shoulder.

This is the man I'm going to kill, Mason thought. It surprised him how easily he could say that to himself. But it was a cold, simple fact. Tyron Harris was walking down the street with no idea that his life was already over.

It would be good to know why he's the target, Mason said to himself. Do a little detective work on my own, for my own benefit, maybe start to figure out how many others are on the list.

They went to the car and one of the two big men got in the backseat with Harris. The other big man-got in front on the passenger's side. The car pulled out onto the street. Mason waited a few moments, then pulled out and did a U-turn. He stayed a half block behind as they drove south.

When they arrived at the mini-grocery in Washington Heights, Mason figured he was about to see the same loop in reverse. He waited and watched while Harris and the two big men went inside. Harris was still carrying his laptop bag. He walked with an easy, confident manner like a man who owned things. Which was probably true in this case. The other men were all business, looking up and down the street for anything resembling a threat.

They stayed only a few minutes. When they came out, Mason took a good look at the first bodyguard. The way his shirt hung off his body, that slight bulge on the right side. There was an automatic in that man's belt.

Mason couldn't get a good sight line on the second man yet. He'd have to wait for the next stop.

The car was pulling out into traffic and Mason was about to follow when he happened to see the manager come out of the grocery. Black, rail-thin, with receding white hair, he pulled out a cigarette and stood there, breathing in the hot air from the street. He lit the cigarette and his hand shook as he took his first drag of smoke.

The car headed down toward Roseland. Mason was guessing they were headed down to the liquor store, but instead they hit another laundromat. As they got out of the car this time, Mason finally got a clear look at the second bodyguard and the large crease running all the way down from his shirt into the left leg of his pants.

Fuck me, he said to himself. That's a sawed-off shotgun.

The two men stayed on either side of Harris, who apparently never let go of that laptop bag. He was a twenty-first-century entrepreneur, and from everything Cole had told Mason about Harris's history, it was clear to Mason that this man Harris was following the exact same blueprint, right down to the bodyguards. Get yourself in legitimate businesses that turn over a lot of cash. Build your base. Start with the places you know, the neighborhoods where you're welcome. Then expand from there.

He was starting to understand why this man was a target.

The only surprise was why Harris was being driven around and doing much of this collection work himself. It seemed like something you'd let your men do for you. Maybe he didn't trust them enough. Maybe he was just that kind of man, hands-on all the way.

Or maybe there was something else going on here. Maybe he was getting back out on the streets, trying to find out if anybody was hearing things.

As he settled in behind the car again, Mason called Quintero.

"I expected to hear from you already," Quintero said.

"Took a while to find him," Mason said. "Now I'm tailing him."

"You see your shot yet?"

"You're fucking kidding me, right? He's got two bodyguards with him at all times, both armed. One with a sawed-off. There's a third man in the car. He might have a fucking bazooka, for all I know."

"Keep watching him," Quintero said.

Then the call ended.

Mason flipped the phone onto the seat and kept driving.

He was back on familiar ground. Sitting in a car, keeping his eyes open. Waiting. Watching. Not getting bored because boredom distracts you. It's all part of what you do when you're setting up a job.

Only now, the job was killing a man. And the waiting and watching were all about the angles. About the numbers. He knew he'd have to take out the shotgun first. That left the other man with the automatic. If you're lucky enough to get them both, then the third man steps out of the car. Or Harris could be carrying himself. Something small and light. Be a big surprise if he wasn't.

There's no shot here, Mason told himself. Not unless I can get him alone.

. . .

The Homan Square police facility, or simply "Homan" to every cop in the city, was once a Sears warehouse. It was renovated in the nineties, along with the rest of the old Sears headquarters, and it was the biggest police building in the city, a redbrick fortress that housed all of the Bureau of Organized Crime units—Narcotics, Vice, Gang Enforcement, Asset Forfeiture—as well as Forensics and the Evidence and Recovered Property Section. Sandoval had been there many times, but usually just to drop off evidence, either for storage until a court date or else to be sent out to the Illinois State Police lab.

It made perfect sense that SIS would be stationed in this building, where they could draw from the best narcotics detectives just downstairs or even other OCD units, if they found a strong enough candidate. SIS had their office on the top floor, of course, with the big windows on the east side of the building, facing downtown.

Few Chicago cops ever got the chance to see this place. Today was Sandoval's chance, but it didn't make him feel lucky.

He rode up the elevator and found the door at the end of the long hallway. The sign outside the door read Special Investigations Section. He walked into a little waiting area and told the receptionist he was there to see Bloome. She was an attractive redhead—it figured that SIS would even have the best-looking receptionist at the front desk. She told him to wait on one of the benches.

This was a secure police building—you wouldn't even get to this floor if you weren't a cop or else a cop was escorting you. But Sandoval still had to sit on the hard wooden bench in the little waiting area like he was an informant off the streets waiting for his meal money. He could see over the half wall into the bull pen of SIS desks, arranged in random clusters. There were a dozen officers walking back and forth between the desks or talking on the telephones. The SIS uniform seemed to be tailored suits with the jackets hanging on the backs of chairs, everyone in dress shirts and ties, a few with suspenders.

Sandoval couldn't help but notice the energy in the room. There was a testosterone-fueled buzz that seemed to hang in the air like the static electricity before a thunderstorm.

Then Sandoval noticed the one man standing still among all the others. He had his suit jacket on and was over by the big warehouse window, looking out at the summer day.

Making Sandoval wait. Making him absorb the atmosphere of this place, where the best cops in the city did their work.

Sandoval felt his blood pressure rising until finally the man turned and came toward him. Sergeant Bloome had that same imperial walk, those cold gray eyes looking out at the world from somewhere above it. As Bloome got closer, Sandoval could see a small black band stretched across the lower two points of the silver star on his belt.

Everyone in the unit was probably wearing one, Sandoval thought. In memory of Sergeant Jameson.

"Detective Sandoval," Bloome said, swinging out the half-wall door and holding it open. "This way."

Sandoval followed him into the bull pen. He took a quick scan of the place, saw three different bulletin boards with photographs tacked on them. Some were mug shots, others were obviously the product of a long-range surveillance camera. All of the SIS cops were giving Sandoval the eye as he walked between their desks, measuring him, forming their own opinions of this outsider who'd been summoned here.

"We'll talk in here," Bloome said, leading him into an interview room. Like everything else, it was newer and cleaner than any interview room at Area Central Homicide. Bloome closed the door behind him and waited for Sandoval to sit down on one side of the table. Then Bloome sat across from him.

"I won't waste any more of your time," Bloome said, making it sound exactly like it was his time that was already being wasted. "One of my men heard you call in a plate today."

"A cop calling in a plate. Go figure."

Even seated, Bloome seemed to be looking down at Sandoval. His expression didn't change. "Tell me why you're interested in the driver," he said.

This guy's got ears everywhere, Sandoval thought. A one-minute exchange on the radio and he's all over it. Which makes me wonder how I would have played this if I knew it would cause such a stir.

Hell, probably exactly the same way.

"You guys don't have anything better to do? Sit around and monitor the radio all day?"

Bloome studied him carefully. "You know what we do here?" he said, nodding toward the closed door. "We've taken four hundred pounds of heroin off the street this year. Fuck knows how many guns on top of that. You want to come down to the evidence room and see?"

"I'll take your word for it."

"We report directly to the supe, and we can take over any case we want. At any time."

Sandoval had already seen it, in the motel room, when Bloome had told him SIS was taking over the investigation of Jameson's murder. That was the rule and it came straight from the superintendent himself—if SIS takes over, you get out of the way. There is no argument, no appeal, no room for discussion. If SIS wants your case, it's theirs.

But there's no way I'm gonna give them Mason, Sandoval thought. Hell, it's not even a case. It's something more.

"The driver of that Escalade," Sandoval said, watching Bloome's eyes, "Marcos Quintero. You think he's part of a case I'm working on. And you want it."

"I don't know anything about your caseload," Bloome said. "But I know you homicide guys usually have your hands full. And Quintero happens to be someone who's already on my radar."

"How do you know him?"

Sandoval watched Bloome working over the question.

"He's a person of interest," Bloome finally said. "That's all I can say."

Sandoval took a moment. He had to decide how to play this. "I'm watching someone else," he said, "and Quintero shows up. I wonder who he is. That's it."

Bloome leaned back in his chair. He didn't say a word.

This is where you keep your mouth shut, Sandoval thought. You wait to see what happens next. Because that might tell you everything you need to know.

"I'm going to bring in two of my men," Bloome said. "Then we can keep talking."

I just told him I was watching someone else, Sandoval said to himself. And yet he's not asking me who that someone is.

Because he already knows.

Bloome was startled when Sandoval stood up. This was clearly something that didn't happen. Ever.

You don't get up and walk out of this room before you're told to do so.

"Detective," Bloome said, "where the fuck do you think you're going?"

"I'm going back to work," Sandoval said as he opened the door and walked through it, never looking back. He could feel a dozen eyes burning right through him as he made his way through the office and out the door.

It was late in the afternoon now. Mason trailed the 300 as it headed back north through Englewood. It pulled over on a street in Wood-lawn and stopped at one of those rent-to-own places where you pay a little every month for furniture and electronics.

Mason watched them pay their visit to the manager, then get back in the car and take off, but this time they went to the express-way and headed downtown. They got off around the Loop and dis-appeared into the late-afternoon traffic. Two times, Mason thought he had lost the car but picked it back up again, until he saw it pull over in front of Morton's Steakhouse.

A second black Chrysler 300 was already parked out front. The doors opened and a woman got out from the back. From forty yards away, Mason could see why a half-dozen other men on the street were already staring at her. She was a perfect blonde with a perfect body, right off a Stockholm runway, the kind of woman only a man like Tyron Harris could afford.

Harris greeted her with a kiss. Then the four of them—Harris, this woman, and the two bodyguards—went inside, leaving the two drivers outside in the cars.

Mason parked the car, got out, and wolfed down a Polish dog at a place down the street, from where he could still see the cars. Unsure whether to call Quintero again, he decided to finish the day with Harris first. Waiting back out in the BMW, he could picture the scene inside the restaurant—bottles of wine and waiters falling all over themselves.

When the party broke up, Harris and the woman came out on the street, followed by the bodyguards, and this time both drivers got out of the cars and met with them. Everyone stood there, nodding and bumping fists. Still all business, but a little more relaxed. Taking their cue from the boss.

The woman got in the car with Harris, along with the bodyguards. Harris's car took off in one direction while the other car went in the opposite. Mason kept his eye on Harris's car and followed it back to the expressway. The sun was going down. He checked the gas tank and realized he didn't have many more miles left.

But he didn't have to go far. They stayed in the local lanes and got off on Forty-third Street. Just a few blocks in, they stopped at an old three-story brick building surrounded by two empty lots. Harris, the woman, and the bodyguards went inside. The driver stayed in the car.

Mason stayed a block away. He didn't want to get too close. With no other cars on the street, he'd be spotted in a second.

So this is Harris's home, Mason thought. It didn't look like much from the outside, but that was probably the point. There was plenty of room on the inside, and a little money could have turned it into something comfortable.

The best part of all was, Mason knew exactly where he was. He was in Fuller Park, which meant he could have gotten out, walked down past the stoneworks to the tunnel on Forty-fifth Street that would take him through the embankment and under the railroad tracks. On the other side of those tracks was Canaryville. A few more blocks and he'd be standing in front of his old house.

They called that embankment the Berlin Wall when he was growing up over there. They probably still did, because things like that don't change. You never went through that tunnel under the Berlin Wall. You stayed where you were, surrounded by your own.

He picked up the phone and called Quintero. He heard a woman's voice in the background, words exchanged in Spanish. Mason gave him the update. He had found Harris's home base. But he was surrounded by bodyguards at all times. Right now, there were two men in the house with Harris and the woman. Another in the car outside, and Mason wouldn't be surprised if that man stayed there all night.

"It's going to be hard to get to him," Mason said. "He's never alone."

"You keep watching him. You find a way."

"Do the math," Mason said. "Wyatt Earp couldn't get to this guy."

"I'll see if I can get you some help tomorrow."

"What are you talking about? What kind of help?"

"You'll know it when you see it," Quintero said. "Then you'll get your shot."

The call ended.

As the street went dark, Mason sat there with the phone still in his hand, watching the house of a dead man.

| 22 |

Mason's time had run out. He would get no chance to kill today.

It was midnight. The one man was still sitting in the car on the street. From a block away, Mason saw the window open and the hot red speck of a cigarette. A blue glow flickered in one of the top-floor windows for a while, then went out. Harris and his woman were in bed. Mason pictured the two bodyguards somewhere downstairs, probably sleeping in shifts.

He pulled away from the curb and drove north. He wasn't sure whether Diana would still be at the restaurant at this hour, but when he came up Rush Street, he saw the Camaro parked out front. He couldn't imagine somebody watching the car all day, but he looped around the block and parked in back just in case. He went in through the back door and found Diana alone in the office, reviewing the day's receipts cashed out by her staff. Her eyes were closed and she had her head propped up with her right hand.

"I'm here," Mason said.

She came back to life with a start.

"Didn't mean to scare you," he said. "You should have gone home."

"Had to close out the day."

"You always leave that back door unlocked?"

"Everybody left. They forget sometimes."

Mason looked around the office, then out the door at the darkened dining room. "You shouldn't be alone here," he said. "Somebody could walk right in."

"You don't have to worry about me, Nick."

Mason leaned back against the frame of the doorway. All he'd done that day was drive around looking for one man, then watching that man. Nothing else. So why was he so tired?

"You still haven't told me why you're here," he said.

She looked at him. "I work here."

"That's not what I meant."

He waited for her to answer. After a few moments, she finally spoke.

"I told you my father worked with Cole. He always fascinated me, from the first time I met him. He had this ... way about him. This *presence*. After my father was killed, he asked me to move into his town house. I was already becoming attracted to him by then, so it wasn't a hard decision. I didn't have any other place I wanted to go. But then I started to see what his life was really like."

She paused for a moment.

"He never tried to hide any of it from me," she said. "There were no secrets because there was never any question of me leaving. Ever. When they arrested him, he told me to stay here. He said he'd be watching me every minute. And that someday he'd be back."

"He's in for all day and a night," Mason said. "Life without parole."

"I'm telling you, he'll find a way."

Mason didn't try to argue with her. On some level, maybe he even believed the same thing.

"In the meantime, I have this," she said, nodding toward the open doorway. "I run this place. It takes everything I've got. It's not the best life in the world. I know that. But it's mine."

She looked up at him. Mason nodded. He understood. Maybe he was the only person in the world who could.

"Come on," she said as she stood up. "It's late."

He followed her to the back door and watched her lock it. She got in her BMW and left him there. He walked around to the front of the restaurant, got in the Camaro, and sat there for a moment. By the time he got back to the town house, she'd be upstairs. He'd sit by himself for a while, maybe out by the pool. He wouldn't be able to sleep. Not tonight.

Especially now, after talking to Diana, hearing about how her life had turned forever. How from one day to the next it would never be the same again.

For her, it was meeting her father's partner, the man named Darius Cole.

For Mason, it was something else entirely.

He drove south, down quiet, empty streets, to the edge of the city. Crossing the Ninety-fifth Street Bridge, he parked outside the fence line, turned the engine off, and opened up the windows to let the night air in.

Five years later, Nick Mason had come back to the harbor.

This is where the railroad tracks came in from the state line and joined the big oval that ran around the Port District. Freight cars were stacked in neat rows in the interior, all lit up with artificial light. On the opposite side, the dark water of the Calumet River flowed into Lake Michigan. The big ships all came here to unload, down here on the ass end of town, just this side of Indiana.

In a city that never put on too much makeup to begin with, this was where the landscape looked its hardest. It was all dirt and iron, and on one side of the shore, there was a great pile of old cars as if the ships had passed by and thrown them off like garbage on the side of a road.

This is where it happened, Mason said to himself. This is where you fucked up your life forever.

The job had been conceived as a misdirection, something you can pull off right under a man's nose because he's watching for something else. When you look at this Port District and all of the freighters unloading, you think, There's only one way this can happen. One of these freight cars will have a certain something inside. Which we'll proceed to unload into these two trucks and then drive to Detroit. Where we'll be paid over a hundred thousand dollars each.

A huge payoff for one night's work, if it was really possible. But, of course, it wasn't. Not even close. The level of security here at an international port—the quarantine area, the cameras, the around-the-clock guards . . . Even if you had someone on the inside, how would you get all that weight moved onto the trucks without anyone noticing within two minutes? That was Mason's first objection when the four of them were sitting around that table at Murphy's. The day they met Jimmy McManus.

McManus wore expensive clothes, he had a gold ring in one ear, and he talked like a man who knew how to do things. But Mason had this guy pegged, first sentence out of his mouth. When he was eight years old and his mother called him in the backyard, the first thing out of his mouth was "I didn't do it!" He was a Grade A fuckup when he was a kid, he was a Grade A fuckup when he was a teenager, and now he was a Grade A fuckup as a man. He was absolutely the last guy you'd ever want on a job. It violated a half dozen of Mason's rules just sitting here at this table listening to him.

"You'll never move that much freight out of the Port District," Mason said to him. "It's impossible."

"What kind of jackass do you think I am?" McManus asked him, and Mason had one or two answers ready. But then McManus laid out the plan.

Just beyond the Port District, after one bend in the river, was the area where sailboats and other smaller craft went for dry dock. That's where the boat would be found. Everyone would be watching the Port District while the trucks left the dry dock and drove right past them.

"So why you?" Mason asked. "They got this valuable shipment coming in, how come they put you in charge of delivering it to Detroit?"

"They need four locals. Four white-faced boys from Chicago who won't look out of place on the dry dock. Who can get the trucks in and out without having to stop and ask for directions."

"You said a hundred thousand. That's each man's share?"

"I get two hundred for setting it up. You guys all get a hundred."

"Then you can forget it," Mason said. "Equal risk, equal pay. A hundred and twenty-five per man."

Looking back, he should have already been on his feet and out the door instead of sitting there arguing over payouts. When McManus gave in, Mason looked at Eddie and he could tell his friend was thinking about it. He'd been sitting back and listening carefully, the way he always did. Absorbing every word and putting it together in his mind.

Mason dragged his friend outside.

"That man's a clown," Eddie said. "But I like the angle. Avoid the hot spot but don't try too hard to hide."

"Don't do this because you want to buy a house," Mason told him. "Do it because you think we can get it done and get out."

"You could do a lot with that money, too," Eddie said. "Think about Gina. And Adriana."

"I wouldn't even consider this if you weren't a part of it. If you walk, I walk."

"You know I'll have your back," Eddie said. "Don't I always?"

"So you're saying you're in."

Eddie looked at him. He didn't have to say it. He was in.

Two days later, the four men arrived at the dry dock with the two panel trucks. McManus had found the trucks somewhere, each one with a lot of miles on it and four bad tires. No shocks left at all. But the trucks were clean and forgettable and that's all they needed.

Mason drove one truck. He had Finn with him because Mason was the only man who could keep Finn calm if things went sideways. That left Eddie driving with McManus. They pulled into the dry dock area just as the sun was going down. They were wearing gray coveralls and baseball hats. The idea was to look busy, to look like they belonged there. You see four men loading up trucks, doing what looks like boring, productive work, you leave them alone.

Mason was surprised when they pulled up to the boat. It had come in earlier that day and was tied up along the edge of the dock and was bigger than what he'd been expecting. It was some kind of passenger ferryboat, at the end of a long journey from Canada, where it had been used for many years in Toronto's Inner Harbour. At least a hundred feet long, it was built to look like one of those old-fashioned paddle wheelers, with the long double-decker canopy and two dozen rows of padded benches.

The four men got out of the trucks and boarded the boat. They started pulling up the pads from the benches and bringing them back down to the trucks. It was late enough in the day that there were no other people around on the dry dock. But not so late that they couldn't see what they were doing. It was Eddie who had taken the time to make up the cover story about how this boat was scheduled to begin its overhaul the next morning and how he and the three other men had been contracted to pull out all of the existing upholstery. Hard, dirty, boring work that nobody else wanted to do. And yes, they were getting a late start on it. It had been one of those days. Rounding up the right crew. Then one of the trucks broke down. And so on. Eddie even had a work order made out to show if somebody happened to wander by and ask for it.

Eddie was good at cover stories and he was a natural-born actor. Finn could play along, but he could be counted on to stay in character for only so long. When the spell was broken, it was broken beyond repair and he would lose his game completely.

Mason kept an eye on Finn as they tore out the padding of one bench after another. He seemed to be doing just fine. It didn't look like they'd have any reason to use Eddie's cover story or to show the work order to any curious dockworkers who happened to wander over. There was a constant thrum of activity over in the Port District, but here at the dry dock it was deserted.

There was a sharp smell in the air. Diesel fuel, gasoline, dead fish. The last light of the day created a rainbow sheen on the surface of the water.

They worked for over an hour. Pulling up the padding was hard work. The pads weighed more than Mason would have imagined and he had to wrap his arms around each one to wrestle it off the boat and into the truck, feeling the rough wood of the backing against his forearms and breathing in the dust from the padding he had to carry so close to his face. When they were done with the padding, they started in on the life vests. These were stacked tightly underneath the benches and stowed in side compartments along both gunwales.

"A hundred twenty-five grand," Finn said to Mason as they were jumping off the boat for the last time. "Not bad for one night's work."

"We're not done yet," Mason said. "Keep your head on."

"I told you this guy was for real," Finn said. "You gotta admit, it's a pretty smooth play."

Mason kept hoping that Finn would shut the hell up. But he knew that Finn liked to keep talking and talking when he was doing a job and that it made him feel better. Like a release valve. So he let him keep going on about the money and what he was going to do with it like he already had it in his pocket.

Mason knew it wasn't that easy. Not yet. They still had to close up the trucks and get the hell out of there. Then drive the four and a half hours, curling south under the lake and through Indiana, then across the wide, flat plain of southern Michigan, all the way to Detroit. They had an address to drive to. Some old building deep in the heart of Detroit that nobody knew anything about. It was the part of the trip Mason wasn't looking forward to. But Finn and McManus were both convinced there was a big player out there who wouldn't think twice about paying that kind of money, especially for two trucks full of old boat padding and life vests that were actually worth about ten million dollars. If it was cocaine, which was Mason's best guess about what they were now hauling in these trucks, that meant about five hundred pounds of the stuff. A quarter ton. Hard to believe they could fit all that in a bunch of old bench padding and life vests, but, damn, if it wasn't a total bitch lugging all of that stuff off the boat. Mason knew he'd be sore as hell the next morning. But the money would make it a lot easier to deal with.

A better house for Gina. Maybe even college for Adriana. That's what he was thinking.

It was just getting dark when they finally slammed the truck doors shut and got in the cabs. Mason had Finn with him again. He could practically feel the man vibrating in the seat next to him. Mc-Manus pulled his truck out of the lot and Mason followed him. The road took them over the railroad tracks and through an old neighborhood of two-story brick buildings.

They didn't notice the car behind them. They didn't know that in that car were two DEA agents, out of a half dozen who had been staking out the Port District that evening, operating on a tip that a major shipment would be unloading at the harbor. They'd made the same assumption that Mason had made when he'd first been told about the job. If it's coming through the harbor, it's on one of the freighters.

The agents were settling in for a long night of surveillance. There was a lot of ground to cover, if you looked at the road and the long fence around the railroad tracks, and even at the waterline itself. There was no reason why you couldn't pull up a fast boat at the mouth of the river, load up, and then take off into the lake.

Nobody paid any attention to the two panel trucks leaving the dry dock. Until Sean Wright and his partner, who were watching the southern perimeter of the Port District, happened to see the trucks rumbling by them. Sean's partner, who was driving, pulled out and followed them. It was an unlikely lead, two trucks coming out of the dry dock, but better to make sure and not get reamed out by their boss if those trucks ended up being something they shouldn't have missed.

Mason kept following McManus as he drove the lead truck down Ewing Avenue. There was a series of three bridges coming up ahead. They would drive under them—two for railroad tracks, one for the expressway. Mason could feel Finn starting to tense up and for once he was just about to tell him to calm the hell down. The words were right there on the tip of his tongue.

That's when he noticed the car following close behind him. One of those dark-colored sedans that look plain and boring and suspicious. He watched his big side mirror for a few seconds, but it was too dark to see through the car's windshield.

They came to the first bridge. Its façade was a low, crumbling band of concrete just inches above their heads. Everything narrowed under the bridge, with rusted-out I beams squeezing in close on either side of the trucks. Pale sodium lights made everything look like a fever dream. Mason checked the car behind him. It was too close. If he even tapped on his brakes, there'd be contact.

McManus slowed down ahead of Mason. It was too narrow for speed. One slight mistake and you're scraping either iron or concrete or bouncing back and forth between both. They came out from under the first bridge and Mason saw the open night sky above them. The reprieve was short-lived as the second bridge loomed, even more dilapidated than the first, with a thin row of high weeds lining the tracks. The first truck was swallowed by the darkness, the sodium lights blinking and flickering now. Mason entered a second later. Another long, narrow passage, Mason holding his breath, waiting for the trucks to pass through into the open air again, already an-ticipating the daylight and the highway overpass beyond. A clear road ahead of them, the traffic light beyond the last bridge already turning green. He saw it all in that moment and let himself believe that they had passed through to safety.

Then a car pulled out in front of the first truck.

There was a service road from Indianapolis Avenue, cutting in sharply to merge with Ewing. An unmarked police car pulled forward and stopped, lights flashing, and everything that happened next was preordained by the basic physics of two trucks with bad tires and bad brakes suddenly trying to stop.

The lead truck hit the car. Mason's truck slammed into the lead truck. The car behind slammed into Mason's truck. A haze of noise pierced Mason's ears, and then there was a slow-motion pantomime that would have been a comedy if it didn't include such sudden deadly force—three more unmarked cars fanning out behind the first, plainclothes officers wearing tactical vests throwing open the doors and streaming toward them. Mason saw McManus already out the open door of the truck in front of him. He was running awkwardly, his head low, on a sidewalk on the other side of the iron rail. A moment later, Eddie came running behind him. Mason saw that his door was blocked by the girders and that there'd be nowhere to go even if he could get out that way. He had to get out the other door.

That's when the gunshots started.

He looked out the passenger's-side window just in time to see McManus fire at the two men coming out of the car behind them. One was hit. The driver threw himself to the ground on the other side of the car.

The screams of a dying man, the truck's windshield suddenly exploding all around him as the cops in front fired on them. Mason went down and tried to take Finn with him. He pulled down Finn's head and saw where the bullet had entered his skull through the left eye.

Mason pushed the door open and Finn fell to the pavement. Mason tried to pick him up, but he was already gone.

Shouts from the officers ahead of him, now using the first truck for shelter. The driver from the car behind him yelling, "Hold fire!" His partner was down. Those few seconds when every weapon was still, Mason saw his one chance to escape. Back to the open air between the bridges, a break in the concrete wall, through the brush and garbage, to a thin strip of land where the power lines were held high by their towers. The foliage had been trampled already by Eddie and McManus. Mason followed their trail to the high grass between the towers but did not see either man in the dark.

He heard more sirens in the distance. Every cop in the city would be out looking for them. He didn't think any of them had gotten a clear look at his face. That was his only hope. There was a line of trees to his right. He went in that direction, knowing that it was east and that it would lead him farther from his home and from where his car was waiting in Murphy's parking lot. But that was miles away and he'd have to find some way to get back there as quickly as possible. Which meant another vehicle.

He didn't know the neighborhood, so he didn't know if there was an easy spot for stealing a car, and he didn't have his tools with him, anyway. He hadn't carried those tools in years. He felt exposed as he came out of the woods and started walking down the street. He passed a storefront church and a liquor store. Some of the signs were in Spanish, and the people he saw walking on the other side of the street all had darker skin. He knew he'd stand out if somebody took a close look at him. The flashing lights of a police car lit the street.

Mason stepped into a parking lot and pressed his body against the wall as it drove by.

He went down another half a block, waiting for more police cars, waiting for the helicopter to start circling around in the sky, shining down its white-hot spotlight.

He held off the thought of Finn's dead body lying on the ground because right now it was all still in the moment and the moment was about getting the hell out of there. He saw the side door of a building open and the light spill out. A man came across the parking lot, stumbling his way to his car. He had his keys out in his right hand and he was singing something in Spanish.

Mason went right up to him, doing things the Finn way for once. You want something, you just take it, without another thought in your head. The man's eyes went wide when he saw Mason coming at him in that parking lot. *"Sangre,"* the man said, pointing at Mason's chest. But Mason was already on top of him before he could do anything else. The man was too drunk to put up a fight. Mason took the man's keys and discarded the man on the ground.

He got in the car, some filthy old beater of a thing, and pulled out of the lot. When he was finally a few blocks down the street, he looked down at his chest and saw the blood. For one second he thought, I've been hit. Then he realized that the blood was Finn's.

A few more police cars raced past him in the opposite direction as he made his way back to the heart of the South Side. He dumped the car a mile away from Canaryville and wiped himself off with a blanket he found in the backseat. As he walked up Halsted Street, he composed himself into something resembling a calm man taking a normal evening walk, then went in through the back door of Murphy's and cleaned himself off in the bathroom as well as he could.

He watched the last of Finn's blood run down the drain.

Then he got in his own car and drove home.

Gina was surprised to see him home so early. She figured he'd be out at Murphy's until after midnight, drinking with his friends.

"I'd rather be here," Mason said to her. "This is where I want to be." He went into his daughter's bedroom and sat there for a long time, watching her sleep. Then he climbed into bed with his wife and made love to her. That night would be the last time.

Now, five years and change later, Mason was sitting in his car, reliving that whole night.

The Port District was right there in front of him, glowing in the night. A turn of the head and there was the dry dock, mostly hidden in darkness.

The newspapers were still stacked in the box on the backseat. He picked them up, switched on his interior light, and paged through them. They were in reverse order, so he saw his own face on the first front page. Being led into the station, his hands cuffed behind his back.

Mason leafed through to another front-page photo, the Chicago police superintendent standing behind a microphone, telling a room-ful of reporters that even though it was a federal DEA agent who was killed, today all divisions and rivalries were forgotten. Today, Sean Wright was one of them.

One more front page. The day after the bust, the trophy shot, with a line of cops standing behind a table, bags of white powder spread out in front of them. He looked at the photo closely. Something didn't look right.

There should be more, Mason said to himself. All those hours we spent dragging the stuff off that boat, this is how much of it actually made it to the police station? Just enough for the photo op.

Mason switched off the light and sat in darkness again. He put the newspapers down and started driving, retracing their escape route. He went down Ewing, the street quiet, with everything closed up for the night.

Why did we come this way? Why didn't we get right back onto the expressway, start making time for Detroit?

When he got to the bridges, he felt the same claustrophobic feeling as the concrete and iron closed in around him. The same cheap sodium light giving everything an otherworldly glow.

The street was empty and he was alone under the second bridge. He slowed down as he got to the exact spot. Here's where Finn got shot. Here's where Finn died, sitting on the seat next to him.

He came out from under the bridge, to the place where the cops were waiting for them. This exact spot. Of course. This is where they were waiting.

He stopped the car in the middle of the street, opened the door, and stepped out. He looked back at the bridges, at this perfect funnel that would bring anyone coming down that street right into your lap if you happened to be waiting *right here.*

That's exactly how it happened, Mason thought. All those cops had to do was sit here and wait for us. Sit here and wait for McManus to lead the trucks into the trap.

He remembered what Eddie had said to him about McManus being out of the truck before the first shots were even fired. He remembered what he had seen with his own eyes—McManus firing only at the agents behind them, never at the cops in front of them. He panicked when he saw the agents blocking his escape.

It was all stacked against them that night. Everyone involved, right down to the man who put the team together in the first place.

Mason, Eddie, Finn... they never had a chance.

Everything else that happened, Mason said to himself, from going to prison and losing my family to meeting Darius Cole and making this deal to come back. And everything I've had to do, killing one man, planning on killing another...

It all goes back to that one night. The night we were betrayed.

23

Mason had two and a half seconds to kill five men.

He had a Glock 20 in each hand, the same type of gun he'd used at the motel room. He'd never fired with his left, but the first two men had to be done together. Take out the first bodyguard, then the second. Easy shots, then move on to the drivers. Keep firing and all five men will be dead. If he does it in two and a half seconds.

Time slowed down as the bullets ripped through the two bodyguards' chests, hearts blown apart before they even knew it was happening. Then the two drivers, each with a gun drawn from his belt and half raised when he brought his 20s together and the men were dead before their brains' signals reached their trigger fingers.

Now it was just the fifth man, Tyron Harris, who didn't have a gun after all, just a laptop bag that he held out in front of him like a shield. Two and a half seconds barely gone, but Mason could take his time. He could breathe and look down the sight of the one gun in his right hand. Finish his job and walk away.

But then Harris's bag was already falling and behind it he saw the two barrels of the sawed-off shotgun. He heard a sound and saw the flash from one barrel as it took away his hands and his guns. Another sound and another flash and his chest was gone. Just enough time left to look in Harris's face as he heard that same sound a third time.

He opened his eyes and sat up in his bed, breathing hard. The morning sun was shining through the window.

It was a chime. A doorbell.

He got up and put some clothes on, meeting Diana just as she was coming down the stairs. It was early, but she was already dressed for work.

"Are you expecting someone?" he asked.

"No," she said.

He went down and opened the door. Lauren was standing on the little cement porch with Max sitting patiently at her feet. As soon as he saw Mason, the dog went past him and up the stairs, into the town house.

"I had my car today, so Max and I thought we'd stop by before work," she said. "I hope you don't mind."

He stood there for a moment, trying to figure out the best way to handle this.

"I thought, from the other night..." she said, her face starting to turn red. "I mean, we talked about me bringing him over... And you didn't come to get Max yesterday, so..."

"Hello, whose dog is this?" It was Diana from somewhere behind him.

"This is Diana," Mason said. "She manages the restaurant."

Lauren looked up at Diana as she came down the stairs. "Um, hello," she said.

Diana gave Mason a look and reached out to shake Lauren's hand.

"This is Lauren," Mason said. "She works at the pet store over on Grant Street."

The two women eyed each other closely.

"I see," Diana said with a cool smile. "And this is her dog?"

"No," Mason said. "Max is mine."

"That's interesting," Diana said. "Were you planning to tell me?"

Mason got quiet. Both women stood there, watching him.

"Can we step outside for a moment?" Mason said to Lauren. Then to Diana, "Excuse us, please."

He guided Lauren outside to the sidewalk.

"I'm working at her restaurant," he said. "I haven't found a new place yet."

"I'm sorry, Nick. I shouldn't have come here."

"I'm glad you're here," he said, trying to keep his voice cool and even. He'd been working so hard to follow his rule about keeping his personal life and his professional life separate, a rule that seemed more vital now than ever. Even if it was more and more impossible. Having Lauren here at the town house and, hell, having her meet Diana... This did not belong on the program.

"I got a lot of stuff going on today," he said. "Would you mind looking after Max for a while longer? I don't want to leave him here all day alone."

"I could probably do that."

"I'll try to stop by your place tonight. It might be late."

Lauren looked at him carefully. "You're gonna call me first, right?"

"Yes," he said. Then he went back in to collect Max, who already seemed interested in the pool. Diana just stood there, watching him. By the time he got Max back downstairs, the garage door was open and Diana was already driving off in her BMW.

"That's your roommate," Lauren said as she watched the car disappear down the street.

"Like I said—"

She put a hand up to stop him. "You don't owe me any more explanation, Nick. I'll see you later."

She gave him a quick kiss and he could feel the hesitation even then. But then she smiled and got in the car with Max.

Mason let out a long breath and went back inside to get cleaned up for the day. A few minutes later, he was in the Camaro on his way to the restaurant. He hadn't gotten the chance to talk to Diana about the cars, but he noticed when he got there that she had parked in back of the building again. There were no parking spots on the street, but when he went in the side lot he got the space closest to the street. Anyone coming by would see the car there.

He went inside and found her in the kitchen.

"Lauren seems like a lovely girl," she said to him. "And Max seems like a great dog. I'm sure you'll be very happy together."

"How much trouble are we in?"

"You're lucky I love dogs," she said, handing him the keys to the BMW.

Mason left the kitchen. He was still shaking his head when he got into her car. Then he settled back in the seat and his assignment came back to him. An almost smile left his face as he started the car and headed out into the day.

When he got to Fuller Park, both of Harris's cars were parked in front of the house. One car had spent the night there. The other must have arrived in the morning to pick up the woman. He watched

THE SECOND LIFE OF NICK MASON

her come out and leave in that car. Harris was back to one driver and two bodyguards.

They all got in their car and left.

He followed them through the South Side again. It was a different set of businesses today, including the barbershop and the restaurant from Mason's original list that they hadn't hit the day before, but it was the same routine. Go in and pay a quick visit, Harris carrying his laptop. There was one laundromat where Mason could actually see in through the window. Harris sitting there at a table with the laptop open, the manager sitting down next to him. The bodyguards standing by, looking serene. Harris gave the man a hug when he stood up, then he and the bodyguards came out and got in the car and went on to the next business.

By the end of the afternoon, Mason had put in another long day of watching. He was starting to worry that they'd eventually clock him. You can only trail a man for so long, no matter how well you do it, before he turns around and takes a good look at you.

The next stop was different. They headed back north, over the river, and parked by a little coffee shop near Homan Square. The three men got out and went inside. Mason saw Harris sitting at a table with two strangers. His bodyguards were at a separate table nearby. Half an hour later, all five men came out together. Mason got his first good look at the men Harris had been meeting with. They were both wearing dark suits. One man was older and acted like he was in charge of the whole meeting. His hair was cut close, so fair it was almost white, and there was something almost paternal about the way he put his arm around Harris's shoulders. There probably weren't too many men around who did that.

Mason had seen enough cops in his life. These were definitely cops.

They stood outside on the sidewalk for a few minutes. Then the two cops got into a black Audi and drove away. Harris and his men kept talking for a moment. Their friendly smiles were long gone. Then they got into their car and left.

Mason followed them downtown, where they parked outside Morton's again. Harris was clearly a creature of habit. A weakness, perhaps, but not when you travel with an army.

Quintero said I'd be getting some help, Mason thought. Whatever that means, I sure as hell haven't seen it yet.

The same woman showed up and looked just as blond and gorgeous getting out of her car after shopping or waxing or whatever the hell someone who looks like that does all day. Harris kissed her and then they all went into the restaurant. When they came out two hours later, Mason was ready for the cars to separate again, but this time they both headed out in the same direction.

Mason pulled out behind them, tracking them through town. They passed right under the expressway. They weren't going back to Fuller Park. They were heading west on Lake Street, into new territory. Then both cars slowed down in the right lane, turned off into a parking lot, and it all made sense.

It was a strip club.

Mason pulled in after them. He parked a row over and watched everyone leaving the cars. Harris and the woman. All of the men. They weren't going to leave anyone sitting here in the parking lot.

A strip club meant noise and confusion and very little light except on the stage. It sure as hell meant distraction, unless these men were from some other planet. Mason stayed there in the car, his cell phone in his hand. He looked down at the screen for a long time. Finally, he called Quintero.

"They're all at a club," he said. "There may be an opportunity."

"Open your trunk," Quintero said. "Lift up the spare tire."

He got out of the car and opened the trunk with the phone still held to his ear. He pulled up the carpeting to expose the spare tire compartment. The tire was secured with a nut, so he had to find the tool bag in the trunk's side compartment to loosen it. He looked both ways down the parking lot, then pulled up the tire.

There was a pair of black leather gloves. There was no gun.

What the hell, he thought. He picked up the gloves and saw the knife underneath. The blade was folded inside, but he knew one push of the button would release it. Six inches long and no doubt razor-sharp.

"Listen to me," Quintero said. "Take a moment, get your head on straight. If you're not focused, you'll do something stupid. Keep your eyes open. And don't do anything unless you have a clean exit."

It sounded like he was reading Mason his own rules. Mason put the phone away. He stood at the back of the car for a long time, looking out at nothing. He turned down the volume in his own head until it was close to silence. His daughter's face came to him, then a vision of her running across a soccer field. He held on to the image for a full minute. Then he started moving.

He tried the gloves on for a moment, just long enough to pick up the knife and put it in his right pocket next to the phone. He took the gloves off and slid them into his left pocket.

Mason knew that the Chicago firearm laws were a joke, with no automatic jail time even if you get caught carrying around a machine gun. But knives? They had that shit covered in this town. Nothing over two and a half inches, nothing spring-loaded, and another vaguely worded law that all but banned open carry. You can carry a Boy Scout jackknife in your pocket, not on your belt, and that's about it.

He paid his money at the door. A long flight of stairs led up to the main floor, with a strip of white light on each step. The music was already loud as Mason started his way up. It got louder with each step, until he reached the top and everything opened up into an airplane hangar–sized area with three runways and a half-dozen other circles of chairs, all facing dance poles. There were maybe a hundred men in the place, every race represented. Women danced on all three runways, but the more private areas were empty except for one in the far corner. Mason didn't have to look for more than a second to see that that's where Harris and his crew were sitting.

The music kept pounding in his ears. The lights were flashing and making everything look not quite real. Mason chose a chair near the middle of the room, facing Harris's corner. One of the waitresses came by and bent down over him, showing plenty of skin. He ordered a Goose Island and settled in to study the room.

Threats. Witnesses. Exits.

One of the dancers drifted over and gave him a little wave. She was wearing only a G-string. That was the law. You keep the bottoms on and you can serve alcohol. Mason gave her a nod and then looked back across the room.

The club's best dancer was on the pole over there. The men were all watching her, and Mason could see the blond woman sitting in the chair next to Harris. Her hair seemed to glow in the half darkness. He saw her smiling, the white flash of perfect teeth, sitting there on the arm of the man who seemingly owned the whole city that night. She was enjoying herself and watching the show with just as much enthusiasm as the men around her.

Mason counted the men. There were five, including Harris. The whole crew. This night out was their big reward for standing around and looking hard all the time or else sitting in a car for hours on end, even overnight.

The dancer who had waved to Mason was on the pole closest to him now. He took out a twenty, didn't want to stand out as the guy who just sat there and never tipped anyone. She caught his eye and came over close, getting down on her knees so Mason could slip the bill into her G-string. She blew him a kiss and went back to her pole.

The music seemed to get even louder. The lights kept flashing. Mason took a hit off his beer and then put the glass down.

This could be the night, Mason said to himself. All I need is for him to be alone. Just for a few seconds. Then I'll get my chance to do the unthinkable for a second time. And he'll never leave this place alive.

As he looked over again, Mason saw one of the bodyguards stand up, walk along the back wall, and disappear behind a partition. The men's room. Two minutes, the man came back. He sat down on the other side of the woman and then Harris himself stood up. The bodyguard was halfway to his feet again when the woman put a hand on his forearm. She gestured to the dancer as if saying, No, keep him right here, put on a show for him.

The bodyguard sat back down. Harris kissed the woman and walked along the back wall alone, retracing the bodyguard's route to the men's room.

Mason stood up.

He made his way to the back of the room, moving slowly. His movements were all careful, perfectly thought out. Don't move like a man on a mission. Don't look over at the party in the corner. Keep looking at the dancers because they're the only reason you're here. If someone spots you, if one of them gets up to intercept you in the bathroom, you're just a customer. A nobody.

The music got louder and louder. The lights kept flashing.

Mason went behind the partition. He paused at the door to the men's room, waiting a moment to see if one of the bodyguards was about to put a hand on his shoulder. It didn't happen. They were all watching the show out there.

One last moment to turn back, Mason thought. One last chance not to be the person who will do this.

Why me? That same question coming back to him yet again. He still didn't have an answer.

But it doesn't matter, he thought. Not now. You made a deal. You signed a contract. You have no choice.

Do your job.

Mason pushed open the door and stepped into the men's room. When the door closed behind him, the volume of the music was cut in half. It felt like he was out of his own body. Somewhere high above, looking down, watching it all happen.

The man at the sink looked much smaller. A small, weak man with no bodyguards to protect him. The gloves were already on Mason's hands. The man hadn't looked up yet. When he finally did, his first glance at Mason was dismissive. A white boy barging into the bathroom, interrupting his solitude. He looked back down and then up again. This might be a tough white boy, judging from the fading bruises on his face. Then he saw the gloves. Which didn't make sense. No sense at all.

Until it did. But then it was too late.

Mason was already on top of him. Harris struggled, trying to elbow Mason in the ribs. Mason stabbed him once in each lung, then the heart. Three rapid jabs, then with one hand closed over his mouth, Mason moved the blade in one smooth motion across the man's throat. A thin line for one second, then growing into a bright red band. Mason held on tight. That's the exact moment he came back into himself. Holding on to the man and watching both of their reflections in the mirror. The man he was holding turned from a drug dealer into a scared man losing his life. A man with a history and a family. A man who grew up in Fuller Park, just on the other side of the Berlin Wall.

Mason kept holding him. His arms were wrapped tight around him. One last embrace. He could feel the man's chest heaving as he fought for breath.

The man's heart beating.

Fast. Then irregular. Then not at all.

Mason felt the man's life leaving his body. Until he looked at his own face in the mirror.

It was the face of a cold-blooded killer.

The blood kept running. Mason let go and Harris hit the sink on the way down to the floor. Mason dropped the knife in the sink, took off the gloves and put them back in his left pocket. Then he backed away from the body on the floor, the blood already pooling on the dirty tile. He checked his clothes. Clean enough. Pushing the door open with his shoulder, he went back out into the noise and lights and didn't look toward the corner. He made himself move at half the speed his body wanted.

Walk slow. Walk slow. Walk slow.

An eternity until he reached the staircase. Down the lighted steps, one at a time. Not looking behind him but expecting the sound of heavy footsteps catching up with him.

It didn't happen. Nobody followed him. Nobody paid any attention to Nick Mason as he pushed open the main door and disappeared into the night.

| 24 |

The brutal murder of an SIS sergeant, then the execution of a prominent drug dealer, both less than a week apart—it all made Detective Frank Sandoval believe that Nick Mason was following a carefully planned hit list. The question was, how many more names were on the list?

It was after midnight again. Sandoval showed his star to the uniform at the door, then went up the stairs to the club. At night, a high-end place like this should be doing big business, but there was no music playing, no customers, no dancers. The place was lit up with an ugly set of fluorescent bulbs on the ceiling and filled with cops.

Sandoval weaved his way through the chairs and runways until he saw a flash of light coming from the bathroom. He went around the partition and stood in the open doorway. It had been propped open with a chair. The body was lying on the floor in an awkward pose no living man ever struck, the legs tangled together and the torso half turned on its side. A lake of dark red blood had spread for three or four feet in every direction, and Sandoval could see the smooth straight line across the man's throat. The man's eyes were open.

A police photographer was standing on the far side of the bathroom, his shoes covered with white fabric. He adjusted his camera setting and took another picture, blinding Sandoval with the flash.

"Weapon?" Sandoval said.

"In the sink," the photographer said without looking up at him. "Don't come in."

The photographer took another shot. Then another.

Sandoval stepped away from the door, around the partition, and back into the main room. He found a young detective from Area North a few feet away, writing something on his pad.

"Anybody see anything?" Sandoval asked him.

"Nothing," the detective said. "Staff said he had a whole posse with him, took over that corner over there. Four or five other black men, depending on who you ask. One white woman. But they were all gone before we got here."

That's when Sandoval heard the heavy footsteps coming up the stairs. Three seconds later, a new group of men spilled out into the room like they were invading the place. A half dozen of them, all in dark suits. It was SIS.

"What the fuck," the young detective said. He went off to talk to the first man he could find until Sandoval saw Sergeant Bloome making his entrance.

"SIS is taking this one," he heard Bloome say.

Sandoval wasn't surprised. They take over yet another case. They stay in control.

"Okay, Sergeant," the detective said. "It's all yours."

Sandoval watched all the other cops follow the detective down the stairs. Even the photographer. Sandoval took half a step forward. Pure physical reaction. Then he stopped himself. In that one instant, he had made his decision.

The first time he had run into Bloome, the man had treated him like nothing more than a nuisance. The second time, he had tried to intimidate him and pump him for information.

This was the third time, and Sandoval wasn't leaving. It was time to face the man. He knew he couldn't outpunch him, but maybe he could wear him down, wait for an opening. Finally get to him.

There was only one answer to intimidation. Exposure.

He took a breath and swallowed. Bloome spotted him and crossed the room.

"Sandoval," he said, "you deaf? Get the fuck out of here."

"I don't take orders from SIS," Sandoval said. "I'm still working my own case."

Bloome paused a moment to consider that. "Not here," he said.

"How come you get so nervous every time you see me, Bloome?"

Bloome raised his eyebrows. Two other SIS detectives, both within earshot, stopped and turned to listen in.

"Look at you," Sandoval said. "Why are you so concerned about me? A dead SIS sergeant, then a dead major dealer, four days apart? You worried about a connection?"

"You think you can stand there and ask me questions like I'm some goof you just picked up off the street?"

Stay cool, Sandoval told himself. Here's where he tries to end it in one punch. The harder he comes on, the more you lay back. That's how you get to him.

That's how you drag this whole thing into the light.

"How many homicide detectives they got in this city right now?" Bloome said. "How many *hundreds* of you guys are out there and your clearance rate is what, forty percent? Fifty in a good year? That's a fucking joke, Sandoval. You guys are an embarrassment. That's why they put us together, so they got some real cops around here who know what the fuck they're doing. I'd let you stick around and watch if I thought you'd learn something."

A few more SIS officers were looking over at them. Sandoval could see it on their faces. Nobody ever talked to Bloome this way.

"Can you believe this guy?" Bloome said, looking around at his men and smiling.

You're getting closer, Sandoval told himself. You can read it in his body language, the way he's tensing up, the way he's standing taller, like an alley cat getting ready to fight. He doesn't know how to handle this.

"Maybe I call your sergeant," Bloome said. "How 'bout we call him, have him explain this to you?"

"Why waste time with my sergeant?" Sandoval said. "Let's go to the captain. Or maybe the chief. Let's have Internal Affairs sit in and make it a party. Then the feds. I bet the DEA would love a look."

"There's no connection between this case and the murder of Ray Jameson."

"Then why are you sweating?"

Bloome stood there, looking at him. You caught him, Sandoval thought. You slipped your way through and you just fucking caught him. Now don't let up.

"Maybe you should call your union rep," Sandoval said. "Lawyer up, tell them everything."

Bloome had a slight smile on his face. "You think you got something? You got that feeling you've turned up a big case? That *rush*?"

Bloome took a step closer to him.

"You're not exactly walking around in a white suit yourself, Sandoval. Everybody knows your partner's dirty. How long would it take me and my crew to find something on you, huh? Five minutes?"

Sandoval held his ground.

"This is our city," Bloome said, looking down at him. "You should know that by now. We run it and everyone else is just a visitor."

"If you're the fucking king of this city," Sandoval said, "why are you soaking through your two-hundred-dollar shirt?"

Bloome waited a beat. Then he took one step closer.

"I'm gonna take an interest in you," Bloome said. "You don't want that, Sandoval, because there's one thing I know about cops. Somewhere in your life, you got a big problem. A weakness. You got people in your life you care about. I'll get to everything, every corner of your life and everybody else around you."

You got him, Sandoval thought. You fucking got him.

"I'm giving you one time-to-walk-away card," Bloome said, stepping even closer so that the two men were just inches apart. "Because I am the last guy you want to put in a corner."

"Wherever you are," Sandoval said, "you put yourself there. Now step the fuck back." Sandoval was ready for whatever came next. One hand on your shoulder. Or two hands.

Then probably every other SIS cop in the room.

"What do you need?" Bloome said.

"What are you talking about?"

"You want the collar? This is a heater case, Sandoval. I'll bring you in, make you the lead. We run it my way, but you can be the hero. They pin a medal on your chest, take your picture, give you a promotion, a nice raise. You'll make sergeant by the end of the year."

Sandoval didn't answer him. He just shook his head. He'd already said no to the hammer.

Now he was saying no to the carrot.

But he was walking away with something a lot better. He had his answer. Bloome had already given away his connection to Quintero. Add to that these two cases and now this attempt to essentially buy him off...

If Bloome had speed-dialed Darius Cole and put him on the speakerphone, it wouldn't have been any better.

"You're making a big mistake," Bloome finally said. "I hope you're not too attached to your career."

Sandoval looked him in the eye one last time.

"Do you even fucking remember when you were a cop?"

| 25 |

Among the thirty parents watching the soccer game, Nick Mason was pretty sure he was the only two-time murderer.

He stood against the backstop again, behind the bleachers, but with the same good angle to see the entire field. He had his sunglasses on even though it was not sunny. It was a gray day, on the verge of being cold, but he couldn't feel it. He stood there motionless, leaning against the rough wood, with his arms folded across his chest.

He kept seeing the face he saw in that mirror in the strip club. It was the face of another man. A man he didn't know.

A man he didn't *want* to know.

But I would do it again in a second, Mason thought, staring across the field. Give me a thousand different chances to get out of that place, to see this nine-year-old girl running around, chasing a ball, for a few minutes every week...

I would do it again. Every time.

The game developed on the field as Nick Mason focused on one player. He kept watching his daughter even when play stopped, even when she went out for a few minutes and stood along the far sideline, cheering on her teammates.

At halftime, some of the parents stood up to stretch or to go have a smoke somewhere far away or talk on their cell phones. Mason stayed where he was, his eyes on his daughter as she sat in the grass and talked to two other players. When the second half was about to begin, a thought struck Mason and it was enough to make him move. He reached into his pocket and pulled out his cell phone. He dialed Lauren at the pet store, trying to remember if showing up at her place the night before had been a definite promise or just a maybe. Either way, he wanted to see her again. He wanted to walk down the street with her and become that other person again, if only for those few hours.

The players were running around the field again. As Mason listened to the phone ringing, he looked for his daughter and for one moment couldn't locate her. Then he spotted her on the far corner of the field, lining up for a free kick. She sent the ball into play and it was quickly cleared and sent down to the other end of the field. Adriana stayed behind, kneeling down on the grass to tie her shoe. Everyone else followed the movement of the ball toward the other goal, but Mason couldn't care less about who scored or didn't score. He was the one man still watching his daughter on the opposite end of the field.

That's when he saw the other man standing there at the edge of the parking lot, about twenty yards away from Adriana.

Jimmy McManus.

He was wearing his tight jeans and muscle shirt again, with the same gold chains around his neck. It took Mason a moment to process the fact that the man was here, in this same park. And now as

McManus scanned the people watching the game, his eyes settled on Mason. McManus nodded to him, then to Adriana, back to him, as if verifying that this was really his daughter. He reached his own conclusion and gave Mason a thumbs-up.

Then McManus took out his cell phone and gave out a sharp whistle. Adriana looked up from where she was still kneeling on the grass and Mason could see a look of confusion on her face. McManus pointed his phone at her and pushed a button. He was taking her picture.

Mason was already in motion.

He came out from the shadow of the backstop and ran along behind the bleachers toward the parking lot. McManus put up his hands, like, what the hell is this, but then he turned and headed back into the heart of the lot. He moved fast, not exactly running, but not exactly waiting around to see what Mason was going to do to him, either.

Mason caught up to him and grabbed him by the collar. He felt at least one of the gold chains coming apart in his hands as McManus escaped and starting running.

McManus was already in the next row of cars over, so Mason cut through a family getting out of their minivan and heard shouts from behind him. He reached McManus just as he was fumbling with his keys, trying to open the door of his bright red Corvette. Mason got a hand on the back of his neck and drove his face into the roof of the car.

Once.

Twice.

A third time.

The noise—bone on metal—echoed across the parking lot as the blood spurted from McManus's shattered nose. Mason spun him around and drove wicked left hooks into his ribs, the kind of punches that break bones and bruise organs, that make you bleed not out but in.

"It's not enough you set us all up at the harbor," he said as he grabbed him by the throat and pulled him back upright, *"now you're taking fucking pictures of my daughter?"*

The next punch folded McManus right in half and he slid down the side of the Corvette. Mason was pulling him to his feet again when he heard the voice behind him ordering him to freeze. He ignored the voice and kept hitting McManus until he felt a great weight knocking him down from behind and then his hands being twisted behind his back and locked tight in cuffs.

Mason lay there on the ground for another few minutes, catching his breath, until he looked up and saw Gina's face among the crowd of people who had gathered in the lot.

He didn't see Adriana. Just Gina, and her face told him everything he needed to know about what she was feeling.

I was just protecting her. He tried to say it loud. I was just protecting our daughter. But she couldn't hear him.

Then he was lifted up from the ground, put in the back of the squad car, and taken away.

| 26 |

It had taken a week for Nick Mason to be back between three concrete walls and a set of metal bars.

The walls of the holding cell at the Elmhurst Police Station had just been painted buff green. And the stainless-steel sink and toilet were immaculately clean. The bench he was sitting on had a pad thick enough to sleep on. It was probably the nicest cell Mason had ever seen.

But it was still a cell.

He looked at his hands, still red and swollen, especially the right hand, where the knuckles were scraped raw. He knew he had hit McManus at least three or four times with that hand. Maybe the car, maybe the ground.

His hands hurt, but there was something else, too. This feeling he had that maybe beating the shit out of McManus wasn't a smart idea, but at least it was *his* idea. For the first time since getting out, he had committed an act of violence because he had wanted to, not because he'd been told to. It belonged to him and nobody else.

That was the moment. Sitting there in that cell, looking at his hands. That's when Nick Mason started to wonder if he could stop being a fucking windup robot and start taking back control over his own life.

He heard footsteps in the hallway. But it wasn't the Elmhurst officer coming to release him. It was Detective Sandoval.

Mason sat up straight on the bench but didn't say a word.

"I heard they brought you in," Sandoval said.

Sandoval dragged the one folding chair from the narrow hallway between the cells and the outer wall, sat down, and looked at Mason.

"There was an off-duty at the game," Sandoval said. "He stopped you before you killed that guy."

Mason didn't respond.

"They're gonna give you a warning about calling the police next time. Then you'll be out of here. But I asked them to hold you a minute so we could talk."

This is just what I fucking need, Mason thought.

"A dead sergeant in that motel room. And then Tyron Harris last night. You've been busy."

Mason stayed silent.

"So now I got you," Sandoval said. "I got Cole. I got your buddy Marcos Quintero. Ex–La Raza. How long's *he* been working for Cole? You gotta have some protection to get out of *that* life. Or did Cole just buy them out?"

Mason leaned his back against the concrete wall.

"I got your housemate, Diana Rivelli, who runs Cole's restaurant. I hope you're watching yourself. Cole finds out you're fucking her, he's not gonna be happy."

Mason shook his head at that one.

This guy wants Cole, Mason thought. More than me, more than

Quintero, more than everyone in the world who works for him. Or ever will. Cole is at the top of the pyramid and this detective will kill himself trying to get to him.

He might arrest ten other people on the way. They'll promote him and give him a medal and take his picture with the mayor.

But he'll never be satisfied until he gets to Cole.

"I put all that together on my own," Sandoval said. "What do you think a whole elite task force of cops could find out?"

"Are we about done here?" Mason said.

"Did you hear what I just said? You ever hear of a group of cops called SIS? They got put together a few years ago to go after dealers. They can do anything they want, Mason. They make big numbers, so nobody gives a fuck. They're walking around with a god card, courtesy of the mayor and the police superintendent. Drag some guy out of his car, beat the shit out of him, take his money, take his drugs. Bust down somebody's door without a warrant? Nobody cares."

"This is Chicago," Mason said. "What else is new?"

"They've been together for seven years," Sandoval said. "What do you think that means?"

Mason looked up at him.

"They made that bust at the harbor," Sandoval said. "That was SIS."

Mason's grip tightened on the edge of the bench. He flashed back to the cars pulling out in front of the trucks. Not regular patrol cars. These cars were unmarked.

"Is that a big surprise? Soon as they got put together, you don't think Cole was smart enough to buy these guys out? It was a business arrangement, Mason. Goes on for years, until it finally goes to shit. And that's where you came in."

Mason kept squeezing the bench pad tight, thinking about what this man was saying to him.

"You know what the most dangerous thing in the world is, Mason? A dirty cop. Nobody's watching him. Nobody can touch him. He can do whatever the fuck he wants. You got a dirty cop in your life, you got a big problem. But you know what's even worse than a dirty cop? A whole fucking *squad* of them."

I saw Harris meeting with them, Mason thought. Those were the guys in the suits that second day I was following him.

"There's a sergeant named Bloome," Sandoval said. "Tall guy, pale, with gray eyes, looks like a fucking Russian border guard. If you see him coming, don't even bother waiting for an introduction."

Mason could see him in his mind, standing outside that coffee shop with his arm around Harris. "Why are you telling me this?"

"You killed his partner, Mason. And you're his biggest problem in the world now. He had to know that Cole sent you. You think Cole can protect you? Twenty-four/seven? You think you can hide somewhere? These guys go anywhere they want. I'm surprised they're not here already. Couple SIS detectives from the city show up, tell the sergeant at the desk out there they're gonna take you back? You wouldn't make it halfway there. You would disappear. No body. Just gone."

Sandoval stood up and came up to the bars. "You're public enemy number one, Mason. If I was a betting man, I'd be taking odds on how long you're vertical. They'll go after your family. They'll go after anybody and everybody close to you. They'll do whatever it takes."

Mason closed his eyes for a moment. He made himself take a breath. Then another. His daughter was out there, riding her bike or watching television or who knows what. But Mason was here, locked up in the cell. They could take her right now, he thought, and I couldn't stop them.

"You got one way out of this, Mason. Me."

Mason looked at him.

"The wolves are loose," Sandoval said. "They're coming after you. I'm throwing you a line here. It's the only way you're gonna live through it. I know you're just a soldier, Mason. You take orders from above. Help me take the whole thing down and I'll help you. Tell me everything you know, I'll send you somewhere they can't get to you. You, anybody else in your life. Whatever it takes. But the offer expires as soon as you leave this cell. You walk out of here and I can't help you."

"The offer was dead the minute you walked in here," Mason said. "I'm not admitting to anything you say I did. But if even half of it is true, you know there's no way I can talk to you."

Sandoval stayed there at the bars for a long moment, waiting for Mason to say something else. Then he turned and left.

| 27 |

The wolves were loose and Nick Mason had brought
them to the two people he had most tried to protect.

Parked on the dark street, Mason watched Gina's house. He'd
come here as soon as he was released from the Elmhurst Police Station after an officer had driven him down to his car. The whole way,
Sandoval's words echoed in his head.

He got out and took a long look down the street in both directions. Then he walked up the driveway. A spotlight over the garage
made an arc of light across the front yard. More lights shone from
inside the house.

The front door opened. Gina's husband came out and closed it
behind him.

"Get out of here," he said. "Right now."

Still in his soccer-coaching shirt, he stalked across the front
lawn. Mason stepped up until he could see the man's face.

"Brad," he said. "That's your name, right?"

The man had two inches and maybe twenty pounds on Mason,

but the muscle was built in the gym, not on the street. Still, Mason had no interest in fighting him. Not tonight.

"I need to talk to you."

"About what? What you did at the field today?"

"Listen to me," Mason said. Then he stopped. What the hell was he going to say? How could he possibly explain this?

"I'm calling the police, Nick. You can't be here."

Mason was surprised to hear his name. He'd never met the man before. He'd never said a word to him.

"You gotta leave," Mason said. "All three of you. Now."

Brad just looked at him.

"Go somewhere safe," Mason said. "Don't tell anybody where you're going. Give me your cell phone number. I'll call you when things change."

Brad listened to every word. When Mason was done, he shook his head.

"What…" he said, drawing out each word, "… are… you… talking… about… ?"

"I can't tell you," Mason said. "You just have to believe me. Take them and go."

Brad took a step away, rubbed the back of his neck and shook his head like he was waking himself from a bad dream. Turning back to Mason, he said, "Haven't you caused us enough trouble?"

"Yes. But, right now, I'm just trying to keep Gina and Adriana safe. And I need your help to do that."

"You know I'm trying to do the same thing, right? I'm trying to protect…" Brad hesitated and took a quick look back at the house. "I'm trying to protect your daughter. You want me to do that, don't you?"

"Yes."

"So let me do that. Whatever this is you're bringing here, you know it's not good for her. This doesn't belong in her life. *You* don't belong in her life."

Mason had spent so much of the past few days hating him, but he knew this man would protect Adriana with everything he had. He'd give his life for her. That was Mason's best chance to get through to him.

"If I was in your place," Mason said, "I'd be just as pissed off. But I'd listen if somebody like me said there was a real threat."

"Then let's go to the police."

This man didn't grow up where Mason did. He didn't live through the past few days. Mason figured his last contact with a police officer in uniform was giving him his license, registration, and proof of insurance when he forgot to slow down at the speed trap.

"You can't take this to the police," Mason said. "You have to trust me."

Before Brad could say another word, the front door opened. A new rectangle of light was cast across the lawn and, for an instant, Mason saw Adriana shadowed against it.

Then he saw Gina taking her away from the door and closing it. That one single moment, it hit Mason harder than any punch he'd ever taken. He had to close his eyes and swallow.

"I need to talk to her," Mason said.

Brad shook his head.

"I need to talk to my daughter," Mason said. "We can do it right here. Wherever you want. With you or with you and Gina. I just need to see her for one minute."

"She's been through a lot today, Nick."

"I'm asking for one minute."

Brad looked toward the house. "She was very upset about what happened at the field. But she thought she recognized you. She was asking if that was you even though Gina told her she'd never see you again."

Another gut punch. Mason took it and waited for whatever was going to come next.

"I'll be right back," Brad said.

He turned and went back into the house, leaving Mason to stand there in the darkness. When he came back out, he walked halfway down the lawn until Mason could see his face.

"One minute," Brad said.

Mason closed his eyes and let out his breath. Then he followed Brad back to the front door.

When Brad opened it, Gina was standing there. With Adriana.

She was wearing pajamas—little elephants in a row, marching single file around her body, one elephant holding on to the tail of the next with its trunk. When he saw her at the field, her hair had been braided. Now it was wet and hanging down to her shoulders.

"Hi," his daughter said to him.

All of the words Mason had thought he'd say to her when he finally got this chance deserted him. His mind was empty.

"Hello," Mason said.

He looked up at Gina. She had her lips pursed tight, one arm folded across her chest, the other around Adriana's shoulder.

"You're a good soccer player," Mason said. "You're very fast."

She nodded.

"Faster than all the boys," he said.

"Except one," she said. "Branden is faster."

Mason smiled.

"I'm sorry about what happened today," he said.

"I saw you chase that man," Adriana said. "He was taking my picture."

"I'm sorry if it scared you."

"He was creepy," Adriana said. "I'm glad you chased him away."

There was a pause. Gina kept watching him closely. He wasn't sure where to go next.

"Adriana," he said, "do you remember me?"

"I thought I saw you at another game, too."

"Do you remember when we all lived together? When you were four years old?"

"Until you went away to jail."

Mason looked up at Gina. "Yes."

"It was just me and Mom for a while," she said. "Then we moved here."

"I know it seems like a long time ago to you," Mason said, "but to me it's just like yesterday. I hope you know how much I hated leaving you and Mom."

"What did you do?"

Mason looked at Gina again. "You know how you mess up sometimes?"

"Yes."

"Well," Mason said, "I really messed up bad. I did something I shouldn't have done."

She nodded and looked up at her mother.

"I just want you to know," he said, "that all I ever wanted to do was to be with you every day. All I wanted to do was be your daddy."

She thought about it for a while. "Did the jail have metal bars?"

Mason almost laughed. "Metal bars for the first four years," he said. "Glass for the last year."

"A glass jail cell? Weren't they afraid it would get broken?"

He smiled again. "It was pretty thick glass."

She looked up at her mother again. Then back to Mason. "I bet you're glad you're out of jail."

He looked down at her. "I am."

"We should go to bed," Gina said.

Mason wiped his face. "Can I have a hug before I go?"

Gina hesitated but then let go of Adriana's shoulder.

His daughter came to him and wrapped her arms around his waist. Mason closed his eyes and rubbed her back.

Then Adriana let go.

He watched her turn around and walk up the stairs with her mother.

Mason watched her until she disappeared. The two men stood there in the entranceway. They didn't say another word to each other. Brad nodded his head and that was all Mason needed. He went back out into the night.

He sat in the car for a while, still feeling his daughter's arms around him. Then he wiped his face again and turned the key.

I'm ready, he said to himself. Whatever comes next, I'm ready.

| 28 |

Holding his daughter for the first time in five years had made Nick Mason more determined than ever to find a way out of this nightmare. It was the one thing giving him the strength to keep moving.

When he was near the city limits, his cell phone rang.

"Restaurant," Quintero said. "Now."

The call ended.

The restaurant meant one thing—Diana and the possibility that she was in as much danger as he was.

She's just as connected to Cole as I am, Mason thought. Sandoval said as much himself.

But she has no idea who may be coming after her.

He gunned the Camaro down the expressway, crossed the Kinzie Street Bridge, and turned up Rush Street.

Quintero's Escalade was waiting in the parking lot. The driver's-side window slid down as Mason pulled in next to the SUV and got out.

"Where is she?" Mason asked.

"She's safe," Quintero said. "Inside, working. Don't worry about her."

"What did you call me for?"

"You need to find that woman who was with Harris."

Mason thought back to the strip club. The blonde who ran interference with the bodyguard and gave Mason his chance at Harris alone in the bathroom.

"What about her?"

"Track her down and give her this," Quintero said.

He reached over to the passenger's-side seat, picked up a black leather carry-on bag, and handed it to Mason. The bag wasn't big, but it was densely packed with something and had to weigh twenty pounds. Mason didn't ask how much money was inside.

"She was supposed to bring something to me," Quintero said. "Now she's disappeared. If you find her, make sure you get what she has and bring it to me right away. Do not waste a minute, you understand?"

Mason thought about the routine he'd seen over the two days of following them. "There's only one place I can think of finding her. If she's not there, I got no idea."

"Then you better hope she's there. Her name's Angela."

"You gotta listen to me," Mason said. "I don't know what this woman has that you want so bad, but I've got something a lot bigger to worry about."

"No you don't," Quintero said. "Stop wasting time, because the same people after you are after her."

Mason didn't bother asking him anything else. He'd been dealing with these cops for years and he must have known what would happen once Mason started doing his job.

Would have been nice if somebody had told me, Mason said to himself as he looped the bag over his shoulder.

"Hey," Quintero said. "Before you go, what the fuck were you doing getting arrested today?"

Mason remembered what Quintero had said to him. That first day, sitting in his car in front of the town house. *You get picked up for* anything, *now you've got two problems. The one you got picked up for... and me.*

"He went after my daughter," Mason said.

"If you were held overnight," Quintero said, "then everything would be fucked right now."

Mason put a hand on the car and leaned in. "Did you hear what I said? It was *my daughter.*"

"What's his name?"

"Why do you want to know?"

"What's his fucking name?"

"McManus. Jimmy McManus."

"The best thing you can do for your family is to do your job," Quintero said. "My job is to handle anything that gets in the way of you doing that. McManus is my problem now."

Mason looked him in the eye. He didn't know exactly what that meant, but it probably wasn't good news for McManus.

"Go find that woman," Quintero said. Then he backed out and drove away.

On his way back to his car, Mason saw a man and a woman walking in through the front door of the restaurant, going inside to sit down and have a nice dinner. Normal, happy people. Diana was inside, doing her job.

I need to tell her, Mason thought. She needs to know about the wolves. Tonight. After I do this.

Mason got back in his car and headed down the street. He took a few breaths, thought about where he was going, and tried to imagine what he might find when he got to Harris's house.

What could this woman have that every dirty cop in the city would want so badly? As he got onto the Dan Ryan Expressway, a squad car came up behind him. Mason tensed up and ran through his options. Gun it and try to make the next exit. Or look for a break in the median so he could turn and go in the opposite direction. But then the squad car blew by him.

Mason let out his breath and kept driving.

When he got to Fuller Park, he slowed down to a crawl as he approached the house. The street was just as empty as the last time he was here, the night he had followed Harris. There were no lights on in the house itself. Both black Chrysler 300s were parked out front, but there was nobody sitting in either of them. No need to provide security for Tyron Harris anymore. He was probably still lying on a metal table somewhere downtown.

Mason watched the house for a while. Then he turned and parked a block down one of the side streets. He turned off the interior light in his car and waited a few minutes. Let your eyes adjust to the dark, he told himself. When you get out, move fast, but not too fast. Look like you belong here.

Mason took out the flashlight from the glove compartment. Then he eased open his door, got out, and closed it quietly behind him. He walked back toward the house—a long minute of feeling exposed and vulnerable.

His cars are here, Mason thought. So where are his men? The house looks deserted.

An old chain-link fence, half-collapsed in on itself, bordered the backyard. He looked up and down the street and then found a spot where he could step over it. Mason went to the back door, gave another look in every direction, then tried the knob. It was locked.

The door window had nine panes of glass. Mason hit the bottom right pane with the heel of his hand, felt the glass break, and heard it falling on the floor inside. Then he reached through to unlock the door.

He pushed the door open an inch and listened. Nothing.

Absolute silence.

He turned on the flashlight and covered most of the lens with his hand so that only a thin beam of light was cast into the kitchen. The first thing he saw was the wreckage. Both doors of the refrigerator were open and all of the contents had been spilled out onto the floor. Every cabinet was open, every dish broken.

Taking another step, he felt a shard of glass break under his foot. He stopped and listened until he picked up on a noise from somewhere above him. A creak. Then another. Could be the house settling, he thought. Probably makes sounds like that all day and night.

He stayed still and waited. He didn't hear another sound. Then, as he swung his flashlight, he saw the door that led down to the basement. He opened it and shone his light down the stairs. The smell of damp air and mildew came rushing up at him.

And something else.

The four bodies were all piled up at the bottom. All black.

Mason knew exactly who these men were.

| 29 |

Mason had to confirm that Angela was not among the victims. He went halfway down the stairs, just close enough to see each man's body, how it had landed and gotten tangled up with the others. There was no woman here.

Quintero said they were looking for her, Mason said to himself. If she was here, then they must have taken her away after killing every single one of these men.

Meaning I got here too late. And now it's time to get the hell out of here.

As Mason went back up the stairs, he mentally retraced his steps through the house, thinking about every surface he might have touched. He didn't think he'd put his hand anywhere except for the back door itself. Simple enough to wipe down the knob on his way out, which was the one direction he was now headed. He grabbed a dish towel from the kitchen.

He opened the back door and was just about to wipe the knob. That's when he heard the voice.

One more thing about these old houses—they have the ventilation system that runs in open ducts between the floors. He could remember living in old pieced-out apartments in shithole houses in Canaryville when he was growing up and how sometimes you could actually see through the vents to the apartment below you. Interesting if the person down there was worth looking at. Not so interesting if it was some drunken asshole in his underwear yelling at his wife.

He heard the voice again. Hoarse and strained, almost unintelligible. It might have been the whimper of an animal. An alarm clock was already going off in Mason's mind. He'd been here too long. Being in the same house for more than a few minutes with four dead men piled up in the basement seemed like a violation of one of his rules. Or, in any case, a really bad idea.

But he had to find out where the voice was coming from.

He started into the main part of the house and saw the ghostly shadows of upturned furniture. The dining room table on its side, all of the chairs thrown around the room and broken. A cabinet of drawers emptied.

Mason stood and listened again. Then he went into the front room and saw thin threads of blood woven together on the floor. Bullet holes in the walls.

He went up the stairs.

A spiderweb of cracks spread out from the center of a huge HD screen, even bigger than the screen in the town house. Everything else in the room was opened up and turned over, but there was no more blood up here. No more bullet holes. Just anger and destruction.

The third floor had two bedroom suites with whirlpool tubs, tile showers, king-sized beds, and everything else you could ever want. Every drawer and cabinet had been emptied.

More anger, more destruction.

But no bullet holes. And no blood.

He got down and looked under the bed in the first room. The closet had been emptied, but he took a moment to kick through the pile of clothes on the floor. Same in the second room.

There was an even bigger pile of clothing in that closet, but there was nobody hiding there. He looked up at the ceiling and started to wonder about the attic.

The voice spoke again and this time Mason could make out a word. A woman's voice, almost singsong now. Saying the same word over and over. It sounded like... *Jordan*?

He waited.

Nothing happened.

But then he looked more closely at the back wall. A wire shelf with a break in the middle was mounted on the wall. He wrapped the dish towel around his hand, grabbed the shelf, and pulled.

Half of the back wall started to swing forward. There was nothing but darkness behind the wall until he swung his flashlight and saw a woman's wide-open eyes.

And the gun barrel pointed right at his chest.

Her eyes got wider and Mason knew her finger was already tightening on the trigger.

A first-time shooter will squeeze the trigger and pull the shot high and right. It's the only thing that saved him.

Mason dropped to the ground as the gun shattered the silence of the room and he felt the bullet pass over his left shoulder.

He rolled away from the closet and came up on one knee.

"Don't shoot!" he said. "Angela, you need to trust me. I can get you out of here."

"Where's Jordan?" she said, her voice ragged.

"How long have you been in there?"

"I don't know. Hours. He told me to stay here. He told me to shoot anybody else who came into the room."

Mason remembered seeing Angela get out of the car at the restaurant and the driver who seemed to double as her bodyguard. He figured that must have been Jordan.

And that Jordan was one of those men at the bottom of the basement stairs.

"Jordan is dead," he said.

He waited a minute and listened to her softly crying. Then he got to his feet.

"Come on," he said to her. "We need to get out of here."

She came out of the closet with the gun still in her hand.

It was a Beretta M9. Probably Jordan's gun. And probably why Mason was still alive. The thing weighed two pounds, with a fifteen-round magazine. If she'd had her own little Beretta Nano, she probably would have shot him right in the head.

"Give me the gun."

She looked down at the gun and then handed it to him. He tucked it into his belt.

Her face and hair were a mess from all of the crying, and from hiding in that little secret compartment for God knows how long. But she was still beautiful.

"Where are we going?" she said, wiping her eyes with both hands.

"Anywhere you want to go."

"Are you sure Jordan's dead?"

Mason had been thinking she was some kind of fashion model from Sweden the first time he had seen her with Harris outside Morton's. This time, he was hearing her talk with the classic flattened-out vowels of a South Sider. This woman was more Stockyards than Stockholm.

"He's dead," Mason said. "They're all dead."

He thought she'd start crying again. But, instead, she looked at him with what seemed to be a sudden hatred.

"I recognize you," she said.

"The club," Mason said. He flashed back to that moment when Harris got up from the table and this woman held back the bodyguard who was about to accompany him to the bathroom.

"Yeah," she said, looking away. "I was there. Now you want to buy something from me."

She went back to her hiding place, bent down in the darkness, and picked something up. When she stood up again, she handed it to Mason. It was the size of a hardcover book. But it was made of shiny black plastic.

"You wouldn't be giving me anything," she said, "if I didn't have this. And you wouldn't give a shit about me getting out of here."

If I didn't give a shit, Mason thought, I'd shoot you and take it off your dead body.

"What is this?" he said, turning the black box over in his hand.

"It's what those cops were after."

"Come on," Mason said, grabbing her arm.

He led her downstairs, but she stopped in the kitchen and demanded to know where Jordan was. He pushed her past the stairs to the basement and out the back door, not forgetting to wipe off the doorknob on his way out.

As they stepped outside, he felt more vulnerable than ever, leading this woman across the backyard and over the fallen-down fence to the street.

"Where the hell is your car?" she said.

"Right down here," he said, fighting off a sudden urge to put her back inside the house. Headlights blinded him as he opened the passenger's-side door and put her inside. By the time he got to his own door, the car was coming up behind them, moving fast. The flashers came on, red and blue lights bouncing back and forth between the headlights. An unmarked police car.

He found the keys and fired up the Camaro. The tires squealed on the pavement as he hit the gas and started running.

30

The cop caught up to Mason by the first corner. The car edged its nose in front of his Camaro and tried to ride him right off the street.

This wasn't the usual unmarked police sedan, either. It was a Dodge Hellcat. Mason couldn't see the face of the driver. He didn't need to.

Swinging his car to his left, he felt the scrape on his driver's-side door as he edged back in front of the other car. The Dan Ryan Expressway was just ahead of them, but Mason wasn't going to head that way. If this guy didn't have help, he'd have it pretty fucking soon and they'd be able to run Mason down if he was stupid enough to get on the open road. They'd put him into the guardrail and then shoot them both. They wouldn't even let him get out of the car.

Mason cut the wheel, made a hard right, and then another right. Angela screamed as she was thrown against the passenger's-side door.

"Hold on," he said.

The two turns had Mason doubled back and heading west. He couldn't see the car behind him, but he knew it wasn't far away. Angela snapped her seat belt on and slid down in the seat, her eyes closed, as Mason gunned the accelerator.

I've got one good chance here, Mason thought as he headed toward Forty-fifth Street. The embankment came up fast and he barely slowed down as he went under the bridge. The Berlin Wall, this same boundary he'd known since he was a kid. The girders flew by, just inches from either side of the car. When he came out on the other side, he was in Canaryville. He was home. Now he had both the fastest car on the road and home-field advantage.

Mason cut down to Forty-seventh, where he'd have some room to run. He passed every car in his lane, swerving into oncoming traffic and then back, hearing a dozen different horns blaring behind him. It was late enough at night, he figured he could just barely make this work.

He looked in the rearview mirror and saw the Hellcat two blocks behind him. Its flashers were still on and some of the other cars on the road pulled over to let it pass.

I need some space, he thought, before I can start using the side streets. He went around the cars waiting at the next red light, coming so close to an oncoming truck that he felt it tick against the corner of his rear bumper. He swung back hard to the right and gunned it up Halsted. It was a good open stretch where he could really fly and he ran through two more red lights. When he looked in his mirror, he could barely see the flashing lights a few blocks behind him.

Time to show you Canaryville, he thought as he took a hard right on Pershing. He looked back to make sure he was clear, threw the car onto the first side street, then took another turn and headed down through the heart of the neighborhood. He knew the streets were narrow here. He had to be careful where he was going. One car backing out of a driveway and he'd be fucked.

But he knew which streets ran all the way through and which streets ran into dead ends. He even remembered the alleys he used as shortcuts when he was a kid.

He went down one of those alleys, working his way past the back-yard garages and squeezing past a dumpster that almost blocked him dead. He finally looped all the way around and pulled into the loading dock of the old meatpacking plant that had been standing there for a century. He wedged the car in tight between two semis. Nobody would see them here. He turned off the car so that even the low, growling idle wouldn't be heard.

He caught his breath for a moment while Angela slid up in her seat and looked out the window.

"Where are we?" she said.

"Someplace safe," Mason said. "We'll let them run for a while."

"They would have killed me," she said. "If they had found me in that house..."

Mason nodded.

She closed her eyes and put her head back against the seat. He could see her whole body shaking. Her hair seemed to glow in the near darkness.

"How did this get so fucked up?" she said. "Jordan was just trying to get me out. To get us *both* out."

It wasn't hard to imagine. The man was assigned to protect this woman. He spends that much time with her alone in a car. He smells her perfume, laughs at her jokes. She starts really talking to him. She sees something in him. Something different.

"He didn't want to be in the life anymore," she said. "We were going to go away together. This was our chance. That's why I..."

She didn't finish the thought. She didn't have to. They both knew the parts they'd played that night.

Mason reached behind him and grabbed the black box from the backseat.

"Are you gonna tell me what that is?"

"That was Tyron's insurance policy."

Looking it over more carefully, Mason saw access ports along one edge, where you could plug in a power supply, and then another cord to connect it to a computer.

Or a laptop.

"He kept records of every meeting he had with those guys," she said. "Every deal he made. Every payment."

"It's a backup drive," Mason said. He pictured Harris, walking down the street with his laptop. Going from one place to the next. Doing his daily business.

"It was more than just the deals," she said. "He had this . . . thing on his laptop. Whenever he was with any of them, he'd turn it on and it would record the whole conversation. Even when the laptop was closed. It's all there."

Mason remembered the coffee shop near Homan Square. The man in the suit, his arm around Harris's shoulders. That conversation, whatever it was about, was stored inside this box, too.

"He thought it would protect him," Angela said, looking down at her hands. "He thought it would protect *everyone*. All of his men. And me."

Mason hefted the thing in his hand. A couple pounds of hard plastic and computer parts, whatever else was in one of these things.

And enough evidence to bring down a whole squad of dirty cops.

"You need to get out of town," Mason said, "and never come back."

"Take me to 2120 MLK. This guy's gonna let me stay there for a few days, then get me out."

No surprise, Mason thought. There will always be a man to help you when you look like that.

They waited another twenty minutes. Then Mason pulled out from the loading dock and went back up the alley. When he got to Forty-seventh, he looked up and down the street, trying to spot the Hellcat or anything else fast enough to chase him down. He made the turn and drove at normal speed, hoping to blend back in. But he was ready to run again. One flashing light and he'd gun it.

He went to MLK and found the address. He pulled over in front of the house and waited for the door to open. When he gave her the bag, she unzipped it and took a quick look at the contents. She let out a breath and nodded her head.

"See ya around," she said as she got out quickly and went to the door of the house.

Mason watched her go inside. Then the door closed behind her.

His cell phone rang. He took it out, expecting Quintero. I got your fucking package, he was ready to say to him. Tell me where you are.

But it was Diana.

"Nick," she said.

One word and he could already hear the fear in her voice.

"Diana, what's going on?"

"They want to talk to you. Nick, get me out of here."

Mason didn't have to ask what she was talking about. He could already feel it burning a hole through the bottom of his stomach.

"Mason," a voice said.

"Who is this?"

"This is Bloome. Bring that hard drive to me. We trade, the two of you walk away."

Mason knew it was a lie. He wasn't going to question it. It wouldn't help him. It wouldn't help Diana.

"Where are you?" Mason said.

He listened carefully as he was told exactly where to go.

"Your men are looking for my car," Mason said. "You have to call them off."

"Already done," Bloome said. "No need to do this in the streets."

"I'm on my way."

He ended the call. Then he pulled out the M9 that Angela had given him. He checked the load. It looked like the clip had been full when she had fired it at him. So with one round in the chamber, that left him fifteen.

Fifteen shots.

| 31 |

As Mason looked down into the depths of the enormous quarry, he was already standing in the crosshairs of a high-powered sniper rifle. His friend Eddie Callahan was waiting in his vehicle by the gate, a Precision Pro 2000 trained at Mason's back.

It felt like he was standing at the edge of the world. There was a four-hundred-foot drop straight down this sheer wall to the quarry's floor. A thin line of cars ran along the highway on the northern rim, tiny pinpoints of light like distant stars. The space between here and there just empty darkness.

They'd been taking limestone from this place for almost a century, grinding it into powder, using it for roads, for cement, to build the skyscrapers of the city. He could taste it in the air as he scanned the canyon for any light, for any movement, for any sign at all that would tell him where they were. Where Diana was.

He had come through at the southeast corner, had gotten out of the car and unlooped the gate's chain. The padlock had been unlocked, as Bloome had told him it would be. He had driven through the swirling dust to the edge, where a vehicle could start the long descent down the narrow shelf cut into the wall.

Mason took a breath and tried to clear his head. His plan was simple. He was going to save Diana. He was going to kill everyone else. Everyone he could find.

The hesitation he felt at the motel, that would be gone. The horror he felt at the strip club, that would be gone.

He would take all of the violence that had been forced into his life by Darius Cole and he would turn it all back on these men.

This is why he chose me, Mason thought. It finally makes sense to me. He didn't want some premade killer from the cellblock. He wanted to make his own.

He saw the raw materials in me even then, sitting across the table from me in a prison cafeteria. Everything he'd ever need.

And now here I am.

Mason shook out his hands and took one more breath. Then he went back to his car.

As he drove down, crossing the city line, he had gone over everything he knew. He knew these cops wanted the black box that was sitting on his backseat. They needed to protect themselves. Once they had that, then they would kill him. They had to eliminate this threat, this soldier Cole had sent to fight in this war.

And then they would kill Diana. No other way to see it. Not only would she be a witness, even more important, she would be the one way they could strike back at Cole. She was his only weakness.

They couldn't touch Cole directly, not if he was sitting in a federal prison two hundred miles away. They could kill Mason, they could kill Quintero, they could kill any man Cole sent to Chicago. Cole would just send someone else.

Diana was the one person in the world he cared about. The one person who couldn't be replaced. Kill her and you've taken the war right to him.

Mason couldn't imagine where the war would go after that. But he knew he'd be a part of it.

And you don't go to war without someone covering your back.

"Where are you?" he said as he touched the Bluetooth headset in his left ear.

"I'm stopped at the gate," Eddie said. "I see you."

"I'm going down. Hang back until I tell you."

Mason had remembered what Eddie had told him when the two of them were catching up over beers in his garage. How he still got to the range once in a while even though he'd been out of the Army for years.

He just hoped Eddie could still hit anything inside a thousand yards.

"You're too far away," Eddie said in his ear. "Too dark to cover you."

"Do your best," Mason said. "Don't get too close."

He was inching his way down the shelf. You couldn't call it a road. It was too steep a drop, with no rail on the side. One slip and the car would go over the edge and fall for five seconds before finally hitting the bottom.

He was glad Eddie was trailing behind him in a four-wheel-drive Jeep.

"Hey," Mason said, gritting his teeth as he kept the wheels dead straight. "While I got a chance..."

"What?"

"Shoot anybody you want. Just not me or Diana, okay?"

He heard a nervous laugh on the other end.

Mason came to a place where he had to make a tight turn and

head in a new direction. He could see nothing past his headlights. When he finally crawled all the way to the bottom, he stopped for a moment and got out of the car to take a look around.

The quarry floor was mostly flat and empty, with dark mounds of broken limestone scattered in the distance. As he looked up, he could barely see the thin line of cars on the highway that passed along the north rim.

He had just driven into his own grave.

"I'm down," he said. "Nobody here."

He got back in the car and drove across the quarry, his car bouncing on the rough ground. As he got closer to the north wall, he saw nothing but a sheer cliff rising forty stories above him. He turned and traced along the edge of it until he found a pass-through leading under the highway.

He found himself in another canyon, just as vast as the first, just as deep, but now there were ponds of standing water all across the floor, and in the far corner, he could make out a dim circle of light.

"Pass-through under the highway," he said, picturing Eddie in his Jeep somewhere behind him. "I'm on the other side."

"You're too far ahead of me. Wait up."

Mason didn't bother answering. As he moved the car forward, his headlights played against the construction vehicles, all standing idle for the night. He weaved his way past a giant backhoe, the tires ten feet high, then a dump truck just as large. He was a tiny figure in a tiny car, a speck moving across this vast chasm. But he kept going. There was no turning back.

Mason still couldn't see why they were doing this here. A quiet place, with nobody else around—that much he got. But they could have done that almost anywhere. Even in the middle of Chicago you find an abandoned house, with known drug traffic. Just like the house in Fuller Park. Bring Mason there. Kill him. Throw him down the stairs with the rest of the dealers. Even Diana. Just two more people in the wrong place at the wrong time. Caught up in something they should have had no part in. Let the uniforms sort it out.

But no, it was all going to happen here. In a fucking limestone quarry.

Mason made a tight turn between two more construction vehicles and saw a circle of light in the distance. It could have been a mile away or it could have been suspended in outer space.

He kept driving toward it, splashing through the standing water, then passing by one construction trailer, then another. The circle kept growing, kept getting brighter. Until Mason came close enough. Stopping his car, Mason stepped out onto the ground.

He stood at the mouth of a tunnel.

The circle was forty feet high. A perfect round hole cut into the side of the cliff. A strand of braided rebar, as thick as a tree, reinforced its perimeter. A half-dozen halogen lamps were mounted around its rim, giving the entrance an eerie glow.

Mason just stood there, looking up in wonder at the size of this tunnel.

"Where are you?" Eddie said.

"Find the tunnel," Mason said. "Can't miss it."

This was the Deep Tunnel he'd been hearing about since he was a kid in Canaryville. Because Chicago was built on a swamp, the sewers and the storm drains would overflow every time it rained hard enough. They'd been working on this tunnel for forty years, so they could bring all the rainwater and piss and shit and fuck knows what else in a giant pipe away from the city and apparently right into this quarry. The whole thing would be flooded soon. Any dead bodies left in this quarry would be swallowed up under four hundred feet of water and never seen again.

Now I get it, Mason thought. This is why they chose this place. He took the gun from his belt.

Then he walked into the tunnel.

The ground had been cut flat here. Flat enough to walk on. Flat enough for a vehicle to drive on. The walls rising on either side and coming together in an arc high above his head, the coiled rebar like the ribs of a great whale. Thick cables ran along the ground on the right. Electricity, water, maybe even air. There were more lights spaced every few feet, but only a few of those were lit. Every hundred feet, there were two bulbs mounted high on the arc, one left, one right, together creating a single ring of light. These rings ran one after another, the lights getting dimmer and dimmer as they stretched off into infinity. Just enough light to see your way through in a nighttime emergency. During the day there'd be workers coming through here, vehicles going back and forth, fans blowing, every light turned on. A busy underground street. Now the place had been given back almost completely to darkness.

He had no idea how far he'd have to walk to find someone. He had no idea how long he'd live.

He walked through great puddles of standing water. It was cold and as his shoes got more and more soaked, his feet started to get numb. He could hear more water dripping all around him. He could smell it in the dense, humid air.

Go back, he said to himself. Get the car, drive it right down this tunnel's throat. Get as much speed as you can. But then he saw a shadow appearing ahead, and as he got closer, he saw it was a great orange-painted crane that had been parked there for the night. There was no way he'd ever get around it.

Mason put the gun back in his belt and climbed up the ladder to the cab. What the hell, he thought. Maybe they left the keys in this thing. But there were no keys. And he had no idea how to operate it, anyway. He jumped back down to the ground.

As he looked back, he couldn't see any trace of the entrance anymore. He'd been swallowed by the earth.

"Nick!"

It was all he heard from the Bluetooth. He was starting to lose the signal.

"Here."

"Can't see... Bad light..."

Shit, Mason thought, looking down the tunnel. A faint ring of light, then full dark. Another ring, then full dark. No matter what kind of scope Eddie's got, how do you see to the other end?

But I'm not letting him get any closer. This is my war, not his.

Mason walked through another puddle of cold water, saw another shadow, this time high along the right side of the circle. As he got closer, he saw that the wall had been cut away and a flight of metal stairs had been set into the rock. He climbed the stairs and went along a catwalk until it came to a door. It was thick metal, with a large wheel in the center, like the door of a submarine. He tried turning it but it wouldn't budge.

He went back down the stairs to the ground. He took a few breaths to reset himself, the air even thicker here, so wet and filled with the smell of limestone it was like drinking mineral water.

"Where the fuck are you?" he said out loud. His voice disappeared into the void, bouncing off the rock walls and echoing in both directions.

He took off the headset and yelled, *"Where the fuck are you?"*

Not a smart thing to do, but he didn't care anymore. He'd come too far. It was too dark in here and Eddie would have to get too close for any kind of shot. Mason's feet were now completely numb and he was choking on the thick air. He knew he'd never have any advantage on these men no matter what he did. They knew he was coming. They'd see him long before he got close. There was no surprise. They were probably wearing their tactical vests, too. They'd be fools if they weren't.

No match for Eddie's rifle, but any body mass shot from Mason's M9 would be blocked by the Kevlar.

So all they have to do is wait for him. Then gun him down.

If that's the way they wanted to do it.

Mason thought about it. Maybe they don't do it that way, he said to himself. Maybe I've got one slim chance.

"I'm right here!" he yelled, hearing the words echo again. *"What the fuck are you waiting for?"*

He waited. He listened. Finally, he heard a voice.

"Down here, Mason! Walk slowly! Hands on your head!"

The words reverberated and could have come from either direction, but he knew they had to be coming from up ahead.

You already made your first mistake, Mason thought. You just proved to me you're gonna do this like a cop.

He put the Bluetooth back in his ear and the gun in his belt, left hip, handle forward. He started walking again. He heard more water seeping down the walls, felt a fine spray of drops hitting his face. A chill ran down his back.

You're cops, he thought as he moved forward from one dim ring of light to the next.

Dirty cops, clean cops—you are all still cops.

And I know cops.

He saw the slight flicker of a shadow in the distance ahead of him. It was impossible to know how far ahead—three lights, a dozen lights—but there was something up there. He kept moving.

The shadow grew as he continued on. It became bigger and then split into two separate shadows. Mason again shook out his hands to release the tension from his body. He took in deep breaths of the cold, wet air.

In. Out. Breathe. Heart rate down.

As he walked through one more passage of complete darkness, he reached over with his right hand and adjusted the gun on his hip.

Right here. Exactly right here.

He was surprised they hadn't stopped him yet. Surely they could see him as he stepped under the next light. But nobody said a word. Nobody moved except Mason.

Forward. Forward. Shoes splashing through another icy puddle. He couldn't feel anything. It was all motion. Reaction.

"I said hands on your head!"

The unmistakable voice of a cop. This is how he'd been trained. He's done it this way a thousand times. Even if he's a fucking mile below the ground, getting ready to gun down a man in cold blood, he's still gonna do it the same way.

It's a routine to him. It's practically hardcoded into the man's DNA. He'll tell Mason to turn around next. To keep his hands on his head. To walk backward toward him until he's close enough. Then to get down on his knees.

"Hear them," said the voice in his ear, the signal almost gone. "I'm coming..."

But Mason knew Eddie couldn't help him now. He reached up, clasped his hands across the top of his head, and kept walking. He started to see the quality of the light change as the walls on either side of the tunnel seemed to bow outward. There was a wide spot here, with another flight of stairs cut into the rock of one wall, accessing another high door. He saw all of this as the two shadows ahead of him resolved into a man wearing a long coat.

And Diana. She was on her feet, but otherwise half bent over and closed in on herself. Mason was maybe a hundred feet away. His eyes darted from one wall to the next, and things were starting to add up for him. A bulldozer sat idle on the left side. The widening of the tunnel had created a large room, where the dozer had been chewing away at one wall. Mason saw that the ground dropped off just beyond the dozer's blade. He couldn't tell how deep it went, but he imagined a pile of rocks and debris at the bottom, pushed over the edge by the machine.

The perfect place to put two bodies.

Bury them there, cover them with more debris. Nobody would ever think to dig it up. And within months this whole tunnel would be filling up with water.

This is why you made me walk all the way down here, Mason thought. You're gonna stand me right at the edge of that pit before you kill me. Not only are you dirty cops, you're dirty cops who don't want blood on your hands.

"That's close enough!" the man said.

Mason kept walking. Eighty feet away now. There had to be another man here. A cop would never do this alone. Mason needed to know where that second man was.

There. He saw that the other man had moved up onto the stairs for a better angle. He had his Mossberg 500 police-issue shotgun aimed right at Mason's body mass.

The next sound, Mason thought. You can't talk and shoot at the same time. The next time you open your fucking mouth.

Wait for it.

"I said—"

Mason pulled the gun and fired. The sound exploded in that closed space, pressing in against his eardrums. He fired at the man with the shotgun first, with not much hope of hitting him from this distance. But he had to take that gun out first. Mason had already thrown himself against the wall as the shotgun blast obliterated everything else in the world. Water erupted where he had just been standing. Mason fired again at the shotgun, just to keep him pinned down, then at one of the lights above. He needed darkness. One shot, then two, and the light was out. Mason was already moving again—forward, not backward—as the shotgun went off again and he heard the wall crumbling just behind him. He rolled on his back and shot at the other light. It was out and now he was hidden. But he needed to keep moving. He threw himself forward again, staying prone, rising up just long enough to fire off two more shots at the shotgun. The man next to Diana found his range and put a bullet in the wall inches from his head.

Mason got up just long enough to throw himself across to the other side of the tunnel, hoping that the dark would be enough to hide him. He heard two pistol shots as he went down as flat as he could against the cables that ran along the right wall.

He caught his breath for a moment, wondering why the shotgun hadn't gone off again. Six shots in one of those motherfuckers and he'd heard only two. He looked up and saw the first man in the classic pose, two hands on his gun, aiming carefully. Diana had collapsed to the ground behind him.

The first man fired. Then again. But the man was backlit. He fired yet again and now Mason took dead aim, fired, and shot the man in the head.

He tucked himself back in against the wall as he heard the body fall.

He waited. He tried to listen, but he couldn't imagine ever being able to hear again. He let a minute pass, then it was time to get up and move. He held the gun out in front of him as he took one step after another, keeping the gun steady. The second man was sitting on the stairs. He seemed to be lying back against the wall as if catching his breath. But as Mason came closer he saw that the shotgun had fallen down to the first step and that the man was holding on to his neck, blood running through his fingers and down onto his vest. He gave Mason a pleading look.

Mason shot him in the forehead, blowing off the top of his head. The blood flew high in the air, far enough to spray Diana's face. She screamed.

Mason went over to her and tried to pick her up. She hit him with her fists and kicked him and kept screaming until he slapped her across the face.

"It's me," he said. "Diana, it's me."

Her eyes met his, but they were still unfocused. She was fighting to breathe.

He picked her up, but she collapsed against him. He pulled her up straight and held her for a moment, his arms wrapped tight around her.

"It's gonna be okay," he said into her ear, not even sure if she could hear him. He could barely hear his own voice. "You're safe."

She nodded her head against his chest.

"Hold on." Mason let go of her hand and went over to the cop on the stairs. He picked up the shotgun and took one more look at the man's dead eyes. Then he went up the stairs and along the catwalk to the door that had been cut into the wall. It was another submarine door, like the first one he'd tried. But this door opened when he turned the wheel.

He pushed it open slowly, keeping the barrel of the shotgun trained on whatever might be on the other side. As he stepped into the enclosure, he saw a caged staircase winding its way high above his head. All the way up to the ground level, he thought. That's how they had gotten down here with Diana.

But there's no way we're going back up these stairs, he thought. With or without Eddie.

There could be more cops up there. Even if it's clear, we won't have a vehicle.

He closed the door and came back down the stairs.

"This way," he said, grabbing her hand again.

They started walking. He knew it was a long way back. He hoped she had the strength to make it. They moved from one circle of light to the next, marking their progress that way even if nothing seemed to change ahead of them. He tried to keep her out of the standing water, but it was impossible. Her feet were soon as wet as his and she started shivering.

"Eddie!" Mason said into his headset, not sure if he had a signal again yet. "Clear!"

"Here..."

"Get out!"

"Going..."

They came to the crane Mason had passed on the way in. He figured they were halfway out.

"Almost there," he said to her.

She didn't answer him. He pulled her up for a moment to look into her eyes. She had gone somewhere else. But at least she was still moving, her body on automatic pilot, so he took her hand and kept walking with her.

More rings of light until he saw where they ended. Where the night sky could already be seen through the last ring and the air was getting fresher with every step.

He looped his arm around Diana's back and held her up for a few more steps.

"Stay here," he said.

He found a dry spot against the rounded wall and eased her down into a sitting position. She folded her arms over her knees and put her head down. She didn't say a word.

"Be right back," he said. "Don't move."

He brought the shotgun up to a ready position and made his way slowly to the mouth of the tunnel. Drinking in the night air, he caught his second wind. One more shot of energy to get him across these last few yards.

Mason didn't want to speak into the headset now. He didn't want to make any sound at all.

He inched his way to the last ring of light, staying low, taking one careful step at a time, each step giving him a better angle on whatever he might see outside. He switched to the opposite side of the tunnel, then back again. Another step, then another. Until he was at the edge and could carefully scan the entire scene.

His car was there. The darkened trailer behind it. The giant construction vehicles still asleep in their places. The far rim of the quarry high above everything else.

Mason took another step, out into the night. He could see along the cliff in either direction. Nobody there.

No Eddie. No Jeep. He was already on his way out.

We're safe, Mason said to himself. This whole crazy fucking thing worked. Which is yet another confirmation of why Cole chose me. He said so himself. I might not even understand it until I saw it with my own eyes. Now I have.

Because here's the simple truth. There aren't many other men who could have done this.

But the thought didn't give Mason any satisfaction. He wasn't even sure what it meant—about what kind of man he really was—but there'd be time to think about that later.

He went back to where Diana was still slumped against the wall. When he bent down to her, she shivered and tried to push him away.

"Come on," he said. "Let's go."

He picked her up and carried her out of the tunnel, across the open ground, working hard to keep his balance, finally getting her to the car and opening up the passenger's-side door. When he put her in the seat and closed the door, she fell back, her head against the window, her hands covering her face.

Mason went around to the driver's side and got behind the wheel. He started the engine and turned on the headlights.

Another cop was standing directly in front of the car.

He had his pistol leveled at Mason's head, and he was smart enough to swing himself around, away from the front of the car, so there'd be no chance of Mason running him over.

Mason had put the shotgun between the two front seats. He played it out in his head as the cop came around to the passenger's-side window, his gun still pointed at him. One move for the shotgun and he'd get it right through the glass.

The cop spoke to him, but Mason couldn't make out the words. Probably something about getting the fuck out of the car. Or, maybe, don't even bother.

The two men were frozen in that position for a single second, just long enough for Mason to have his one last hope. That second ended when a .338 Lapua Magnum round tore through the man's body, going through the Kevlar like it was toilet paper. The man fell onto the windshield, the blood already streaming from his nose and mouth.

Then a movement. On Mason's left. A face, vaguely familiar to him in that fraction of a second, then pure reaction as he picked up the shotgun and fired. The blast was louder than any so far, a spike in each ear, as it sent buckshot and pebbles of glass at the man who had appeared at the driver's-side window. Diana kept screaming as Mason put his foot down on the accelerator and the tires threw limestone dust high in the air behind them. The dead man slid off the windshield as the tires found purchase, the second man down on the ground somewhere behind them, as Mason weaved around the construction vehicles at impossible speed, sliced through the ponds of water, drove through the pass-through into the other section of the quarry, and then climbed the long, sloping shelf up to the access road, fighting every inch of the way to keep the car from falling off into the abyss below.

She had stopped screaming by the time Mason exploded through the gate. She had no breath to scream anymore. No strength. She had nothing left.

But Mason did.

| 32 |

Mason didn't know where he was driving. He didn't even know which direction. He was just getting away from the quarry as fast as he could. Drive the fuck away, he told himself. Don't stop until you're somewhere safe.

Diana was slumped in the seat next to him. Her eyes were open, but they weren't focused on anything at all. He grabbed her arm and shook it.

"Diana!"

She didn't respond.

"Diana! Are you okay?"

As Mason made a quick turn, she was thrown against the side of the car. Then she fell back to the same position. She was still staring at nothing.

"Answer me! Are you okay?"

She inhaled a long breath, ragged and sputtering. Like a diver breaking through to the surface. "Let me out!"

"No."

"Let me out! Let me out right now!" She grabbed his arm, her fingernails digging into his skin. "Pull this car over, God damn it!"

He jammed on the brakes and brought the car to a skidding stop on the side of the road. Diana was thrown forward in her seat, then came back hard. She grabbed at the door handle.

"Listen to me," Mason said, reaching over and trying to pull her hand away from the handle. He looked outside, had no idea where they were. Still outside the city somewhere. A darkened warehouse on one side of the road, an empty field on the other. *"Will you fucking listen to me for one second?"*

First she was comatose. Then she was clawing at the car door like an animal trying to escape its cage.

"You need to calm down," he said.

She took a few more gasping breaths before she could speak again. "You want me to calm down?" she said. "I was just kidnapped, Nick. I was kidnapped and taken down a fucking tunnel. And then you came and you . . . you . . ." She tried to find the right words. "You killed four people right in front of me! You killed four cops, Nick! I've got their blood on me!"

She showed him the sleeves of her shirt. The white fabric was sprinkled with bright red dots. He didn't want to point out that the same blood was all over her face.

And he didn't feel like telling her that he'd only killed two of them. Eddie had killed the third.

As for the fourth . . . He flashed back on the fraction of a second he saw the cop standing there on the other side of his car window. He could see the man's face and those cold gray eyes. He could see the man's tactical vest. Then the explosion from the shotgun, aimed right at the man's chest.

That cop was probably still alive.

He'd only seen the man once before, from a distance. But he knew exactly who it was. Sergeant Bloome.

"That's their *blood*, Nick! And you're telling me to calm down?"

"Fine," Mason said, letting go of her arm. "If you want to get out, get out. They'll find you and they'll kill you. But at least you'll be out of this car."

She was still breathing like she couldn't get enough air. Mason put the car back into gear and kept driving.

"There's only one safe place for you right now," Mason said, trying to put some calm into his voice. "And that's with me."

"Are you crazy? Every cop in this city will be looking for you."

"No," Mason said. "That's the last thing they want. They arrest me, they start asking questions. They start asking questions, they'll want to know what I was doing there. They'll want to know what *you* were doing there. And they'll *really* want to know what Bloome and his men were doing there without backup."

"What *was* I doing there?" she said. "What did they want from me?"

"They want something I have," Mason said. "And then they want us dead."

Her breathing was finally settling back into a normal rhythm. But her hands were still shaking.

"Where do we go?"

"Not home, not the restaurant," he said. "They're not safe."

"Then where?"

"I don't know," he said. "That's what I'm trying to figure out."

They were heading straight back to the city, so he turned and cut to the west until they were in the forest that ran along the canal. He turned onto a gravel road leading off into the trees, the branches scratching at both sides of the car. He came to a fork and went left, then to another fork and went right. All the way into the middle of the forest until the ground rose and the road ended in a clearing.

Mason stopped the car. Diana had her head back on the seat, but her eyes were still wide open. I wonder if she'll ever be able to close them again, Mason thought, without reliving this night.

"Where are we?" she said.

"Nowhere," he said. "Good place to be."

"How does this end?"

"I don't know."

"My house?"

"Gone."

"My restaurant?"

"Forget it."

"What about *my life*?"

"That life is over," he said.

She shook her head and looked out at the trees.

"This goes back to Darius," she said. "Those cops..."

"They were in business with him."

"But he's *always* owned cops," she said. "As long as I can remember. I'd see them parked outside on the street. Darius would send Quintero out to talk to them, give them their money. He hated cops his whole life. He'd tell me stories about what they did to some of the kids on the streets when he was growing up. But he said you had to learn to use the thing you hate the most. 'Tie your wagon to the Devil's tail,' he said."

"This one got loose," Mason said. "So Cole had to respond. That's why I'm here."

"I was doing just fine until you got here," she said. "It wasn't the exact life I wanted, but I was making it work."

"This was not my idea, Diana."

"You brought this on me."

He felt like he was about to say the wrong thing, so he got out of the car and walked away. He looked up at the stars in the moonless night. To the east, he saw a great smudge of light in the sky. This city where he came from. This city where nothing would ever be the same again.

We need to go somewhere, he said to himself. We need to go somewhere safe where we can figure out our next move.

Which means one thing. There is one man out there who told me to come to him with any problems. He remembered his exact words. *You need something, you call me. You get in a situation, you call me. Don't get creative. Don't try to fix anything yourself. You call me.*

That's his job. He couldn't have made it any more clear.

He took out his cell phone.

He's the only man who can help us, Mason thought. So why am I not calling him?

He heard the car door opening behind him. Then he heard the scream. As he wheeled around, he saw Diana halfway out of her seat, one foot on the ground. She was looking at the side-view mirror. At the blood on her face.

He went over and pulled her up from the car. He wrapped his arms around her and held on to her as she sobbed into his chest.

"It's going to be okay."

"What are we going to do?" she said. "Where are we going to go?"

"I know a place we can go," he said. "It'll be safe there."

He picked up the phone again. He dialed Eddie.

"Thank you for what you did," he said. "You saved our lives. Now we're coming to your house."

There was a long silence on the other end.

"You can't bring this here," Eddie finally said. "I'm glad I got a chance to help you out. You know that. But whatever this was, you can't bring it into this house."

"You can open the door," Mason said. "Or I can knock it down."

| 33 |

Sergeant Vince Bloome stood over the dead body of his friend and fellow SIS detective, trying desperately to figure out how the hell he was going to explain any of this.

Detective Sandoval's question came back to him.

Do you even fucking remember when you were a cop?

He'd been a Chicago cop for the past twenty-nine years, including sixteen in Narcotics, then seven in SIS. But, right now, he didn't know the answer to that question.

He went over to where Jay Fowler lay on the ground, got down on one knee, and turned the man over. His eyes were open. Shot from behind, Bloome thought. One of my best friends in the unit. One of the few men I'd even think about asking to be here tonight.

Bloome's head was still ringing. He felt sick and dizzy, unsteady on his feet. Feeling along his right shoulder and neck, he came back with blood on his hand. He'd been hit by some scatter from the buckshot and by some glass. The Kevlar vest had taken most of it.

Squinting in the near darkness, he scanned the construction vehicles, the cliffs, the empty road that ran along the top. Then the ring of the tunnel, casting the only light in this whole place. The door to the trailer was still open behind him, but they had left the lights off. There was nobody else here.

He looked back down at the dead man's face. Fowler had been part of SIS for five years. He came out of the Narcotics unit, just like Bloome had. He was young, he was ambitious, he wanted to be a rock star cop. And that meant SIS. He'd found Bloome in Homan Square, had walked right up to him in the hallway, told him he'd be part of the team someday. Bloome had remembered him. When they had an opening, Fowler was the first man he called.

He was married now. His wife's name was Joanne. Everybody called her Jo. Jay and Jo. She was seven months pregnant.

I did this, Bloome said to himself. I brought this man here. He will never see his own child.

Bloome stood up and tried moving his neck, felt the muscles tightening, the skin stretching over something hard, embedded just under the surface. He stopped testing it.

"Reagan," he said out loud. "Koniczek."

The two men inside the tunnel. Bloome knew they were dead. He knew by the simple math of a dozen gunshots and Mason and the woman somehow walking away.

They were dead.

Walter Reagan. John Koniczek. He knew their wives, too, just as well as he knew Fowler's. He knew their kids.

None of these men should have been here.

Bloome spotted his gun lying on the ground, went back over and picked it up. He brushed it off before holstering it and, as he did, he remembered the day he bought it. Chicago cops have to buy their own weapons and he had picked out a Sig P250, chambered with .45

ACP shells. It was the only weapon he'd ever carried, even today when it was no longer on the approved list. If you already had one, they let you keep it.

He remembered the first time he had fired it on the streets. Just a few years in, on a West Side buy-and-bust, some low-level runner taking a crack at them as he fled down an alley. Back when they had no idea what they were doing. When their best idea for finding the traffic was looking for white buyers in the wrong neighborhoods or picking up junkies and turning them into informants. Trying to work their way from the bottom up. And never getting anywhere.

Things didn't get much better when Bloome joined the Narcotics unit as a detective. It still felt like a losing battle every day. But then he got partnered with a detective named Ray Jameson. A former college wrestler with permanently mauled ears and a personality as big as his body, he was a human wrecking ball when it came to police work, a perfect counterpart to the cold, machinelike precision of Vincent Bloome. These were two men who never should have gotten along, not for five minutes, but it was Bloome's couch that Jameson chose to sleep on whenever his wife threw him out of the house. And from the moment Bloome and Jameson started working cases together, it was obvious their individual strengths formed a perfect combination to get things done on the streets.

Bloome and Jameson were putting up good numbers, but the overall picture in Chicago was getting worse every year. More drugs, more violence. More pressure on the mayor to do something about it. Anything.

That's how SIS was born. Bloome and Jameson were two of the first men to walk into that empty space on the top floor of Homan, already talking about how they'd lay out the office. Desks here, where the sun could come through these big windows. Interview rooms along that wall. It was time to get to work.

From the beginning, everything was different if you were a member of the new team. You dressed better than other cops. Tailored suits, leather shoes, long topcoats in the colder months. You worked harder. You worked longer. It was part of the team ethos that you didn't even bother keeping track of your hours. You didn't put in for overtime. You didn't complain if you worked all weekend and didn't see your family. The job itself was your reward.

As SIS detectives, Bloome and Jameson could go after anybody they wanted, at any level. They didn't care about the little shit anymore. Low-level dealers were just stepping-stones to the suppliers above them. By the end of their first year together, they were putting together major cases, working them for weeks at a time. Making the arrests that got you photos with the mayor and profiles on the six o'clock news.

That was the payoff, right there. That's why the young guys like Fowler and Reagan and Koniczek wanted to be a part of it.

Bloome remembered the feeling he'd get whenever they'd select their next target. It might have been nothing more than a name and a photograph on the bulletin board at that point, but this man was the target and that meant he was going down. Didn't matter if the man would eventually confess or keep his mouth shut. Didn't matter if they'd get full-color video of the crime or one unreliable witness. Bloome would look at that face on the board and *know* he was on his way to prison. It might take an hour, it might take a week. But the man had a date in the courtroom no matter what they had to do to make that happen.

Sometimes that meant shortcuts. He remembered the first time he saw Jameson put false information on a police report. They picked up a dealer just before he put a bag in his car. On the report, the bag was already in the trunk. Bloome had some misgivings about it at first. All the years he'd been in Narcotics, he'd never lied on a report. Not once. But Jameson took him aside and asked him a simple question: "Was that bag going in his car?"

"Yes," Bloome said.

"Does the case get complicated if we stop him before that happens?"

"Yes."

"Is there a small chance he walks because of that?"

"Yes."

That's all he had to say. They were getting the right result, even if that meant a white lie.

Not only did they make the case, they both got commendations.

It was Bloome's first lesson in how the normal rules didn't apply to them anymore. Not to SIS.

He remembered the first time he broke down a door without a warrant. The first time he searched a car with no probable cause. It was all a new part of doing good police work, taking weight off the streets, making arrests. Nobody ever questioned the shortcuts. They were making their numbers and Chicago was becoming a safe, more drug-free city. That's all that mattered.

He remembered the first time Jameson took money off a dealer. Money that the dealer wouldn't miss, Ray had said. Money he'd make back in eight hours. Money that would sit in a metal drawer downtown for a few months until maybe somebody else took it.

All that unpaid overtime they were putting in. This was just a little compensation. Totally justified.

THE SECOND LIFE OF NICK MASON

Bloome didn't sleep that night. He thought they'd catch up to him.

They never did.

It got easier the next time. Easier again when it was two or three cops working together.

You *had* to take the money then. You were part of the team and it would make everyone else nervous if you didn't.

The suits got more expensive. You started seeing manicures and hundred-dollar haircuts. You started seeing the cars taken from the dealers parked in the lot outside, gleaming in the sunshine. Mercedes, BMWs, Audis, Porsches. Usually black, always fast.

Nobody said a word. In fact, it was more high-profile arrests, more commendations, more pictures with the mayor, more detectives from around the city wanting to be a part of SIS.

And then came Darius Cole.

It was Jameson who first brought up the name, based on a recorded conversation between two high-level dealers. Bloome remembered Cole from his first year in Narcotics and the airtight RICO case the feds had put together to put him away for two consecutive lifetimes. It seemed impossible now that a man who'd been in prison for years could still have such influence in Chicago, two hundred miles away. But Jameson put Cole's name on the board and the two men got to work.

While Bloome and Jameson were putting together a case on Cole and the men who worked for him, those same men were busy putting together a case on Bloome and Jameson. They knew everything about the two detectives. Where they lived. Where their children went to school. Every case they'd ever worked on. Every bribe they'd ever taken. Until the day Cole contacted them both directly on a prison guard's cell phone and gave them a choice. I'll make you fucking rich men or I'll make you fucking dead men. Your choice.

They took the money. Every month, in an envelope delivered by one of Cole's men, an ex-gangbanger named Marcos Quintero. At first, Cole was also giving them tips on members of rival organizations, which led to even more arrests than before, their reputations in the unit rising even higher.

We're still doing good police work, the two men told themselves. And yes, making some good money on the side. Everybody wins.

But Cole's tips eventually turned into requests for favors. Then those requests started to sound like orders.

When Tyron Harris came along, the first man who actually looked smart enough to take over Cole's territory, Jameson tried to make a new deal. End the relationship with the man in prison, start fresh with this new kid, somebody we can break in the right way. Somebody who won't make so many demands.

Cole can't touch us. That was the idea.

Now Jameson and Harris were both dead. And here I am, Bloome said to himself. Look at where I'm standing. Look at what I was prepared to do to protect myself.

If Jameson was here, Bloome thought, we'd talk this over, see if we had any chance to make this look right. Three dead cops in a quarry, three members of the most elite unit in the city . . . in the middle of the night, with no backup. Nobody else knowing anything about the operation. How do you explain that?

Bloome could already see himself giving his version of this story to Internal Affairs. Then the superintendent. Then the mayor. Then a federal prosecutor in open court.

So it better be one fuck of a story.

He looked down at Fowler again.

Or else it better be a fucking mystery why the three of you guys were down here alone.

I don't know if I can do that, Bloome said to himself. These are the three guys I trusted the most, now that Jameson is gone. That's why they were here tonight.

But Bloome knew he had to sell them out to save himself. He had to go get his neck cleaned up somewhere. Get rid of this vest. Then play dumb about this night when they ask about it tomorrow. And every other day for the rest of his life.

That feeling he had whenever they had a target identified, that cold chill in his gut, knowing they were going to put that man away... Bloome had that same feeling now. But for the first time, he was on the other end of it.

Bloome knew that Mason had the evidence to put him away forever. Those recordings, all of their conversations with Harris . . . Mason would take them right to the man who sent him here in the first place. And Darius Cole would now have the power to destroy him.

The war was over.

If he lets me live, Bloome thought, Cole will own me. For the rest of my life. Anything he tells me to do, I'll have to do it.

Even if I get to Mason, or Quintero, or anyone else he sends... I'll never be able to touch Darius Cole.

We thought that prison would keep us safe. It keeps *him* safe.

Bloome walked toward the tunnel. He had to see his other two men one more time. He felt smaller and smaller as he took each step toward the giant ring of light. Then as he disappeared into the earth, walking through the first puddle, the line came back to him one more time. That question that Sandoval had asked him.

Do you even fucking remember when you were a cop?

|34|

Eddie Callahan promised Sandra he would never do any-
thing that would put him in handcuffs and take him away from his
family again. He had promised her when he proposed to her. He had
promised her when the police came to question him about the harbor. He had promised her when their twin sons were born.

Tonight he had broken that promise and put everything at risk.

Eddie had already locked up his sniper rifle in the gun cabinet. It
was an H-S Precision Pro 2000 with a Leupold Mark 4 scope on the
rail. Good thing he'd already had the scope sighted on the range because he wasn't getting any practice shots tonight. Now he was waiting for Nick Mason to show up at his front door.

He picked up some of the toys off the floor. He was about to get a
rag and wipe off the coffee table when he said to himself, What the
fuck am I doing?

It was after two o'clock when they finally got there. If Eddie had
any hopes of letting Sandra sleep through it, they ended as soon as

she came padding out into the living room, wrapped up in her white robe.

"What's going on?" she said. Then she saw Eddie holding open the door, his old friend Nick Mason walking into her living room, and then a woman with blood on her face.

The last thing Mason needed was another scream, but that's what he got.

"What are you..." she started to say when she was done screaming. "Eddie, what are they doing here?"

"They're coming in," Eddie said.

"No they're not! What the fuck are you—"

"Sandra, calm down! They need our help."

"*You* called him before," she said, coming over to Mason and standing in front of him while she tightened the belt on her robe. "That's why Eddie left."

It had been five years since Mason had seen this woman. She'd gained a few pounds, but otherwise she hadn't changed. Never mind the friendship between the two men or everything they'd gone through growing up, Sandra would never see Mason as anything but the one man she needed to keep her husband away from at all costs.

Not that he could argue that point tonight.

"He needed my help," Eddie said to her.

"In the middle of the night? Where did you go?"

"Never mind. Sandra, will you—"

"Eddie helped me," Mason said. "That's all you gotta know. And now I need something else. From both of you."

"I'm calling the police," Sandra said, crossing the room and picking up the phone.

"No cops!" Eddie said, taking the phone from her.

"Eddie, give me that fucking phone!"

"Listen to me," Eddie said to her. "I'm only going to say this once. Our house?"

He gestured at the four walls.

"We wouldn't have this house if it wasn't for him. We wouldn't be married. We wouldn't have our boys. Everything in this house, everything you see, everything in our entire fucking life, we owe to that man. *Everything.*"

Her mouth hung open. She didn't even try to respond.

"This woman needs to clean herself up," Mason said, nodding to Diana. "Then she needs to sleep. You need to take care of her because she's been through a lot."

Diana gave her a thin smile. She looked like the most exhausted person who ever lived.

"Nobody can know she's here," Mason said. "You'd only be putting your family in danger."

Sandra's mouth was still open.

"Nick," Eddie said, "it's okay. We got this. Don't worry."

Mason turned to face his friend.

"Promise me," he said to him. "Promise me for both of you. Diana needs to stay here with you. If you don't hear from me in three days, you need to get her out of town. Don't take her to an airport. Don't take her to a train station. Just drive her the fuck out of town. Get her a car somewhere. Pay cash. Then you can come back."

"No," Sandra said, finally finding her voice. "We can't do this. You have no right—"

"You have no right to say no," Mason said. "Not tonight."

He turned to his friend and said, "I need this, Eddie."

Eddie's eyes went from Mason to his wife, then back to Mason. "Of course," he said. "I told you I'd do anything for you."

Sandra wrapped her bathrobe even tighter around herself. She swallowed hard and nodded her head once, but she didn't look at him.

Eddie's two kids appeared in the hallway. They were both in their pajamas, a Chicago Bears helmet on each boy's chest. They came over to Eddie and held on to either leg, looking up at Mason like a monster had invaded their living room.

"Jeffrey and Gregory," Mason said. "Right?"

"That's right," Eddie said.

Mason got down on one knee and looked at the boys. "I have a daughter," he said to them. "Her name is Adriana."

The boys both retreated behind Eddie's legs.

"Sorry if we woke you up," Mason said. He got back to his feet and gave Diana a quick hug.

"Stay inside," he said to her. "I'll call as soon as I can."

"What are you going to do?" she said.

Mason took out his cell phone and looked at it. He'd received a dozen phone calls over the past few hours, all from Quintero. All of them unanswered.

"I'm going to end this," he said.

| 35 |

Nick Mason waited for Frank Sandoval to arrive. He had
done everything he had been told to do. Now he was going to do
something else. Something for himself.

He was too tired to sleep. Too tired to close his eyes. He had seen
too much since the day he had stepped through those prison gates
from one life to the next.

The benches in Grant Park were all arranged in a great circle
around the fountain. The water hadn't been turned on yet. The air
was cold, so he had his arms wrapped around himself. The black
box was held tight between his forearm and his chest.

He had nowhere else to go. He waited there through the last
hours of night until the dark horizon of the eastern sky started to
lighten. A change almost too subtle to see unless you were watching
for it. Black to something almost black and then to something almost purple. Mason sat and waited motionless through a hundred
more shades until the sun finally started to rise.

He heard the traffic starting to hum on the roads surrounding the park. The city coming back to life for the day. He heard someone whiz by on the bike trail behind him.

He waited a few more minutes. The sun came up and sent its light across the surface of the lake. The boats all slept, covered and anchored in place. Nothing moved in front of him until he saw the man walking toward the fountain. A black silhouette against the blue dawn.

Mason stood up, stretched himself, worked the pain from his body. He walked over to where Sandoval waited for him.

"What am I doing here?" Sandoval said.

He was dressed in a dark blue windbreaker. Not his usual rumpled suit jacket. He wasn't wearing a tie. His face was unshaven and his eyes still looked like he'd just gotten out of bed five minutes ago.

"I told the guy at the station five thirty," Mason said, looking at his watch. "You're two minutes late."

"Go fuck yourself."

"I thought you might want this."

Mason handed him the hard drive. Sandoval took it and looked it over.

"Don't take it to the station," Mason said. "Don't check it into Evidence or you'll never see it again. That's very important. Don't tell any other cops you have it."

"What is it?"

"Take it home," Mason said, "and make a copy. Make ten copies. Then go through everything. You'll know what to do next."

Sandoval looked around them at the empty park.

"You brought me all the way down here, at the crack of dawn, to give me a hard drive?"

"You told me there's nothing more dangerous than a dirty cop. Here's your chance to take down a whole squad of them."

Sandoval just stared at him.

"I know your real target is Cole," Mason said. "But you'll never get to him through me. This is what you get instead."

Sandoval looked at the box again. "Who exactly are we talking about here?"

Mason didn't answer.

"There were three SIS detectives found at Thornton Quarry," Sandoval said. "Someone on the road heard gunshots and called it in. Do you know anything about that?"

Mason shook his head. "Haven't seen the paper today."

"Were you there?"

"Read the official report, Detective. Whatever it says, I'm sure that's exactly what happened."

Sandoval kept staring at him. "Wherever you got this," he said, "I don't understand why you're giving it to me."

Mason couldn't tell Sandoval the real reason. He'd been told by Quintero to bring this black box to him. To nobody else. Cole would be expecting it. He'd use it as a bargaining chip. A threat to have in his pocket. To make these cops get back in fucking line.

That was the order. Mason disobeyed it.

He was taking the cops down because he wanted to. For his own reasons. It was personal. He was ending the war on his own terms.

And he had no intention of ever taking another order again.

"Let's just say I hate dirty cops as much as you do."

"Why not give this to the feds?" Sandoval said, holding up the box.

"In what universe do I go looking around for federal agents, Detective?"

"This is going to make me a pariah," Sandoval said. "You know that, right? I'm not Internal Affairs. I'm Homicide. I'll be back on a seven-man team, working with the same guys every day. What do you think's gonna happen to me when they find out about this?"

Mason didn't bother trying to convince him he could stay anonymous. He knew that would be a lie.

"They'll know," Sandoval said like he was reading Mason's mind. "Cops talk to each other. I'll be the most hated cop in Chicago."

"Maybe you will," Mason said. "But I think this is why you became a cop in the first place."

Sandoval turned away. He looked out at the water for a while.

"You gotta understand something," he said, still facing away from him.

"What is it?"

Sandoval turned back.

"No, I mean you *really* need to understand what I'm about to tell you."

"I'm listening."

"This changes nothing between us," Sandoval said. "Absolutely nothing."

"Not even half a day's head start if I ever decide to run?"

"Absolutely... nothing."

"I didn't think it would," Mason said.

The two men watched each other. They waited for something else to be said that would bring this to a close. Sandoval had a disk full of evidence to sort through. Mason had one more phone call to make.

"I'm still gonna take you down," Sandoval said.

"You're going to try," Mason said.

Sandoval nodded to him. Then he walked away.

| 36 |

Mason sat in his car on Lincoln Park West. He'd been there for two hours and still hadn't gone inside. Instead, he had parked his car on the street and just watched the place, looking up at the high windows of the beautiful town house and thinking about Darius Cole sitting in his cell at Terre Haute.

His driver's-side glass was still gone. There was a crack on the passenger's-side window, another on the windshield. But he had bigger problems to solve that day.

He picked up his cell phone and called Quintero. It was answered on the first ring.

"Where are you?"

"I'm around," Mason said. "Listen to me. This is important."

"Where is it?"

"I don't have it."

"What do you mean you don't have it?"

"Somebody else has it now," Mason said. "You'll read about it in the paper."

There was a long pause on the other end of the line. Mason could hear the sounds of power tools in the background. Quintero was at the chop shop.

"If this is some kind of fucking joke..."

"I need to talk to him," Mason said.

"That's not going to happen."

"Okay, fine," Mason said. "Visiting hours start at eight o'clock on Saturday morning. I'll be first in line."

"That would be a big mistake."

"Then make it happen," Mason said. "Today."

He ended the call and tossed the phone on the seat next to him.

Yet another order disobeyed, because now Mason was doing something he should never do, putting everyone at risk. Himself, Quintero, Cole, even some prison guard who'd have to supply the illegal cell phone.

But it was the only way.

He sat there and waited. He watched the town house. He watched the street. People were walking through the park, enjoying the day. Families were on their way to the zoo.

An hour later, the phone rang. It was Quintero.

"I'm going to give you a number to call," he said. "This is a one-time event."

"Just give me the number."

He waited for it, then ended the call without saying another word. His heart was pounding in his throat as he dialed the number and waited.

"Who is this?" a voice said.

"Let me talk to him."

"Is this Mason?"

Something about the high pitch in the man's voice made him

think about the undersized guard who came to him in the yard that day, just over a year ago, to deliver that first invitation to come meet Darius Cole.

"Let me talk to him," Mason repeated.

"Hold on," the man said. Then his voice became distant as he took his mouth away from the phone to say, "You have ten minutes, Mr. Cole."

Mason pictured the man, two hundred miles south of him, taking off his reading glasses before putting the phone to his ear.

"This is not a smart phone call," Cole said. "What do you want?"

"I can't do this anymore."

"That's not how this works, Nick."

"I've done everything you asked," Mason said. "Things I never thought I'd do."

"Until last night," Cole said. "What were you thinking?"

"I did that for myself," Mason said. "Way I see it, we were already even. Whatever I owed you, I'm paid up."

"You don't get it, Nick. For you, there is no 'even.' There is no 'out.'"

"Listen to me—"

"No, listen to me," Cole said. "I need you to keep doing what you're doing. And if you ever disobey me again—"

"I can't do it," Mason said, his grip tightening on the phone. "Even if that means going back to prison."

"Before another word comes out of your mouth," Cole said, "think about what you're going to say."

"I'll serve out the rest of my sentence right now."

"What do you think would happen if you really came back here?"

"I'd finish my sentence. One day at a time. Like anybody else."

"No, let me educate you. You remember how I said you was able to move around this place—between the whites, the blacks, the Latinos—without ever compromising yourself? How much I admired that?"

"What about it?"

"It won't be that way if you come back. All three of those worlds will turn against you. Even the whites. *Especially* the whites. You'll be fair game for any man. Anytime. I'll make a fucking game of it. Whoever fucks you up the most, I'll make sure that man gets taken care of. Anything he wants, anything his family wants. Do you hear what I'm saying, Nick? You come back here and you'll be passed around this place like toilet paper every single day for the rest of your life. And believe me, I'll make sure you never get out of this place again. Even after I'm dead, you'll still be here."

"There are some things even you can't do," Mason said. "I'll do my twenty, if I have to, and then I'll walk out."

"Nick, who you think goes down for those first two jobs you did? You don't think I'm ready for *anything* that can happen? You'll be wearin' both of those jobs around your neck like a fucking bow tie. Your twenty years will turn into two hundred."

"I'll take my chances."

"I'm not sure your ex-wife will want to roll the same dice, Nick."

Mason felt the bottom drop out of his stomach. He put a hand on the steering wheel and started pushing on it until the muscles in his arms were drawn taut.

"She has no part in this," he said, knowing even as he said it that it was untrue.

"She was *always* part of this," Cole said, "and so was your daughter. From the beginning. You need to listen to me very carefully,

Nick, because everything that happens to you, it'll be doubled for them. Every time you're beaten, every time you're violated, you'll know that the exact same thing will be happening to them. *The exact same thing.* Times two."

Mason closed his eyes. He couldn't breathe. He couldn't make a sound.

"Those twenty years you were gonna work for me just turned into a lifetime sentence," Cole said. "And don't ever fucking call me again."

| 37 |

Mason got out of the car. He was trying to breathe. He
was trying to draw some air into his lungs and *breathe.*

No, he said to himself. Then he said the same word over and over
a hundred more times.

He walked down the shoreline for a hundred yards until he realized he still had the phone in his hand.

Then he threw it as far as he could out into the water.

He kept walking. Until the walkway made its big curl at North
Avenue Beach and came to a dead stop. He turned around and
looked at the buildings rising high above the water without really
seeing them.

"What the *fuck* did I expect?" he asked himself out loud. "Did I
actually think for one fucking second…"

Then he started moving again. Fast. Back up the walkway, up the
beach and through the park. Back to his car.

He got in and gunned it. He drove across town to the West Side,
to the address on Spaulding, past the big storage warehouse and the

asphalt yard and the boarded-up houses. He could see the place better in the daylight. It was practically in the shadow of the Cook County Jail.

The chop shop.

He pulled up in front of the garage door and pressed on the horn until the door finally started to rise. Mason drove through into the bay. The two Latinos stood there, watching him.

"Where is he?" Mason said as he got out of the car.

The Honda Accord they were working on was already halfway taken apart. The whole front end had been removed from the frame, then the doors and windshield had been taken off. When the seats were out, they'd cut out the entire dashboard, saving the air bags. That's what they did here every day, but now they just looked at him.

Until their eyes shifted and Mason knew there was someone behind him.

He felt the hand on his right shoulder. When he turned, Quintero hit him in the mouth. He was already tasting blood as he grabbed the man by the throat and threw him against the car.

When Quintero swung at him again, Mason ducked and drove his head into Quintero's chest, sending him backward into a workbench. Tools rattled and fell crashing to the floor.

"Is that all you got?" Mason said to him. "I fought guys tougher than you in junior high school, you fucking gangbanger piece of shit."

Quintero came at him, faking another swing at his head and then sucker punching him in the gut. Quintero had him lined up for another shot to the face, but Mason got an arm up to block him and drove him back, all the way into another bay, and pinned him against the car in the bay.

They both stayed there for a moment, holding on to each other. At such close range, Mason could see every gray hair, every line in the man's face. Those extra years on Quintero, hard years of service to one man, doing fuck knows what. In that one moment, Mason couldn't help wondering if he was looking at his own future.

"You stupid *güero*," Quintero said. "I've been putting up with your shit from the moment I drove you up here. Your questions. Your attitude. Getting thrown in fucking jail. But now, *today*, you crossed the one line you can't cross."

Mason pushed himself away and caught his breath.

"If you ever disobey him again," Quintero said, "if you ever fucking call him and disrespect him . . . I swear to Christ, I will take whatever he tells me to do to you and I'll make it last twice as long. Do you hear me?"

"I hear you," Mason said. "All you ever do is talk."

"And yet you never fucking listen. I told you, you got a problem, you come to me. That's why I'm here. How come you still don't get that?"

Mason looked at him. What the fuck, he thought, this man honestly sounds offended. Like I betrayed him.

"Just stay away from me, Quintero. And stay the fuck away from my family. I don't care what he tells you to do. I swear to God, if you go anywhere near my family, I will kill you. I will not hurt you. *I will kill you.*"

"You don't want me fucking with your family, don't give me a reason."

"No," Mason said, wiping the blood from his mouth. "Reason or no reason—today, tomorrow, any day of your fucking life—you touch either of them, your life is over."

Quintero brushed off his shirt. "He owns both of us," he said. "Don't you see that?"

"No," Mason said. "He doesn't."

"*Somos hermanos*, you and me," Quintero said. "We are brothers."

They stood there in the garage for a long time while the other men went back to work.

"You need another car," Quintero finally said, nodding toward the blown-out window in the Camaro.

The car they'd just been leaning against as they tried to kill each other was another jet-black American muscle car.

"It's a 1964 Pontiac GTO," Quintero said. "With the Bobcat engine."

He threw Mason the keys.

| 38 |

Nick Mason sat on the edge of his bed, listening to the rain outside, waiting to see if Cole would change his mind and send his "brother" to kill him that night.

He had defied the one man you don't defy. But he wasn't going to run away. He wasn't going to hide. If Cole decided that extending his contract wasn't enough of a punishment, Mason would be ready. He still had the M9, with six shots left. That would be enough.

He kept waiting. The rain stopped. Finally, he got up and went out to the pool. As he turned the corner, he felt the impact against the back of his head. He dropped the gun as he went down, then saw it kicked away from his reach.

When he looked up, he saw Jimmy McManus standing over him. He was holding his own gun in his right hand.

He was in his customary tight jeans and muscle shirt, with some new gold chains around his neck. He held the gun a little too casually, like it was one more accessory in the overall fashion statement, that of a man right out of the movies, a man you do not fuck with.

But the bruises around both of his eyes, the shattered nose Mason had given him, turned that statement into a lie.

"This is quite a place you got," McManus said, gesturing with the barrel of the gun, pointing at the pool and everything else around him.

"What do you want?" Mason said, getting to his feet and rubbing the back of his head. McManus backed away from him.

"I'm here to settle things," he said. "It's like I told you last time. It's the loose ends that hang you, Nickie boy. And you are one hell of a loose end."

Mason took a step toward him. McManus flinched and tightened his grip on the gun, the barrel trained on Mason's chest.

Mason had seen this man fire his gun in a blind panic while he was running away from that truck at the harbor. But this was different.

Facing a man. Ending his life. Something most men cannot do. It takes another kind of man.

A killer.

Mason knew that now.

"Go ahead. If you really have it in you."

He looked Jimmy McManus in the eye and waited.

McManus swallowed and tightened his grip again. He raised the gun to eye level and sighted down the barrel.

Mason waited.

They say you never hear the shot that kills you, but it rang in Mason's ears.

McManus stood there for one more moment, his neck bent at a strange new angle. Blood came running down his face, between his eyes. Then he fell forward into the pool.

Mason watched the pink swirl growing around the body as it turned clockwise in the water. Then he looked up.

Marcos Quintero stood twenty feet away, a gun in his right hand. Quintero gave Mason a slight nod of his head.

Mason stared him down for a long time before finally nodding back.

| 39 |

Chicago Sun-Times

CHICAGO COPS INDICTED IN DRUG SCANDAL
CONSPIRACY, ROBBERY, EXTORTION, KIDNAPPING,
DRUG DEALING AMONG CHARGES

By Denny Kilmer, Staff Reporter

The United States Attorney's Office unsealed an indictment today charging seven members of the Chicago Police Department, all members of the elite Special Investigations Section task force, with RICO conspiracy, robbery, racketeering, extortion, kidnapping, drug dealing, and a number of other charges. The indictments come after a five-month joint investigation by the FBI, DEA, and the Chicago Police Bureau of Internal Affairs and represent one of the biggest corruption cases in the history of the city. More suspects may be charged as the investigation continues.

The investigation may also shed light on the unsolved shooting death of SIS Sergeant Ray Jameson, as well as the deaths of SIS Detectives Walter Reagan, Jason Fowler, and John Koniczek, who were all found gunned down at the Deep Tunnel outlet in the Thornton Quarry. Those homicides have been the subject of an ongoing investigation conducted by the Illinois State Police and have generated intense media attention due to the mysterious circumstances surrounding those deaths.

The names of those officers arrested and charged are:

Sgt. Vincent Bloome, 58 years old, 29 years on force, 7 years in SIS. Det. John Fairley, 42 years old, 17 years on force, 5 years in SIS. Det. William Spiller, 35 years old, 12 years on force, 5 years in SIS. Det. Michael Harrison, 34 years old, 8 years on force, 3 years in SIS. Det. Brian Jaynes, 31 years old, 7 years on force, 2 years in SIS. Det. Hayward Baylor, 29 years old, 6 years on force, 2 years in SIS. Det. Edward Coleman, 29 years old, 5 years on force, 2 years in SIS.

The seven officers charged are all members of the Special Investigations Section, otherwise known as SIS, an elite task force of narcotics officers put together in 2009 in response to the rampant drug-related crimes plaguing the city. Those officers were given broad leeway to conduct their own investigations and reported high arrest rates in every year of the unit's existence. Many of those arrests are now being called into question, and civilian complaints against many of these officers, including claims of illegal seizure and use of excessive force, compiled from the task force's inception in 2009, are now coming to light.

Investigators have cited an unnamed Chicago police officer for his role in providing key evidence used to put together these indictments. That officer's name is not being released to the public, but an anonymous spokesman stated that "the evidence shows a clear and consistent pattern of corruption,

STEVE HAMILTON

with regular cash payments made to the officers by high-level suppliers in exchange for protection against arrest and prosecution." Those cash payments were described as ranging anywhere from $5,000 to $50,000.

The same source states that, aside from detailed records of transactions between police officers and dealers, there were also several hours of recorded conversations. He went on to say that "these recorded conversations between various members of the SIS task force and one supplier paint a chilling portrait of police officers on the take, for sale to the highest bidder."

Chicago police superintendent Garry McCarthy issued the following statement:

"I stand with Chief Rivera and Mayor Emanuel in expressing my condemnation of the actions taken by these rogue individuals and my profound disappointment in how these actions may reflect upon the more than 12,000 other members of the Chicago Police Department who perform their duties every day with integrity and honor. I want to thank the officer who came forward with information crucial to the exposure of these crimes. And I encourage all members of the force to consider this a great example to follow as we continue to work with the FBI, DEA, and our own Bureau of Internal Affairs to pursue those involved in corruption."

In a press conference immediately following this press release, Superintendent Garry McCarthy announced that "all SIS investigations and other related activity will immediately be suspended, pending resolution of these charges." He went on to say that "As of now, SIS is no longer in business."

The District Attorney's Office has also informed the Chicago Police Department that, as a matter of prosecutorial discretion, it would no longer rely on testimony from Sergeant Bloome or Detectives Fairley, Spiller, Harrison, Jaynes, Baylor, and Coleman. As a result, there are no open active cases involving these officers.

No officials contacted at the United States Attorney's Office were willing to speculate on the possible prison terms that may result from the charges leveled against these members of SIS, but the sentencing guidelines for these charges mean that, if convicted, the officers would be serving literally hundreds of years in federal prison.

The unnamed source with access to the evidence gave his own prediction about the eventual resolution of this case:

"We've had more than our share of bad cops in this town. But these guys are the worst. They'll do more hard time than all the rest of them put together."

EPILOGUE

Mason walked down the wet sidewalk, a dark silhouette in the rain, with a million lights all reflected in the slick streets. It was one of those nights when the air turns heavy and cold, chilling your skin no matter how many layers you wear.

The rain kept falling. Mason was alone. As he walked, he watched the ground in front of him with haunted eyes. The eyes of a soldier who's been to war. A man who has seen too much.

A man who will never be the same again.

He didn't care that he was soaked right through his clothes. Not tonight. He kept moving until he came to the store at the end of the block, its interior lights making the windows glow in the darkness.

Max saw him first, his tail already wagging as Mason stepped inside. Mason stood there, dripping in the doorway, his white shirt plastered against his chest.

Lauren looked up from the counter. She was just about to close the store, already had the apology lined up for this last customer of the day. But then she saw Mason's face.

She caught her breath. He had a new bruise around his left eye. A scrape along his jawline. For a long moment, neither of them said a word.

"I'm here to pick up Max," Mason finally said. He went to the gate and put his hand down on the dog. Max kept wagging his tail.

"You bought him," she said. "He's all yours."

"Glad you're here. I wanted to—"

"What's really going on?" she said. "Just tell me that."

That stopped him dead.

"Every time I see you," she said, "you're covered in bruises."

"I wish I could tell you," he said, "but I can't. Not right now."

"Then take Max and go."

"Lauren, listen," he said, coming closer to her. "You've got every reason not to let me into your life. But I'm asking you..."

He paused. He'd been so afraid of letting her in. Now he needed the right words to make her stay. But those words weren't coming to him.

As Lauren waited, she didn't want to look at him, didn't want to remember the one night they'd spent together. She'd been thinking about him way too much since then. How many times had she looked out these windows and wondered if she'd ever see him again?

"This was a mistake," he said at last. "I should just—"

"Do you sell drugs? Is that where you get your money?"

He forced a smile and shook his head. That would be an easier life, he thought.

"So tell me the truth," she said. "Who do you work for?"

"I can't answer that."

She looked down at her hands and didn't say anything for a moment.

"Your arrest," she said. "I read about it. The paper said you were sentenced to twenty-five-to-life. With no chance for early parole. How can you even be here, Nick? How can you be out?"

"It was a bad bust," he said. "They had to release me."

"Bad bust meaning you weren't there that night? Or bad bust meaning—"

"I didn't kill anybody, Lauren."

It was the truth, Mason thought. For that night, at least, it was the truth. I wasn't a killer.

Not then.

Never mind the men I've killed since I became a "free" man.

"The other man who was killed that night," she said, "trying to get away..."

"A friend of mine."

She could see it in his eyes. How much it still hurt him.

"I'm just trying to understand," she said. "I don't know anything about you."

"I'll never put you in danger," he said. He wanted to believe it.

"I don't think you can promise that, Nick. Not the way you live."

It was her biggest fear, that he was involved in something terrible. Something she could never understand or accept. He hadn't said one thing yet to make her believe anything else.

"Whatever you think we can have," she said, "it won't work. You know that, right?"

"I want to be with you, Lauren. I don't know how else to say it. This other thing in my life... I'm trying to get out of it. Every single day."

He didn't know how he'd ever do it, but he would keep watching, and waiting, and somehow he would find a way to get his life back.

"Can you do that? Will you ever be out?"

"I don't know."

It was the truth. He had no idea how long it would take. Or how much his freedom would cost him if it ever came.

"Because if you could…" she said. "I mean, if you really could—"

Mason reached out and touched her hand before she could finish. He knew he was asking for too much from her. Being with him would be signing the same kind of contract that he had with Cole. With no chance to read the words. No idea what would happen from one moment to the next.

He had no right to ask her to live a life like that. Like his.

He took a leash from the rack and opened up the gate. Max came out into the center of the store just long enough for Mason to hook the leash to his collar. He opened the door and led the dog out into the rain. When he was half a block away, he heard the footsteps behind him.

He turned and looked at her face, already wet from the rain.

He put his arms around her and kissed her right there on the sidewalk. They walked up Grant Street together, with Max on the leash beside them. By the time they got to the town house, all three of them were soaked.

Mason took Lauren into his bedroom and they took off their wet clothes.

"I need you to be honest with me," she said as she touched his chest. "You don't have to tell me anything you can't tell me. But no more lies."

He nodded his head once. Then he lifted her up in the air with both arms and put her down on the bed. They wrapped themselves together and it was better than the first time, because it wasn't about five years of hunger waiting to be released. It was about being together and wanting to make it last.

Lauren woke up first. The sun was coming in through the windows of Mason's bedroom. The storm clouds were gone. She lay there for a while, watching him sleep. Then she got up and went into the kitchen to make breakfast.

Diana came down the stairs. She was dressed for work. Dark suit, a white shirt today. Her hair pinned up.

"Good morning," Diana said with that same careful, cold edge in her voice just like the first time the two women had met. With a hundred other things left unsaid.

Lauren watched her pick up her black leather bag, then head for the stairs. There would be no breakfast, no conversation. Not even another word. Then she heard Diana's BMW starting, the garage door opening and closing, the car accelerating down the street.

We don't have to be sorority sisters, Lauren thought, but as long as you still live here… it's just another complication. One more thing to be worked around if we're going to make this work.

Maybe I'm fooling myself. This whole thing is impossible.

But then Nick was there in the kitchen with her. He came up behind her and wrapped his arms tight around her waist.

We have to try, she said to herself. Somewhere in the middle of this crazy mess, we have to try to find a real life.

They spent the rest of the day together, walking down to North Avenue Beach and the outdoor hamburger stand at Castaways, the restaurant that was built to look like a big blue steamboat. One more piece of classic Chicago, and for one fleeting moment, it made Mason think that maybe this city was big enough, and good enough, to find a new life in.

And maybe even find a way to include Adriana in his life. Bring his daughter to this same beach, on another day, just as perfect as this one. Watch her swim and then wrap her up in a towel. Sit on the sand and watch the sun go down over the lake. He still had the soccer games twice a week. Still keeping that part of his life separate. And safe. But if I ever find a way to get my life back, he said to himself, I can have more.

I can have everything.

As they were walking back to the town house, Mason stole a quick look at his new cell phone. He'd thrown the old one away, but, of course, it could never be that easy to break the connection. He had a replacement the next day and now it was right here in his pocket to remind him. I can think anything I want, he realized, but it all gets obliterated with the simple sound of this phone ringing.

It could be five weeks. It could be five days. Hell, it could be five minutes.

This is the dreamworld, he thought. This seemingly normal life, walking down this sidewalk with this woman at my side. When the phone rings, I'll open my eyes and see my real life again.

I'll go right back to that waking nightmare.

He put the phone away, but Lauren caught the look on his face. Neither of them said a word about it, but it hung in the air between them for the rest of the day.

They had dinner together that night and made love again in his bed. They watched a movie on the big television, wrapped up on the couch, pretending to be a normal couple on a normal night.

The phone sat on the table, just a few feet away. It stayed silent. But they both knew it was there.

After midnight, Mason woke up and felt for her beside him. She was gone.

He got up and went outside and found her sitting by the pool. She was wrapped up in his robe, curled up in a chair, looking up at the night sky. She took his hand and stood up. He kissed her, then sat in the chair and pulled her down to him. He held on to her, the warmth of her body holding off the chill of the night air.

He looked up at the same stars until she finally spoke.

"What's going to happen next?" she said.

He didn't answer. He knew he'd have to tell her someday. Everything he'd done. This man he killed with a gun, this one with a knife. God knows what else he'd have to do between today and that day. He wouldn't be able to keep it all inside him forever.

But for tonight, there was nothing he could say to her. He had to keep doing his job, whatever he was told to do next. He had to follow every order until he finally saw his chance to get out. Until then, letting her into his world would mean making her a part of it.

He wasn't ready to do that.

Not yet.

They were having lunch at a place on Addison Street the next day, sitting at a table outside. Mason looked across the street and saw the black Escalade parked there. The driver's-side window slid down and he saw Quintero's face.

"Who is that?" Lauren said, following his eyes. She saw the man sitting in the vehicle, saw the tattoos and the sunglasses and the easy way he rested his arm across the steering wheel. Watching them and not caring if they noticed.

Then he took off his sunglasses and nodded to her. She swallowed hard and looked away. Mason stared at the man and thought about what this could mean for them. He knows we're together, Mason said to himself. He followed us all the way up here to her neighborhood. He knows she's in my life now.

"He's part of this," she said. My first glimpse into this other life, she thought. This other life that touches both of us.

This other life that will begin again, at any moment.

"Yes," Mason said, keeping his promise to her. No more lies.

When Lauren woke up the next morning, she lay next to Mason and traced her finger along the lines on his face, memorizing him. Thinking about the bet she'd made on this man. That he was a good man in a bad situation. That all of the uncertainty and all of the wondering were a price worth paying to be with him.

Then the phone rang.

Nick's eyes opened. He looked at her first, then he sat up and grabbed the phone off the night table. He sat with his back to her as he listened, never saying a word. When the call was done, he put the phone down.

She sat up in the bed. "Nick..."

He got up, still silent, and put his clothes on.

She wrapped the covers around herself and watched every movement he made. This is it, she said to herself, the moment I've been dreading. I can't ask him where he's going or what he'll have to do. All I can do is wonder how long he'll be gone and what new scars he'll have when he comes back.

If he comes back at all.

Mason came over and kissed her. He stood there for a long time, looking down at her in the bed.

He checked his watch.

"I have to go to work," he said.

Then he was gone.

ACKNOWLEDGMENTS

I want to thank Shane Salerno for believing in me and for doing more than any one person could ever be asked to do to make this new series a reality. Thanks, also, to Edward Tsai, Don Winslow, and everyone associated with The Story Factory.

I'm grateful to Ivan Held, Sara Minnich, and everyone else at G. P. Putnam's Sons.

Thanks to Chicago police detective John Campbell for all of the technical assistance. And continuing thanks to Bill Keller and Frank Hayes.

And, as always, I couldn't do anything at all without Julia, my wife and best friend, and Nicholas and Antonia, who both amaze me more and more with each passing day.